CHERRY'S WAR

AND

THE FLYING NIGHTINGALES

Cherry's War

And

The Flying Nightingales

Janina Clarke

This is a work of fiction. Names, characters, places, incidents, and dialogues are products of the author's imagination or are used fictitiously. Any resemblance to actual persons, living or dead, events or locales is entirely coincidental.

ISBN: 978 0 6458 0397 6

janinaclarke.com

DEDICATIONS:

For Kerry and Jessie, with love

My mum Jessie, is the woman under the Wellington bomber in chapter nine. She spent much of the war working on Wellington bombers in a hangar at Sywell Aerodrome, Northamptonshire. Fixing and 'Doping' the bombers during WWII so they could be flown another day. Thanks for your service mum.

Table of Contents

CHAPTER 1 - July 1940, Portsmouth

The bombs fell, with the air raid sirens moaning up and down the city. The siren rose and fell, rose and fell, wailing like a banshee which people believed was the foretelling of death. The Heinkel, a German aircraft was the only thing similar to it. It terrified people when they heard that noise bearing down on them.

The first body that Cherry, the young warden, came upon was already dead. A bomb had penetrated the side of a house at the end of the street but had hit it with so much force that the person in the kitchen hadn't stood a chance. Cherry lifted bricks off the body and found a young child by her side. There was so much brick dust in the air and on the bodies, that it was difficult to see how old the child was. The side of the house had collapsed in on itself, with part of the roof. The rest of the roof hung precariously. Cherry, called out to her father with a trembling voice. The smell of bombs, heat, and smoke filled the air making her cough.

'Here, here Papa!'

The warden hurried over, saw the two victims covered in bricks, and looked up at the debris dangling above them.

'The rest of the roof might fall any minute. Are they alive?'

His daughter shook her head. A sob caught in her throat. 'Let's get them out of here tout de suite, Cherry.' He picked the child up and put it on its mother's belly and lifted her shoulders. Cherry picked up the legs of the woman and they levered mother and child carefully onto the stretcher he had brought with him. She noticed there was hardly a rip in the woman's stockings, although there was blood on her forehead.

'I think it was quick Cherry. We must be grateful for small mercies.'

'I think it's Mrs…' she stuttered not wanting to say her name.

'Now then, never mind,' said her father. 'Don't think about it, let's get them and us out of harm's way before the whole lot comes down.'

Through the smoky haze Cherry and her father stumbled over the rubble to where an ambulance was charging down the street swerving to avoid the bricks and shattered branches strewn across the street. The ambulance squealed to a halt alongside them.

The hum of bombers was fading in the distance, but fires had broken out in all parts of the bombed area. The ambulance driver jumped out of her van and called over to them through the smoke haze.

'Hello! Is that you Warden Caldwell?'

'Yes here!' he waved to her, beckoning her to come over. She jumped over shattered pieces of bark and scattered pieces of branches and bricks.

'Are these the only casualties?' she asked the girl. But Cherry was staring down at the bodies, it was her first dead body and she felt a bit stunned to see the woman lying peacefully. It might be she was asleep. The child face down on his mother's stomach did not move either, it couldn't have been more than six months old. They both had not moved since she had been there.

'I'll check,' he hurried around the house, shining a torch and calling out.

Cherry watched him go, unable to say anything to the ambulance driver. A compulsion made her look down at the victims.

'Come on, let's get them into the ambulance,' the older woman said, urging her along, sensing that Cherry was struggling with her emotions.

Cherry strained lifting the heavier end of the stretcher into the ambulance. The driver pulled the stretcher into the ambulance and bent over the woman and her baby.

'Is she...you know?' Cherry asked the ambulance driver, who was checking the woman's pulse, and the small child on her stomach. She shook her head.

'Sorry love, did you know her?'

'Oh...' a sob caught in the young girl's throat. She cursed inwardly her quivering voice. As a new assistant warden to her father, she did not want to show any emotion to those more experienced around her. Her father had a remarkable long-serving reputation in the neighbourhood and she didn't want to let him down by crying.

'Yes, I've seen her at the grocers. She was expecting a year ago, which was the last time I saw her.'

'Is this your first death?' the woman asked her gently. She nodded, the tears starting to fall down her face silently. Her father returned.

'No. No one else here. I don't know if the husband is still at work or if he's joined up. I'll find out,' he said to the ambulance driver. She nodded and shut the back doors of the ambulance. 'I'll get these back to the hospital then.'

The warden put his arm around his daughter.

'You did well. It's hard the first time.'

'Does it get any better?' Cherry asked, rubbing the back of her hand across her eyes.

'Yes,' he said, lying. It had never got any better for him.

'You must've seen so much death in the trenches Papa, it must be easier now...'

'Not really,' he said. 'Get yourself off home now. I think that's the last of the Luftwaffe tonight.' And he coughed as the smoke drifted from the docks where the fires were still burning. The fires in the distance lit up the horizon as he watched his daughter walk wearily down the street silhouetted against the burning backdrop of a city on fire.

CHAPTER 2 – Joe

The air raid the next day came early, it was scarcely half past six. Cherry, walking back from her shift, quickened her step and muttered, 'Damn.' She hurried down the road. The siren sounded across the city, one district starting it, another picking it up and sending it onwards until the whole world seemed to echo.

Cherry hurried on towards her house as the siren groaned its way into silence. The bombers would be on them in an instant.

A figure in uniform stepped out from behind the tree which was in shadow at the side of the house. The evening summer sun had already disappeared as ominous dark clouds were closing in above them. The stranger made her heart jump, it wasn't a uniform she recognised. Her heart thudding, she called out to the man.

'If you want Warden Caldwell he's out.'

'I've not come to see him. I thought Bill might be home,' the young man said in an American accent.

'Bill?' Her mind was in turmoil.

'Yes, he invited me here,' he looked up at the house from the tree where he stood. The dark wood seemed to squeeze in on them making the house look smaller in the dark.

'Bill's not here. When did you see him?'

'We became friends at the Services Club in Marble Arch. He said if I had a spare afternoon to pop in and visit.' She could see his face and recognised the uniform now as he stepped into the light.

'But Bill's at Tangmere.'

Then she wondered if he was a spy and was trying to get information from her, she had seen a poster on the bus about spies with a warning.

'I'm the only one here,' she said and thought how odd this sounded and how it made her vulnerable. Even though he was young and good-looking and had the King's uniform on, it didn't mean he was trustworthy.

She heard an ominous sound overhead like a giant swarm of bees. There was a distant muffled shudder of explosions coming their way.

'You'd better come in. We have a shelter inside.'

Cherry led the way up the short gravel drive towards the front door where it was dark. The clouds had gathered and it looked ready for a downpour. She didn't fancy getting wet. She unlocked the front door. An explosion sounded a few streets away, and drops of rain started to plop on the ground.

They plunged into blackness. Most of the windows were boarded up and the curtains pulled across. She grabbed a torch and slammed the front door shut behind him. The torch went out momentarily, she shook it. Her heart pounding away.

While the stranger examined the hallway, Cherry looked at him and saw a tall, olive-skinned young man, in a brand-new RAF uniform. He took off his cap, he had thick dark hair. Catching her eye, he smiled.

'Joe Taylor at your service ma'am.'

Cherry was tickled he called her ma'am in his American accent. 'You have an RAF uniform on.'

'Eagle Squadron. Americans helping out you British. I met Bill socially and he invited me here.' He looked around. 'I hope it's alright.'

'Yes, of course,' she said politely. 'Is Bill due home this weekend? Only my mother knows things like that. I'm not told anything.' She said tartly. 'It's Friday, so I suppose he may be home today if he has a forty-eight-hour pass. At the moment he doesn't get much time off.' I sound nervous, she thought.

The man stood there not sure what to do. 'Well, I don't like to impose, I can go after the bomb passes over.'

'Bomb*ing*,' Cherry confirmed. 'You really are new here, aren't you? Portsmouth and Southampton are prime targets for the Luftwaffe.

In case you haven't noticed we have a Royal Naval base here in Portsmouth. So, Jerry likes to drop his bombs over our heads as often as he can.'

The house shuddered as a bomb exploded not far away. The rain fell heavily outside and he didn't want to go now and get his new uniform soaked.

She led him into a larger room that looked like his parlour at home. She turned on a lamp on the piano. There was a sheen on her auburn hair as she turned her head in the soft light. She took his breath away. He was just looking for a good time, he knew Bill had a sister at home. But he wasn't sure how old she was. He was curious and at the same time homesick. Trust him to turn up in the middle of an air raid.

Cherry sat down on the sofa and indicated he sit opposite her. The mention of her brother's name calmed her somewhat. For all she knew he could have been a madman out to harm her. She had heard of such stories happening in London. Surely not here in this place where she had grown up. With a uniform on and looking clean-shaven and tidy, he didn't look like a murderer. Her mother would have a fit if she knew she was socialising with a stranger, in their dark, empty house. And he was an American at that. She turned on the lamps next to him and on a small table.

Joe pointed at Bill's photo on the piano. 'I know he's at RAF Tangmere, he told me he might be home today or tomorrow. I just thought I'd visit as I'm new to the area. He was the only friendly face I met last weekend. You're a bit suspicious of us Yanks, aren't you?'

He sat on the sofa leaving a gap for her to sit next to him. 'We haven't started ops yet. We're still in training. So, I thought I'd make the most of time off. I wasn't sure where to go. I don't know anyone here in Britain.'

She sat next to him because he invited her to. There was a grandfather chair in the corner of the room and a stool at the piano where she could have sat. But that would have looked as if she were scared of him. She tried to sound relaxed. She sat down next to him and turned to face him. He showed the expressions of a young and eager man, in his early twenties. His lithe body and olive skin had grown up in a sunny climate. While her skin felt pale and wan next to him. He leaned forward and leaned his elbows on his knees, and she thought he's not as relaxed as he makes out.

'My father was in the Air Force during the last war. Then emigrated.'

'Oh? Where is he from?' she asked trying to sound friendly. But the question stumped Joe because he frowned as if trying to remember. There was an awkward silence.

'I'm not sure if Bill is home this weekend,' she said quickly. 'He would've rung Mother if that were so.' She was aware she sounded formal and stiff. Whereas he sounded relaxed and at ease. Only his movements leaning forward, then looking back at her, showed he was uncertain about something.

'I heard about you from Bill. He said to come and visit. We met at the Services Club in London I was on a forty-eight-hour pass then. We became friends. Having the same background and interests and all...' He had repeated what he'd told her before, perhaps he's more nervous than I am, she thought.

She felt a bit shy and didn't know what to say in reply.

'Where is your mother?' he asked suddenly.

'Oh, she's with the WI...Women's Institute, selling jam and vegetables or something.'

'Gosh, you British women do a lot to support the war,' he said, looking at her again. She felt her heart bump. 'My mother doesn't work and neither do my sisters. Although one's finishing school soon.'

'We've been at it longer than you have. We're used to the chaos of war now.'

She secretly wondered what her mother would say if she knew she was entertaining a young stranger-and a good-looking one at that.

It sounded as if the bombs were exploding in the next street. They heard a whining sound then a massive explosion and the ground shook underneath. Cherry jumped.

'They must be aiming for the docks but they're hitting us instead! They're not very good aimers.'

Joe looked alarmed, although he tried to act relaxed on the sofa.

'It sounds like a bigger raid than last time. They seem to be lasting longer these days,' she said, feeling like she should fill in the gaps of silence.

He admired the way she took the bombing all in her stride. Suddenly some plates fell off the wall. He jumped up.

'We've had nothing like this where I am.' He sat down again. 'I've been given a Hurricane, it moves pretty fast.' Then he stopped talking as if he remembered he shouldn't be saying these things.

'Incendiaries. I should go outside and put them out,' she said. 'If they smoulder they can set the rest of the garden and house alight if they're nearby.' She stood up and went back into the hall. Picking up a warden helmet hanging on a hook, she tucked up her hair and unbolted the back door. Joe was hot on her heels. It had stopped raining. An array of fizzing lights and small fires were burning independently around the garden. The air smelled of ash and almonds.

'Grab the hose and bucket,' she pointed to them by the back door.

Within an hour, he had pumped water on several incendiaries in the back garden and in the next-door neighbour's garden. Cherry had thrown sand on the smaller ones smothering their fires. They looked up into the darkness.

'Welcome to my country.' She said smiling at him. She was oblivious of the black smuts on her face. He rubbed her face clean with a cloth. They stood smiling at each other. He wondered if he could kiss her now, with that young innocent face looking up at him.

The explosions sounded further away. Cherry looked up at them in the distance, she was oblivious to Joe watching her face intently.

'They're destroying the buildings by the coast where they can be seen better next to the water and full moonlight.'

They stood looking at each other. The smell of cordite and smoke filled the air. There were flashes of light to the north and the drumming noise of the German bombers fading on the horizon.

'I think they've passed over, looks like they're going north to some other poor sod's town,' he said as he wiped a smear of black across his face.

His hands and uniform were dirty. Cherry's face, hands, and clothes were black with soot.

'What?' she suddenly giggled. 'You sounded like my brother there.'

'Oh, it's Bill's fault. He taught me that.'

She suddenly felt an attachment through Joe to her brother. 'I haven't seen Bill for ages,' she sighed.

'You're close?'

'Yes, he's my big brother. I miss him,' she sighed. 'Thanks for helping Joe,' she said quickly. 'Let's go inside.' She led the way and they washed their hands in the kitchen sink. Joe tried to brush as much dirt off his uniform as he could.

'We deserve a drink,' she led the way back into the living room.

'It's gotten dark,' he said.

'Close the door and turn on the light. It's all right the kitchen windows have blackout curtains on them.'

'Will there be another wave of bombers?' he asked.

'Sometimes. Usually.' She poured out a large brandy for each of them.

'We deserve this.' She raised her glass and they clinked their glasses together.

She led him into the drawing room, which was filled with chairs and sofas.

He liked the way her hair shone like gold under the lamp. She was pretty. Her eyes were grey and had a charming candid expression. She looked very young and stiff. Very English, he thought. Not like the girls back home. In place of the frills and wide belts and glamorous skirts worn by American girls, his blitz companion was in a brown sweater and skirt. At least she wore silk stockings, but her shoes were as heavy and low-heeled as a man's.

She sat opposite him on the sofa. He moved and sat next to her.

'You are an amazing young lady,' he said, putting his arm across the back of the sofa.

'Tell me more about meeting my brother.'

She felt the heat from his thigh as he moved against her. She thought him too friendly too soon. She looked at him feeling awkward with a glass of brandy in her hand. She gulped it down. Was it to give her Dutch courage? She admired his physique and his informal manner. But he was getting a bit too informal as he drank her father's brandy.

Before he had a chance to answer, a huge explosion sounded nearby making the ceiling lights rattle and dust from the war sprinkle over them. She pointed over to some open doors.

'We sometimes shelter in there.' She pointed. She picked up a torch and led the way.

The room was big and old-fashioned and in the middle was a large billiard table.

'Quick!' she crawled under the table and he crouched his six foot one and crawled in beside her. The sounds of the bombing outside were muffled by thick curtains but then they heard shattered windows. They huddled underneath the table.

'I thought they'd gone over,' he said.

'We didn't wait for the all-clear to sound,' she said. 'I usually do…' She felt guilty, she had been so absorbed by this stranger that her senses had disappeared with her inhibitions.

'Perhaps we were a bit quick….' He didn't finish. She was thinking, *he* was a bit quick.

The blitz continued to rage outside around the house. Broken glass sounded nearby as someone's windows were blown out.

'I think it's wonderful you've come here to England to help us out,' she said suddenly in a warmer voice.

He beamed a wide smile at her. When she smiled back it was as if her face was transformed.

'You should smile more often,' he said. They looked at each other in a friendly way. They were huddled under the table, while an orchestra of destruction went on across the sprawling darkness of the city. People all over England were doing the same thing. Huddling in damp cold shelters or under the stairs, in cellars or under the kitchen table, listening to the blitz, which had been going on every night in cities around Britain.

Tonight, it was Southampton and Portsmouth's turn.

People had become accustomed to the bark of the Bofor guns, and the roar of the thousand-pounder, they knew the light scattering noise of fire bombs, the rattle of machine guns, and the drone of enemy bombers. They listened and identified the sounds with a kind of stoic acceptance. Her new companion was becoming attractive, the brandy probably helped. She looked at his outline under the billiard table.

'Where is your father?' he suddenly made her jump to the present.

My father's a warden with the ARP or Air Raid Precautions - he's busy during the night. Mother is out most of the day.

'What do you do?'

She swallowed, it sounded like a cop-out.

'I'm a volunteer warden and I help my father.'

'Oh? Do you fight fires?'

'I help the public during the raids, I'm not working tonight. But I want to be a nurse, only you have to be twenty-one. I'm not old enough yet. So, I'm thinking of joining the RAF like my brother. He's a pilot. And they don't take female pilots. So the next best thing will be a medical orderly.'

'I would think a medical orderly would be good training for a nurse.'

'I wonder when it'll all be over. It seems it's only just starting here in Portsmouth.'

He looked at her as if waiting for her to say something else. This was the first adult who had actually listened to her for ages.

'I'm receiving first aid training... and I look after my little brother when he's not at school. The school is half-bombed from last week. But they're still managing to keep most of the children there. Those that aren't leaving for the quieter countryside.' She knew she was talking too much about herself.

'What do you do as a volunteer warden?' he asked.

'I started training last month as soon as I was eighteen. We're first on the scene if a building's been bombed. We dig out the injured, check people are still alive..'

'Or dead?'

'Yes.' She swallowed, she didn't want to think of that.

'Well, you're a game girl! Many of the girls I know in Texas don't even work. They get ready for a husband as soon as they leave school.'

'War changes things.'

'I haven't come across a girl like you before,' he exclaimed.

She glowed and went pink. Finishing off her brandy her head was woozy. Her chest went out.

'You British girls are game for anything.'

'We have to be. It's called serving your country. Just like you're doing.'

'I just want to be in the thick of the action. We're kicking our heels doing nothing at RAF...where we're training at the moment.'

'We would rather not have this war. But it's been a godsend for us women.' She was warming to his questions. 'Some women work in the fields and grow crops and look after animals, they're known as the Women's Land Army. Women work in munition factories making bullets and bombs. A friend of mine works in Southampton shooting down bombers with anti-aircraft guns. Well, the men shoot. She does the calculations.'

She held her breath looking at him, wanting to talk to him forever. He watched her animated face in the torchlight under the billiard table. She felt elated, somebody other than Bill was listening to her dreams for the future.

'I should go.' He shifted under the billiard table and banged his head.

'Won't you stay? At least until the all-clear.'

'Your parents...'

'Father won't mind.'

'I'd mind you spending the night talking with a strange man if you were mine. Come to think of it – I wish you *were* mine.'

He took her in his arms. Cherry had wanted him to do that. She had kept thinking about it, imagining what it would be like if he kissed her. She had found herself looking at his mouth, the lips firm and full. Now, as he closed his arms around her she gave a kind of sigh as she shut her eyes. She snuggled closer, giving and receiving passionate, exploring kisses. How beautiful he tasted, she thought. Her mind began to blur, she could no longer think, she could only feel.

Between kisses, he made choking sounds, half exclamations.

'Christ, you're so-oh, God!' He began to pull up her sweater and putting his hands into her brassiere, he exposed one of her breasts. She came spinning back to earth.

'No. Please. No.'

She pushed her hands against his chest but he stayed where he was and still held her.

'You don't want to make love?'

'No. Yes, I want to. I just haven't done it before.'

He rubbed his face against hers. Scratching her skin.

'In that case, you shouldn't.'

Her body throbbed, she felt giddy, she wanted to be kissed again.

'It's your fault I behave badly, you're such a luscious female.' He ached for this unusual, brave girl. 'I haven't met anyone like you before,' he said again.

'I haven't met anyone like you before either.' She smiled at him.

There was the sudden loud noise of a slammed door.

'Damn. That must be my father.'

Guilty as a schoolboy, Joe buttoned up his jacket. Cherry pulled down her sweater and smoothed her hair. They crawled out from under the billiard table. Just as her father's hoarse voice called out from the kitchen.

'In here, father. Mother hasn't come home, but this is Pilot Officer Joe Taylor who came in out of the air raid. He's a friend of Bill's.'

Her father put a bag on the hall table. They walked out of the sitting room. He wore the W on his tin hat and a long mackintosh that was wet. He hung them up on the hall stand.

They stood there awkwardly, Cherry trying to calm her breathing as her father went into the kitchen.

'It was good timing it rained after the raid,' he said. 'Some of the fires went out on their own. But some houses were hit in Duke Street. We had a few casualties.' He looked at Joe who was adjusting his jacket.

Her father had a hint of a French accent. He was not happy about his daughter being in a room with a stranger. 'It was close to our house. How did you fare?'

'Oh, fine Papa. Joe helped me put out the incendiaries outside and then we took shelter under the billiard table. Did you rescue anyone tonight?' Cherry asked, trying to deflect an argument that might ensue; her father was very critical of foreign military men.

'Yes, but they were down the air raid shelter, only one person dazed by falling masonry.'

Why had they both come out of the sitting room straightening their clothes? The frown settled on his brow and stayed there until suddenly the all-clear sounded in the distance.

Cherry fled into the kitchen to deflect the awkward silence. 'I'll make tea.'

Joe shifted uncomfortably and tried to make small talk. 'I came to visit Bill. But no one was here. Cherry took pity on me as the bombs started falling.'

'Where are you stationed? How do you know my son?'

'Oh Papa,' Cherry admonished him sticking her head around the corner. 'Leave it out. You shouldn't ask where someone's stationed. He only popped by to see if he could catch Bill.' It sounded strange even to her.

Mr Caldwell followed her into the kitchen and sat down at the table. She indicated for Joe to do the same as he stood awkwardly in the doorway. She poured the tea. Mr Caldwell noticed she had a flushed face as she passed them both cups of tea and Joe sat down.

'Papa was born in Nantes in France but came to England as a young man. Which is why he has a bit of a French accent. He served in the French army in the First World War.'

Joe looked confused and winced as he drank the first sip. He tried to say something polite but the tea was too hot. He choked.

'Oh?' coughing he said, 'Excusez-moi.'

'You speak French?' her father suddenly smiled at him.

'My grandmother was French. She emigrated to the States in the 1900's. She spoke French with me and my sisters when I was small. But I don't remember very much. My sisters all speak French.' Joe slurped his tea, he concentrated on drinking it without spilling too much in the saucer.

After a declaration of French connections, Mr Caldwell was warming to him. Joe continued to tell them about his sisters. Cherry watched her father, he's re-thinking his first impressions of Joe. That's good. I wouldn't want him to dislike him.

Without looking at Joe Mr Caldwell addressed Cherry.

'Your mother is still out? Where's Tommy?'

'He went with her after school to the village hall.'

'How was your shift this morning on your own?'

'Uneventful. Then it kicked off when I got home. But we were able to put out the incendiaries.' She looked at Joe again.

'You timed it right then. But a bit of experience will do you good.'

'I know what to do Papa. I've been with you often enough.'

He looked up at the kitchen clock.

'I'm surprised they're not home yet. It's dark.' He sipped his tea.

Cherry looked at her father. Worry lines spread over his forehead.

'I'll go and look for them,' she stood up. Joe stood up at the same time.

'No. I'll go.' Her father stood up and put his warden's helmet on again.

'All right,' she said. Joe hinted he should leave too. He was still embarrassed.

'No need. Not yet.' She put a hand on his, as her father went out.

'You seem young to be a warden,' he commented.

'I'm eighteen, and I'm going to join up. My father fought in World War One at seventeen.'

'Join up?'

'The Women's Air Auxiliary. It's the RAF like you and Bill. I've always wanted to join the women's side since Bill joined up.'

'Do your parents know?'

'Heavens, no. My mother thinks I should stay at home and look after my brother until I get married. I couldn't think of anything worse.'

He smiled and squeezed her hand. 'I'd like to see you in a blue uniform.'

She smiled at him across the table.

'I have to go back to base tonight,' he said. 'But I could ring you tomorrow. Perhaps we could meet up next week?'

'I should like that.'

The front door opened and voices filled the hall. It was dark save for the kitchen light. There was no hall light because of the blackout. They had been in trouble with showing lights at the start of the war and Mr Caldwell had taken out the light bulb so that Tommy couldn't turn it on by accident.

'I should leave too.' Joe stood up. Mrs Caldwell pulled off her hat and Tommy came running in and barrelled into Joe in the hall.

He grinned staring up at Joe.

'Blimey a yank! I thought it was Bill.'

'Tommy!' her mother shouted. 'Don't be rude.' She shook her umbrella outside as she came in. She turned on a small lamp next to a door on the other side of the hall. Now he could see her. He noticed the resemblance of mother and daughter. The luscious auburn hair swayed as they moved, the highlights were like caramel swirling in chocolate but Cherry's hair was longer.

'I have to report at seven tomorrow morning so I'll have to go back to base tonight.' He took Cherry's hand and kissed it. She'd never had her hand kissed before. She looked at his shiny black hair as he bent over her hand.

Tommy whooped, 'The French do that, don't they Dad?'

Everyone ignored him as his parents hung up their coats, and Joe held her hand looking into her eyes.

'Shall I call you tomorrow?'

'Yes please.'

He gave her one last look, smiled at her, and called 'Au revoir!' to her father, as he set off down the path to the train station.

CHAPTER 3 - The next day

'Oh no, mum, that's not fair. Take Tommy with you. He's being really annoying,' Cherry pleaded with her mother. Mrs Caldwell grabbed her handbag and tucked her coat around her ready to go outside into the wind. The sky was threatening rain.

'I have the WI meeting,' she said with irritation in her voice. 'And the chairs to put out. I'm sure you can help out by looking after him. After all, you don't have a proper job yet. I'll only be gone a couple of hours.'

'But I do have a proper job.' Cherry scratched her arm. 'I'm supposed to be helping Papa today.'

'He can do without you.'

Cherry gasped. 'Did you tell him that?' She stuttered, upset. 'That's not fair! I'm scheduled to help him today.'

'Don't answer back. My work is just as important as your father's. And anyway, you owe it to me after what you did...'

Cherry stared at her mother. She couldn't believe that she had brought up that old excuse again.

'Oh!' Cherry gasped. 'That's not fair. Are you going to hold that against me for the rest of my life?' And she burst into tears. She turned away so that her mother couldn't see how much that comment had hurt her. It took a few moments to struggle with her emotions. She swung round to face the passive look of her mother watching her. She wondered why her mother was such a cold, emotionless woman. What had her father seen in her? She swallowed and breathed in steadying herself.

'I didn't say it wasn't important. All I'm saying is - take Tommy with you. He can help put the chairs out.' She felt her heart pumping, her mother had a habit of deliberately trying to upset her just to get her own way.

'It's not convenient having a child there. We like to talk, women-talk. He shouldn't listen to things like that.'

Cherry could feel herself getting angry, she raised her eyes to the ceiling. She felt like saying, then don't talk about women-things in front of him, but she wouldn't win this argument, she never did. She'd spent many years arguing with her mother who organised things to suit herself. Since starting volunteering as an assistant warden with her father, she had completed some shifts, but if her mother wanted her to babysit Tommy, and she was due to work with her father, her mother won, her father had given way each time. Cherry felt her emotions simmering beneath the surface, and she tried to hold back the tears. Mother still treated her like a child. She was an adult now, she was eighteen for goodness' sake. Tommy was treated better than she was, and she felt very resentful. Kicking the table leg she slumped down onto the chair, she felt defeated. She couldn't outwit her mother, she knew that. But she had had plans today, she really should try to stick up for herself. Mother was doing a typical job of scuppering her plans at the last moment.

'You act like my work is not important. I'm eighteen now, I'm an adult!'

'You help your father, you can help me by looking after Tommy.'

Cherry looked at him out of the corner of her eye from the kitchen. Tommy slid up the stairs looking through the banisters and smirking, he dangled something through the bars to goad her. She was starting to hate the drudgery of looking after her little brother every day, when her friends were doing exciting things with their life, like joining the Women's Auxiliary Air Force or Women's Royal Naval Service.

What mischief was he planning for her now? He was always naughty when mum wasn't around because mum would give him a 'back-hander,' and he knew that Cherry wouldn't do that to him.

'Please take him with you. I have plans today.' She wanted to wait for Joe's telephone call, as he'd promised. She was looking forward to that. He hadn't telephoned her yet, it was nearly midday. She was sure he'd said he had another few hours' leave

'Absolutely not.' Her mother said, tying up her coat with an aggressive action.

'I always have to stay in and look after him. You won't let me do anything I want to do,' she heard herself whine. 'You only let me be a volunteer Warden so you could keep me at home.'

'Lots of people are doing their bit, and staying at home. It's called being patriotic,' her mother snapped.

'You're trying to keep me here to look after Tommy so *you* don't have to. And I'm not allowed to do what my friends are doing.'

'You're too young anyway,' said Mrs Caldwell shrugging it off. 'You have to be twenty-one to be a nurse. A young girl shouldn't be allowed to see a man's parts.'

'Ha! You know what I mean. Joining the WAAF so I can be a medical orderly, so I can learn the basics for nursing.'

'You have to learn to look after your brother before you go off looking after other people. Anyway, you have a lot to learn about looking after others when you couldn't even look after your own sister!'

It was like her mother had slapped her in the face. Cherry felt the tears spring up in her eyes.

She took a deep breath and straightened her spine.

'I was seven. How was I supposed to look after a five-year-old on my own near a river? Where were you?'

Her mother glared at her, stony-faced. She'd never dared stick up for herself like this before, for fear her mother would retaliate. This time her mother almost shrugged her shoulders. Cherry could hardly believe it.

'Like I said before, you're far too young to leave home.' Mrs Caldwell opened the back door and grabbed her handbag.

'I'm eighteen, and all my friends are joining up.'

'No, they're not. You're far too young, you're only just eighteen.' And she whisked herself out of the door.

'How would you know? You never let me bring any of my friends home!' She shouted after her mother, watching her retreating figure down the garden path in a buzz of frustration.

'You don't appreciate what I do. I clean for you and look after him!' She pointed at Tommy who was watching from the kitchen with interest. 'You go out enjoying yourself every day. What have I got to look forward to?' She gulped back a sob. Her mother wasn't listening because she slammed the back gate and shot off down the street. The rickety gate rattled in its position.

Cherry felt anger and exasperation rise in her chest.

'I'm joining the WAAF. Don't say I didn't warn you!' Her comments were caught in the wind because her mother was already at the bottom of the street and turning the corner. Cherry stormed back into the house.

Cherry knew her mother wouldn't take any notice of her protests. What her mother said was law, and she wasn't used to people crossing her. The truth was that she had never taken any of her school friends home after school, because her mother wasn't warm and welcoming like her friends' mothers were. Her mother was stubborn and cold. How her brother Bill and Sid had joined up without her mother stopping them she couldn't understand, because they were the apple of her eye.

Cherry went inside and then sighed as a giggle behind her came from her brother. A wet flannel hit the back of her head.

'Ouch!' it hadn't hurt, but Cherry was angry with herself for being taken for granted. She had been minding Tommy for years. He was the youngest now and nine years old. Tommy took after his mother for definite. He had a confident personality. Whereas she was like her father. 'Cherry's a chip off the old block', she had heard her mother tell the neighbours one time. 'And he's a walkover.'

'That's obviously what I am too,' she said to herself. Well, I'll show her!'

When she had expressed a desire to spread her wings and do something to help the war effort, her mother had said no, her father had just agreed with his wife because he couldn't cope with the conflict.

Her school friend Rosie had previously told her she was too soft, before dashing off to join the Women's Royal Naval Service. 'The trouble is Cherry you're too nice. What my parents called weak and watery. People walk all over you.' Rosie had left in the Spring to join the WRNS. The government was advertising for young women to join up and help their country.

'I know. I know.' Cherry had said to her friend.

'You're a walkover for anyone. Even at school the rough kids picked on you.'

Although friends since Infant School their parents were very different. Cherry's house was larger than Rosie's, as she had pointed out. 'But your mother's so much nicer.' Cherry had replied.

'You have to be tougher. Don't let them take advantage of you,' Rosie had told her.

'I know. But it's all right for you to say because your mother is normal. She's nice to me. Not like mine,' Cherry had replied.

'Even Sidney got you to run errands for him when you were young, remember?'

'Yes. Yes. He said he'd give me a ha'penny but he never did.'

Rosie had leaned into her. 'That's it exactly. You know what to do. Now don't let her run your life and grow a backbone.'

Cherry teared up, her friend put her arms around her.

'Sorry,' Rosie said immediately. 'It had to be said. Now make sure you do it. Promise me.'

'I will.' She nodded and wiped a hand across her eyes. 'Bill always stuck up for me when I was in the Juniors, do you remember? He would always fight my corner for me,' she said to her friend.

'That's true. When I come back on leave, I want to hear a different story. I'll write to you when I have time. I'll send you my address and you can write to me.'

Rosie had written to her during her WRNS training in July. Cherry had recently received a letter explaining how marching in the rain had been tough, and how a bomb had missed the WRNS quarters and hit the edge of the parade ground. It had been exciting but no one had been hurt. The war was getting closer.

She wrote back to her friend just a bit jealous that she was serving in the WRNS. Rosie was only six months older, and Cherry hoped that in a few months, she would be serving her country too. Cherry discussed it with her father when she was with him during the night shifts, hoping to get him on her side.

'I yearn to serve my country, Papa. Just like Bill and Sidney. Can you get Mother round to our way of thinking?'

'I'll try, but you know when your mother sets her mind to something you can't shift her.'

'But if you stick up for me Papa, she'll see that *she's* the only one thinking that I should stay at home.'

'It won't make any difference my dear, once her mind is made up... and anyway, she doesn't want her only daughter leaving her,' he said plaintively. 'I don't want you to leave me. À qui je parlerai? Who will I talk to?'

'Mother? Try talking to each other. You keep missing each other at night anyway Papa. You're always out working. Mother just wants a cheap babysitter for Tommy so it doesn't disrupt her busy schedule.'

Nothing ruffled her father easily, but he puffed on his pipe even harder. They were sitting in his allotment shed with the pot-bellied stove alive in the corner. Her father often came in here to rest between raids instead of going home. He once told her it was quieter than at home. Cherry was determined to try and encourage her mother to let her join the services.

Well, she'd show them. There was nothing to keep her at home now. Although she had learned a lot as a warden it was time she left and spread her wings. After all, she wasn't even getting paid as a volunteer. In the Royal Air Force, you got paid!

There had been no phone calls today as promised from Joe. She'd had a gradual sinking feeling in the pit of her stomach as the day wore on. When she returned home her mother was in the kitchen, they did not speak to each other and Cherry wandered outside into the back garden imagining what life would be like for her when she joined up. She ignored Tommy shooting down his imaginary enemy aeroplanes, playing on the dried-out yellow lawn. She could see the sea in the distance. At night she saw the sky light up with cluster bombs and hear the clacking of the fire engine when the docks were targeted by the Luftwaffe.

The summer sun was overhead. The birds twittered and flitted amongst the hedgerows in the next field where their garden ended. She looked out into the distance from the shade of the lilac tree. It smelled wonderful. There was a crash inside, it made her jolt, it sounded like Tommy had dropped a water jug on the floor. She forced herself to close her eyes and listen to the buzz of the bees around the lilac.

Then she heard it. Opening her eyes, she caught an aeroplane coming towards them from the horizon. First, there was a sound of droning in the distance, then she saw black specks in the sky. Were they enemy planes? Then she recognised the sound of Merlin engines rising and falling as they came closer. It was a Hurricane, but the plane behind looked different. It was a Messerschmidt. She had learned about British and German fighter planes with Bill and had felt pleased that she could recognise the outlines of each aeroplane and the sound of engines from a distance.

That could be her brother up there. Bill, the eldest of her siblings, and a pilot at RAF Tangmere, was one of the few who was defending Britain's shores by battling the Luftwaffe.

Cherry made her way to the beech tree at the bottom of their garden. The wire fence had been broken down over the years and no one had bothered to fix it. She stepped over it into the farmer's field. Very often the sheep that were grazing in there came into their garden, which was why there were no plants and hardly any grass left. Unlike their neighbour next door, whose fence was reinforced and flowers flourished in their garden. The childless couple had lived there for years. Cherry had no one to play with until she went to school, even then she wasn't allowed out as she got older and so didn't make friends as easily as the others. Today, there were still no children to play with in the house next door. Tommy still had no one to play with,

Cherry's parents relied on their daughter to fill the gap.

Cherry felt desolate, she felt her father could help her more if he tried. Francis Caldwell was a quiet, thoughtful man, who had returned to England from France with his English mother when his father had died. The next year he was sent to Ypes with thousands of other young men who joined the local artillery unit. On return he had fallen in love with Cora. He had thought she was the most beautiful woman he had ever set eyes on. Nine months later a baby boy was born with red hair. They had married quickly so that the child could be baptized and they named him William, after Cora's father. They settled in a village overlooking the sea not far from Portsmouth and Cora's parents. Bill was born first, then Sidney a year later. Cherry was born two years after Sidney and then another girl, whom they called Cecily. Cecily died when she was five but although Cherry was with her at the time, she couldn't remember the events leading up to Cecily's death. Her mother had told her that she had fallen into the river. She had never missed an opportunity since then to blame Cherry for her death. Tommy was born two years after Cecily's death, almost like a recompense. But Cora Caldwell did not have the same connection with Tommy as she had had with Cecily.

When her mother returned later that day, Cherry was trying to read with Tommy. Her mother opened the door and threw a backward glance at her youngest.

'I hope you've behaved?'

'It took him a while to calm down.' Cherry answered for him. 'The trouble is he can't read like I could at his age, and he gets bored just playing tin soldiers all the time. He needs someone to read with him.'

It was a dig at her mother, but her mother ignored her. Mrs Caldwell had never been one to read with her children, whereas Cherry's Papa had loved reading with them at night, it had been his job to put them to bed and tuck them in. Now he was too busy at night when the Luftwaffe came over to read to Tommy, and Cherry felt Tommy was missing out.

Mrs Caldwell did not comment, she was still smarting from their encounter when she left home earlier. Tommy had been spoiled by his siblings while he was growing up. He flashed a cheeky grin at his mother and then tore himself away from Cherry and ran outside into the sunshine. Mrs Caldwell just couldn't be bothered with trying to get him to behave. Her answer to everything was to smack him in frustration.

'Mother, I need to talk to you now please,' Cherry tried to sound calm. She took a deep breath. She had rehearsed what she was going to say to her.

'You know I want to join the WAAF.'

'I thought you wanted to be a nurse.'

'I'm not old enough. I told you yesterday I have to be twenty-one.'

'Forget it, Cherry, you're not old enough to leave home. No daughter of mine is going to war.'

'But that's not fair, my friends are joining up, and my brothers have.'

'When you're twenty-one. That's fair enough. Not at eighteen, you're too young.'

'But Bill and Sid joined up in their teens.'

'That's different, they're boys.'

'Anyway,' Cherry said sulkily. 'Being an ARP is dangerous enough. You didn't say anything when I joined as a warden.'

'That's different. Your father is one, he keeps an eye on you and you work in the same area.'

'You must've known what I was going to get faced with as an ARP. I pulled dead bodies out of a bombed house the other day. Why be squeamish over me joining the WAAF?' she said, remembering the shock and sadness she felt when she came upon the dead mother and her baby. It brought back unhappy memories of her sister's accident. But the emotion was lost on her mother. Cora Caldwell ignored her, turned on her heel and walked off.

That was typical of mother, she thought, she doesn't know what to say so she just leaves. Cherry felt frustrated.

She chased her mother along the hall towards the stairs. 'Why do you always run off when you don't know what to say?'

'It's bad enough with your brothers away at war. Didn't we discuss this last week?' her mother was at the bottom of the stairs and with her foot on the first step, she said. 'It's not seemly for young girls to join up and to go to war.'

'Where did you get that rubbish from? You've been listening to the neighbours again, haven't you?' Cherry felt her hackles rising, the resentment she had been building over the months, and the recent serious air raid on her town had jostled her into making a decision.

'You just want me at home to look after Tommy. You shouldn't have had children if you can't be bothered to look after him yourself!' she said trying to stand up tall next to her mother, which was difficult because her mother was in high heels.

Her mother swung round and with a resounding slap hit her across the face. Cherry was stunned and wobbled on her feet, she reached out and held onto the wall. There was a shocked silence after the slap. Her mother hadn't hit her before. She had smacked Tommy many times but had never hit her older children. Cherry rubbed her cheek, the red mark getting redder by the minute.

Tommy looked up at them, his mouth open, he'd been playing with his toys on the floor. This was the best view of an argument between mother and daughter he'd seen in a long time.

'That does it!' Cherry shouted at the back of her retreating mother, who hurried up the stairs. 'I'm definitely going now. There's nothing for me here. If you think for a minute you can keep me here looking after your child, you've got another think coming!'

Spurred on by the shock of the slap and the emotions running rampant in her that week, she came to a decision. She would join up and not tell her mother.

Cherry gulped back a sob, her hand still on her flaming cheek and rubbing it. She didn't want to cry in front of her mother and brother. But she couldn't stand by and do nothing. She couldn't wait to leave home and start to enjoy life. She thought of the American pilot who had kissed her yesterday – she wished he would call her on the telephone. He hadn't rung yet even though she had been here all day waiting for his call. She decided she would take action. She grabbed her handbag and stormed out of the front door, making sure she slammed it in the process. She had obtained a new confidence. Mr Caldwell was walking up the path, and she ran past him.

'Cherry! Where are you going in such a hurry?' he called after her.

She didn't answer him. She decided to go into town. Joe hadn't called her and she was fed up with waiting. Never one to be patient, she decided to go and join the WAAF right now in town at the recruitment hall. That'll show Mother, she thought.

Cherry hurried down the street, just as Mr Caldwell walked into the house and heard the telephone ring in the living room. He'd just finished an exhausting watch. He would let his wife answer it for a change, it was bound to be about work. It had been put in, especially for his job

Mrs Caldwell answered the ringing telephone.

'Hello ma'am, this is Joe Taylor. Could I speak to Cherry please?'

At the sound of an American voice. Mrs Caldwell curled her lip and put the phone down.

Still smarting from her argument with her mother Cherry arrived at the local RAF recruitment office, as the sun came out. She looked up at the posters of a smiling woman in uniform plastered on the wall outside. It read:

'Help the RAF. Join the WAAF today.'

She held her head high and swung the door back as she walked confidently through.

CHAPTER 4 – RAF Tangmere August 1940

Cherry saw two specks coming towards her low and fast. The lead was a Spitfire the one behind chasing it. Cherry screwed up her eyes towards the sun as they came in from the sea. The whining of the Spitfire Merlin engines could be heard now as the planes swooped across the field before her. A Messerchmidt 109 was on the Spitfire's tail. They banked left then right, the Messerschmidt dogging its every move. Then they disappeared. With an intake of breath, she heard the rat-a-tat-tat of guns in the distance and heard the droning and whirring of the Spitfire's engine as it rose and fell, rose and fell, climbing and spiralling in its efforts to evade being shot down. Her head ached from straining her eyes into the bright sky. She realised this could be Bill. Please let him get away, she prayed to herself.

The Spitfire swooped up into the sky with the enemy's plane on its tail, she could no longer hear the guns. They were just specks. As they flew towards the airfield, she saw the Messerschmidt was in front and the Spitfire was on its tail. The experienced RAF pilot had managed to get behind the enemy plane by doing a loop. Now he was doing the chasing. She heard the rat-a-tat-tat of guns firing as they shot out of sight.

Most of the other Spitfires in the squadron had landed. One mechanic at the bowser pointed up at the dog fight, two pilots had just climbed down from their aeroplanes and stood looking up too, with their parachutes around their ankles.

Cherry stood still, not daring to breathe, as she suddenly saw some Spitfires in the east coming off the sea towards them at high speed. Perhaps this was him? She hadn't seen him for months. Her anticipation was high but so was her anxiety after what she saw happening in front of her.

Three aeroplanes appeared on the horizon, their shapes getting larger as they flew toward them. Cherry identified the sound of the Merlin engines, three more Spitfires were lining up one by one to come into land. Each plane landed with a light bounce, their engines making a last-minute roar as they taxied to a halt a few yards away from Cherry onto a yellow area of dry grass in front of Dispersal. They hopped down from their Spitfires, their parachutes hanging ungainly around their knees. Bill wasn't among them. Her smile faded, she had anticipated his arrival too much. Now all she could do was worry until he'd landed.

She started to perspire, the worry lines showing across her brow. The summer had been hot so far and was getting even hotter now it was

August. It hadn't rained for a long time, and September promised to be a scorcher too.

Cherry scanned the horizon to see if any planes were lagging. Her mouth was dry and she had an increasing headache. She was beginning to think coming here had been a bad idea. The RAF chaps walked towards the Dispersal hut where they usually hung around waiting for the next call to scramble. She could tell they were eyeing her up. One of them she recognised was Pilot Officer Eddie Trenchard. His shock of strawberry blonde hair stood out as he took off his cap. He had been with Bill to their house last year. She pushed a lock of hair up into its bun. She wished she had brought sunglasses with her.

Eddie Trenchard whistled over at her and she responded with a wave and hurried towards him. She moved with the freedom of youth, lithe and effortless. Her cheeks were bright red from the sun.

Eddie looked worn out. His face was tanned from spending hours in the sun. He had two white rings around his eyes where his goggles had been.

'Hello stranger what are you doing here?' and without waiting for a reply he said, 'Waiting for Bill?'

She nodded. 'I'm waiting to tell him I'm joining the WAAF next week. I want to see him before I leave. Otherwise, I may not see him for a while…'

'Does the Commanding Officer know you're here?' He indicated towards Dispersal.

'Well, no, I haven't actually told anyone I'm here. Although they let me in at the main gate.'

'Well, you're lucky. Good job you're not a spy,' and he winked at her and ground out his cigarette on the floor. He took her elbow, and he guided her away from Dispersal towards two empty chairs in the shade of a big oak tree.

She blushed as many of the pilots returning from their sortie were going into Dispersal and looking over at them.

'Don't mind them. They won't say anything unless I do.'

'About?'

'About you. In case you haven't noticed, unless you have a uniform on, they'll chuck you out. Unless you have the CO's say-so you shouldn't be here.'

'Oh.' She realised what he meant then. She stood up and looked uncomfortable. 'They let me in.'

'Sit down, don't look guilty. That's because you look about eleven. I'm sure if the CO comes out, I can vouch for you. You want to stay to see Bill, don't you?'

'Yes.'

'Well sit down then, and look natural. Let's not rub their noses in it. If you keep a low profile, you're more likely to see your brother, if you know what I mean?'

She nodded. They were out of view of Dispersal windows and in the shade, she started to breathe normally.

'Once you're in the WAAF you'll know what they accept and what they don't, like gaining entry to one of the most important RAF stations in the south.'

Cherry was suddenly quite pleased with herself, pretending to be a little innocent at the main gate got her in after all.

'So, you finally joined up, well I bet Mater and Pater weren't too pleased.'

Cherry blushed. 'What makes you say that?'

'I met you last summer, remember? Before any of this kicked off.' He lit another cigarette and took a deep drag as if his life depended on it. Perhaps it did, she wondered, as she watched him grip his cigarette tightly between his yellow fingers. Then she remembered she had been very vociferous in her plans to join the WAAF. Her parents hadn't taken her seriously. But she remembered Eddie listening to her intently and nodding with her when she told him about following her hopes and dreams in the RAF, as a young girl she'd been eternally grateful. The women's services were desperate to fill the void now that the men had left, it seemed natural that women would be encouraged to join up.

'I would have liked to join as a pilot. Apparently, the RAF don't think women should fly.'

Eddie grinned at her and tapped a cigarette out of its packet as he leaned back in his chair.

'And did you ask them if you could be a pilot?'

'Of course. But the WAAF officer looked at me as if I'd gone mad.'

He chuckled and looked at her up and down.

'I hardly recognised you...You've grown some.' His admiring glance took in her appearance. 'But socks make you look younger.'

He looked down at her brown bare legs with little white socks and sensible shoes.

'Nice legs. Tanned. You can't get nylons? Shame about the shoes,' he smiled and took another desperate drag of his cigarette.

Cherry pulled her skirt down lower.

'I can't afford nylons. Anyway, they're hard to come by. And I can't afford fashionable, high-heeled shoes either. Where have you been living? Oh yes in the middle of the countryside,' she said tartly. 'Sensible shoes last longer, so my mother says. And anyway,' she shrugged. 'It's easier to climb over bomb holes and rubble in the streets. I wouldn't get very far in high heels.'

Eddie smiled and put an arm on her shoulder.

'Of course they are, I'm teasing you. I'm used to seeing my mother in them that's all.'

'Where does she live? It must be away from the bombs, in the middle of nowhere. She can't live in the city because the Germans are bombing them.'

Eddie had the grace to look abashed.

'As it happens, she lives in a big house in the country. I think she wears sensible shoes when she's out walking the dogs. And no...she's never had to walk around bomb craters. At least, not yet.'

Cherry felt self-conscious. She was proud of her legs. She was athletic and had been a fast runner at school. Eddie laughed at her.

'Oh, no need to be self-conscious. Sorry, Cherry, it's not every day we have a lovely young woman in our midst. I'm just making the most of it...you, I mean. Don't be so serious.'

She smiled at him and tried to relax.

'I'm glad to see your friendly face, even though you are teasing me. Anyway, where's Bill?'

'I saw him fighting a Messerschmidt.'

So, her guess had been correct, it had been Bill in the dog fight. She swallowed and went pale.

'Don't worry about him. Not many Luftwaffe manage to beat our Bill. So, when are you leaving?' he asked her.

'I'm being sent for training at Duxford, a place in North London.'

'Lucky you - not far from the city then.'

'Not sure if that's a good idea. I don't suppose we'll go into London.'

'Make the most of it.'

'I may not be able to. For one thing, we don't get paid for the first two weeks.'

What are you up to there?'

'Nursing orderly.'

'Ah, I remember your passion for being a nurse.'

'I can't train to be a nurse in civvy street until I'm twenty-one. I'm not old enough yet.'

'Well, you're doing the right thing. We need young lasses like you helping our pilots on the ground. And Cherry...If you can, go into London. Do it. Enjoy yourself. You never know, you might never get the chance again. God knows what'll be happening tomorrow. We could all be speaking German.' He puffed away on his cigarette.

Cherry looked shocked. He stood up and stretched.

'Are you staying?' he asked her.

'Here? No. I just popped in to see Bill before I catch the bus home.'

At that moment a lone aeroplane appeared above the horizon. Cherry watched it, a frown etched on her forehead as it came closer. It landed with a light bounce on the runway, everyone looked and saw a line of bullet holes running down the fuselage.

'There he is,' said Eddie. 'Looks like he's been in a scrap.'

The Spitfires Merlin engines made a last roar as Bill taxied to a halt a few yards away from Dispersal. He faced it back into the wind ready for the next urgent take-off.

They stood up and walked towards her brother. He pulled back the canopy and saw his sister, a big smile showed on his face. He climbed down the parachute between his legs.

'What are you doing here?' he called to her. Without waiting for an answer, he unhooked his parachute giving it to a member of the ground crew who ran up to help him.

'Hey, look at this!' he showed a penny in the palm of his hand, it was a peculiar shape.

'Look at this! If it hadn't been for this penny, the bullet would have entered my leg!'

The penny was inverted and the imprint of the bullet was left behind. It had stopped the bullet, but there was still some blood coming from a small wound at the top of his thigh.

Eddie whistled admiring the penny.

'Are you hurt?' Cherry asked concerned, eyeing the blood seeping from his thigh.

'Oh no, it's just a scratch. I'm off to the doc to get him to look at it. Did you see the dog fight?' he asked Eddie, who shook his head.

'It was touch and go. He hung onto my tail, but I managed to spiral out and come under him.' His arm wound up and around showing how he'd done it. 'Then he was in front and I shot him in the tail and he came down over the sea!' He was high on adrenalin. He laughed when he saw his sister's worried frown.

'Don't worry ol' girl. You develop a rubber neck if you want to survive. I tell you I look around me all the time.' He limped away from them.

'Where are you going?' she called after him.

'To see the CO then to the doc.'

'I'll come with you,' she said.

'Goodness, you can't do that!' he said. 'The other chaps will laugh.' And Bill Caldwell limped off towards the Dispersal hut.

Cherry sighed as she watched his back disappear in the distance.

'I wanted to talk to him about joining up.'

'Why would you want to do that? When you could settle down with a handsome pilot, like me, and have lots of children?'

She frowned and looked darkly at him, to see if he was joking. He laughed when he saw her face. Her expression spoke volumes. Then she went pink with embarrassment.

'Ha ha, Cherry your face gives your feelings away every time!'

Now she was angry. 'Why do you pilots have this attitude? People worry about you and all you do is develop this devil-may-care attitude towards death?'

'Death can happen at any time. It's the only way we know how to survive. Time is short and we have to live life to the fullest. Shall I take you out tonight?'

Cherry was momentarily distracted by his question. But continued her line of thought.

'The newspapers make it out to be a glamorous job. My mother would have a fit if she knew how it really is. She tells her friends in the WI that Bill shoots the Luftwaffe down daily. They don't truly report the number of RAF killed.'

'Reports are exaggerated Cherry. Reality is very different.'

'But people should know the truth!' she exclaimed.

He stopped and turned to her. 'Would that be good for public morale though? The Express is trying to instil confidence in the public. If the public aren't on our side we can't win.'

She turned to face him and looked into his tired blue eyes. The breeze picked up his hair and ruffled it. He ran his fingers through it. His freckles showed sensitive skin, but his attitude was anything but sensitive. She knew he and her brother had a strange black humour, they talked about life between them as if it was a show. But he was serious when he said; 'It's the job of any prime minister to fudge the truth, if the public knew we had our backs to the wall there would be widespread panic. We've a few experienced pilots who protect us from annihilation from the Messerschmidt. Germany has been building its armaments for years leading up to this day. We hadn't - until Churchill had his way. But still, if they keep shooting us down at this rate, we won't last.'

Cherry suddenly felt depressed. 'Well, that's not very patriotic, saying we're not going to last out! Anyway,' she said suddenly tired of the discussion. 'I'll wait for Bill before I go anywhere,' and she planted her feet firmly and crossed her arms, a grim look on her face.

He took her elbow and led her towards his car.

Eddie smiled at her. 'I have a better idea. Let's go to the pub.'

CHAPTER 5 – The Battle of Britain

Bill sat in the sun in his chair, his eyes were closed. He was tired. Dog tired. His whole squadron was exhausted and it needed replacements. He was touched his sister had come to see him yesterday. He was glad she was joining up. He had told her to do it and not worry about their parents. She had gone off happy enough. He just hoped he lived long enough to see her again.

In one of the hottest summers ever recorded 43 Squadron of Group 11 Tangmere, had one of the toughest jobs at present, trying to stop the Germans from destroying shipping in the English Channel and airfields in the south of England. The south-east was taking the brunt of the might of the German air force, and Bill felt desperate. If losses continued like this, they would lose the battle, he only had five of his original crew left from the beginning of the year.

The Germans knew that the British had radar stations and often targeted them, but causing minimal damage. What they didn't know was that their RDF – Range and Direction Finding, was a chain of communications linking airfields with a central place where enemy aircraft were plotted day and night. A telephone call could be at Dispersal within minutes.

Bill was proud of this RAF development but the truth was that there were too many of the enemy coming over day by day and not enough RAF numbers. Pilots were being shot down with alarming regularity. They had already lost four hundred valuable aeroplanes since he'd been at Tangmere, and they'd lost 153 good pilots at Dunkirk in May. Goodness knew how he had escaped death, more by luck than judgment. More experienced pilots were needed quickly to fill the breach.

Desperate duels were fought high in the cloudless summer skies over southern England and valuable fighter planes, like the new Spitfire, and the old war horse - the Hurricane, were being lost. The Germans were already massing invasion barges and boats, he had seen the activity building on the other side of the Channel with his own eyes. He had flown over the French coastline through a barrage of anti-aircraft guns only last week and had reported back what he had seen.

German U-boats were sinking the British Merchant Fleet carrying valuable cargo, including food around the coasts of Britain. Food shortages were becoming common and there was talk of rationing.

Suddenly the telephone rang, and everyone who had been lounging woke up all at once, alert.

‘Scramble!’ the Commanding Officer shouted, slamming the receiver down.

Pilots leapt up from their seats and ran to their aeroplanes.

‘Get up! Get up!’ Bill shouted to the newer pilots, who panicked and looked confused.

Crew and pilots were scrambling everywhere. Pilots jumped into their planes and careered off over the grass in an effort to take off before being shot down by enemy planes. Bill looked up mid-run as he heard the blood-curdling banshee scream of a Stuka nose dive ahead of him. The two Spitfires angling to take off in front of him exploded into pieces as the Stuka unleashed its bombs on the squadron's newest Spitfires and newest recruits. Bill felt sick, it was the two young pilots. Why hadn’t they had any warning from Bentley Priory?

The trouble was the radar stations could only look outwards and once the enemy aircraft were inland it was up to the Royal Observer Corps to identify enemy aircraft and report to central control.

Bill shook his head as the ground crew tried to put out the fires on both Spitfires. What a waste of life and aircraft, he thought. A group of Stukas had slipped under the radar and caught the RAF with their pants down, he couldn’t believe what the bastards had done in five minutes.

The enemy aircraft had already disappeared, and black acrid smoke wound its way up into the sky from the station. Ground crew helped pilots into their aeroplanes and sent them on their way. Within minutes the squadron was airborne.

Up in the air, the squadron grouped behind their leader ready for action.

'This is yellow leader. You're too slow! We should be up in three minutes!' The CO shouted over the radio.

'Red group you take the left. Blue group you take the right. Follow me the rest of you!'

The Merlin engines rose and fell, as they got into line at the side of their leader.

'If you go any slower Sandy ol' boy, you'll get your arse shot off!' Eddie called over to the plane on his right.

'Not before you do, ol' boy!' Sandy shouted back.

'Enemy ahead, twelve o'clock!' someone shouted over the radio.

'Break!' said the CO.

Bill pushed his control stick hard left.

Messerschmidts swooped down on the unsuspecting Spitfires. Within seconds the rat-a-tat-tat of the Spitfire's .303mm guns were firing on the enemy. Messerschmidt after Messerschmidt, Spitfire after Spitfire went down in plumes of smoke. Sometimes parachutes billowed down slowly to earth, and an aeroplane exploded in a ball of flames.

People watching from the hills in the distance likened the planes dropping out of the sky like birds. Farm workers from the fields looked up to see white streaks in the sky, they stood and watched for a few minutes then carried on working.

'On your tail Robert!' Bill warned the pilot to his right.

'Watch out to our left Sam!' Dicky shouted as he dived to counter-attack an enemy plane which had appeared on his tail and was opening up its guns. There was a wisp of smoke, and the next instant a long trail of black smoke plumed out behind Sam's plane. After two seconds Sam bailed out and his parachute opened. The plane exploded in a ball of flames just beneath him.

'That was a close one Dicky. Did you get him?' Bill asked him over the radio.

'Yes, let's hope Sam doesn't die of hypothermia down there!' He watched the parachute billow and a few seconds later the figure disappeared from view in the green expanse of water below.

'Well, it's up to you now old boy,' Bill said to himself, and his eyes scanned the cold waters below in search of a fishing vessel. If one didn't find Sam soon, he could die of cold. The English Channel was freezing, it wouldn't be long before the pilot had hypothermia. It was summer so he had high hopes he would last until a vessel picked him up. The trouble was it was like looking for a pin prick in a haystack, let alone a needle, and that was if the winds didn't pick up and drag him down.

The squadron was flying over the Channel below them, and for the next few minutes, the air was pierced with the rat-a-tat-tat of bullets.

Suddenly a Messerschmidt appeared from out of the sun in front of Bill. It was a tactic used by the Luftwaffe to frighten the living daylights out of any new pilot. Bill dived quickly avoiding the bullets from the Messerschmidt and pulled up underneath the enemy. But the enemy was experienced and pulled up sharp doing a loop and coming back down on Bill's tail. Relentlessly winding and diving, twisting and turning, the Spitfire managed to get out of the firing line through the sheer skill of its pilot. Bill knew he had an experienced Luftwaffe pilot in front of him, because once he got him in his sites and fired his bullets, the Messerschmidt disappeared and appeared behind him again. Bill had to dive again to get out of his sights. He felt a judder as a bullet hit the tail of his Spitfire. He swung hard right and managed to lose him amongst the clouds. Coming round in a corkscrew Bill sighted the Messerschmidt no doubt looking for him over to his right. This time he was behind it, and he gave it all he'd got with his guns.

'Here's one for you Hitler, you bastard!'

Some bullets pierced the fuselage of the enemy plane and a plume of white smoke streaked from its tail, as it took a nose-dive down towards the sea. Bill saw the small white ball open up into a parachute below him, the pilot had bailed out just in time. Ten seconds later the plane hit the sea and exploded into a thousand pieces.

As Bill landed at the airfield for the second time that day, he limped over to Dispersal quickly. He could see Dicky waiting at the door for him. There were no other pilots who had yet returned.

'What's happened Dicky?' he was trying to read the expression on his friend's face.

'The CO's copped it, Bill. He was shot down over the coast. I saw him go down in a ball of flames...he didn't stand a chance.' He swallowed, his face pale. 'That's the last of the old boys left from Dunkirk. There's only you and me, oh and Eddie, left. I reckon you're next in line to take his place.'

Bill contemplated for a minute. He hadn't expected to be the Commanding Officer within a few months. His face was grim. This wasn't what he'd hoped for or even dreamed of when he joined up. The Luftwaffe had been underestimated, and they had pounced on the retreating Allied soldiers on the beach at Dunkirk. They'd caught the RAF with their pants down during the evacuation. But he was determined it wouldn't happen again.

Would any of them survive? The deaths of friends and comrades were happening all too quickly. He knew he hadn't got the experience of being a commanding officer. He didn't want to be a CO. Pilots didn't tend to live long nowadays anyway. He resigned himself that he must speak to his sister about his personal effects, and what to do if anything happened to him. It was no good putting it off any longer. He would instruct Cherry, because his mother would get emotional anyway and refuse to talk about death. Papa was always busy. Which is why he didn't gone to see them on his 24-hour pass last month. Instead of resting as they were supposed to, he went to London with Eddie and the other pilots and drank champagne with a load of Americans from Eagle Squadron. They could be killed at any time, they realised that. It was time to live life to the full.

That evening the squadron drank heavily at the Unicorn public house in Chichester, and the next day Bill awoke with a hangover to fight another day. Realising that his squadron leader was dead and he had been promoted in his place.

CHAPTER 6- Their hardest day

As the new squadron leader, Bill sat looking out of the Dispersal window at another balmy summer's day. It belied the storm that was to come. Daily they were flying to meet the enemy. The aim was to get into the skies before they got caught 'with their pants down,' as he told the new fellows of his squadron. It happened to Biggin Hill last week. The pilots and their aeroplanes were shot to pieces by enemy fighters before they could even get down the runway.

The Spitfires were all lined up today at RAF Westhampnett, it was an emergency landing airfield for RAF Tangmere where Bill's squadron were waiting patiently. Today, it was peaceful. The flight engineers were buzzing over some Hurricanes in the Tangmere hangars, a field away, like bees to a honey pot. The Hurricane had been the work horse, but the new Spitfire had become the thoroughbred.

Bill knew a storm was brewing. It was perfect flying weather – the Luftwaffe would make the most of this. He could imagine them on their way, taking to the skies in rows and rows of fighters and bombers. He had lost some good friends and some jolly good men. As he looked out of his open window the bees hummed and the birds twittered amongst the tree tops. Who would think they were in the thick of the war with the Luftwaffe? The Luftwaffe was beating them hands down - it was four to one in the sky. Bill absent-mindedly waved a lone bee away from his face which had flown in the window. He looked at his men, the few who now made up his squadron. They were all waiting for the signal. The sudden ring of the telephone with a voice at the end from Bomber Command who would tell them to immediately 'Scramble.'

There was Dicky, his best friend, who was pretending to read a book in the morning sunshine but was listening with half an ear for that ring of the telephone. Life was like that nowadays, you pretended to be relaxed and not care too much when all the time you were keyed up ready to spring into action. He and Dicky had joined up together, just before the outbreak of war, although the threat had been on the cards. They couldn't have foreseen what was going to happen. They were glad to sign up and looked forward to defending their country. And now – well, so many lives were lost, and so many of their friends were here one day and gone the next.

Then there was Sandy, which was the colour of his hair, a larrikin, always playing jokes on people. Tim, who was the youngest at nineteen, a mop of brown hair flopping over his face as he lounged in a chair and was reading a book called War and Peace. He was a clever lad and told his parents he wanted to fight the Germans, he didn't want to read English at Oxford. They weren't very happy about that.

'My parents are hoping I'll continue with my studies after the war's over,' Tim had told them.

'He'll be lucky if he lives that long,' Bill had told Dickie. Bill was twenty-four years old and felt like an old man. The truth was they were on a knife edge, any one of them could be gone at anytime.

Another thing, he didn't like the way Eddie and his sister were getting pally. Flying Officer Eddie Trenchard was also one of the original Dunkirk pilots, he was known as a 'Jack the Lad' and a 'Hooray Henry' and spent his spare hours in the evening drinking, socialising, and spending copious amounts of money. He came from a privileged background and was the same age as Bill and Dicky.

Eddie had gone home with Bill one day to Southampton when thick fog had stopped them from flying. Bill had taken Eddie home in his car. Bill had been a bit worried about bringing him to meet his family. Eddie could charm the birds down from the trees and Cherry had only been seventeen at the time. Eddie preferred to go home with Bill instead of going home to his family estate, where he said he wouldn't see anyone.

'Mater is always out doing some fundraising or some such thing'. He gave Bill some petrol vouchers (of which he seemed to have plenty) so Bill relented. His mother and his sister had succumbed to Eddie's charm as soon as Bill took him home. His mother was tickled pink when he flattered her straight away.

'Why, you didn't tell me this was your mother, Bill! Cora, you look like his sister.'

'Don't get pulled in by him Cherry!' he had told his sister, while he was flattering their mother. 'He's a pilot. So not marriage material.'

'Who wants to get married anyway?' Cherry said innocently, assuming her brother had meant her. 'There's too much to do for women with this war. Now's our chance to do more for our country.'

Bill saw evidence of Eddie's womanising with every female when the officers went to the pubs and clubs of London. A twenty-four-hour pass was difficult to obtain. Yet somehow, they managed it. When they managed to get to London, they spent their time drinking, dancing and flirting with the ladies. Pilots were very attractive in their uniforms and were free with their money. Their motto was live for today for tomorrow you could be dead.

Bill brought himself back to the present. The grass was yellow and dry, there was smoke coming from a bonfire somewhere. Bill sat in the shade with his chair. On the back two legs he leaned against the wall of the Dispersal hut, but within reach of the telephone to Bomber Command. His boots were hot, he had his flying jacket on. Billy, and Rob were playing chess together in their shirts, their flying jackets slung over the backs of their chairs. For some of them, it was too hot to wear them, but at 10,000 feet it was freezing. They pulled them on when the time to scramble had them running for their planes.

Bill looked over at two new recruits who had joined straight from university to replenish the squadron. They were kicking a football around. Other men were reading or dozing in the shade. The average of the squadron was twenty-one years of age.

Someone was listening to the wireless, it was the prime minister's voice broadcasting to the nation:

'The battle of France is over. I expect that the Battle of Britain is about to begin. Upon this battle depends the future of Christian civilisation…'

Someone shouted, 'Turn it up!'

Churchill's voice boomed out across the airfield. Everyone stopped and looked.

'Let us brace ourselves to our duties, and so bear ourselves that, if the British Empire and Commonwealth last for a thousand years, men will say, This was their finest hour.'

Suddenly the telephone rang, Bill's heart jumped. He looked at it and everyone seemed to hold their breath as he reached out for the receiver. Dicky sat up quickly looking at him with anticipation. Men stopped playing football and board games, whilst Bill with hands shaking, swiftly picked up the receiver.

'Dispersal,' he said crisply.

'Tea's up!' said a cheerful voice at the other end.

Bill replaced the receiver and realised he had broken out into a cold sweat.

'NAAFI's coming round with the tea,' he told the others mildly, trying to calm his heart rate down. He sat down heavily and heard the sighs of the rest of the pilots as they tried to relax again. How many more false alarms? How much longer could they carry on trying to remain ready to go up at a moment's notice and be ready to die? His eyes searched the clear blue cloudless sky, the temperature was climbing and it wasn't yet midday.

The hot clear summer days made it ideal weather for flying over the North Sea from Germany to England. More Heinkels, Stukas, and more Messerschmidts came over in swarms, their engines humming like hungry bees ready to bomb the British airfields and attack the merchant shipping bringing food and supplies from across the seas.

The hot days of August melted into September. Cherry joined the WAAF and left home for basic training at Duxford.

Meanwhile, Bill and his crew were fighting their own battle up in the skies above the airfield. Climbing rapidly to gain height, a gaggle of 109s came out of the sun making their way downwards towards the squadron who were trying to climb to gain the advantage. It was too late.

'Break!' Bill called over the com as soon as he saw them.

Aircraft scattered like fireworks. Diving to the left Bill found a Messerschmidt on his tail. He swayed right and left trying to shake off his pursuer. As he pulled up from a dive, he saw his number two and four go down to a barrage of bullet fire from the enemy. Archie lost his tail and was on fire as he disappeared downwards. Sam shed pieces of his Spitfire on the way down towards the sea. Then from out of the sun another Messerschmidt came straight at Bill. Even before he had time to manoeuvre Bill felt the hits on his aircraft. The Spitfire started to go into a dive. His instrument panel and fuel line were useless. Smoke was billowing behind him. He looked down and found blood oozing from his thigh. He suddenly found himself flying on his own in the clear blue sky. He realised he had been hit by shrapnel, there was blood coming from his shoulder too. But he was more bothered by the fact that he had seen two of his friends plummet to the sea below him. He tried to manoeuvre the stick so that he could see Archie and Sam's planes and see what had happened to them but the stick would not move. The plane started to go into a dive. He tried to pull back the cockpit roof - it was jammed. He had seconds to get out if he wanted to survive.

The sweat was running from Bill's face as he struggled with his canopy to try and free it. The seconds ticked away.

The 109 flew over him to ensure his kill. It was so close that in an instant Bill saw the planes painted on his fuselage with crosses through them. The enemy pilots' score.

CHAPTER 7 – October 1940

Cherry was halfway through her training in Duxford when she received a letter – it looked like Papa's handwriting. The nursing orderly recruits were living in an old RAF house near Duxford airfield and were going to and from Cambridge Hospital.

At last, a letter from home. Running upstairs to the room she shared with six others she sat down on her bed to read it. There was no one in the room which was a blessing because it was noisy when everyone was there.

She was enjoying her course and this week was learning about giving medical aid and caring for the sick and injured. She loved the training it was what she had always wanted. And she was happy. Her mother had written to her last month asking her to come home.

'You are needed more here - Because God's work starts at home,' her mother had written.

Cherry had scoffed at that. Not likely, she thought, I'm not being your slave. She knew she'd done the right thing leaving home. She was learning new skills all the time and developing a friendly camaraderie with young women her own age. She was learning how to treat people and deal with emergencies. In the evening the trainees were tired, because they seemed to be cramming so much information. The girls read over their notes in the evening, and asked each other questions ready for a test. At last, she felt she was learning something. She felt she was finally doing something for her country.

Cherry thought that the letter was from her mother, but this letter was in her father's handwriting. It was unusual for him to write unless it was something urgent. She ripped open the letter in haste. It was short but the words jumped out at her from the page.

'Sadly, your brother Bill...Missing in Action.' She drew in a sharp breath. She was shocked. Her brother had been an experienced pilot. She hadn't expected him to be shot down. But the sad truth was, the odds of surviving the Battle of Britain, as Churchill had called it, were small. Bill had gone missing in action over the English Channel. No one saw him bale out. No one was able to say what happened to him. The letter had taken three weeks to get to her from her father, and the sensor had opened it, read it, and resealed it, she could tell by the way it didn't stick and was crumpled.

Cherry read the letter and felt numb. Why hadn't her parents rung her on the telephone? They could have spoken to her CO and she would have passed the message on. She was upset to think they thought it wasn't worth calling her on the telephone straight away. She imagined that it was her mother's idea not to tell Cherry about her brother until later on. She started to become angry. For the rest of the day she simmered and fumed, blaming her mother for all the resentment she felt about the sad news.

After training had finished for that day she hurried to a telephone box, and rang her parent's telephone number. Mr Caldwell picked up the telephone on the third ring.

'Cherry! Are you all right?' his tone changed she had never rung them during the day before.

'Are you all right?'

'Father!' she almost shouted down the telephone. 'What induced you to write me a letter instead of telephoning and telling me about Bill?'

'Ah...you got my letter.'

'Yes. And it took three weeks to get to me!'

'Oh well if I'd known it was going to take that long we would have telephoned you.'

'You should have done that anyway Papa! I'm upset that I was the last one to find out about Bill.'

'I didn't know you were allowed to take personal calls,' he replied weakly.

'Pa, my brother may be dead. Of course I would be! You could've tried the CO here. You knew which hospital I was at, didn't you?' she tried not to shout at him as emotion overcame her. She tried to calm down, her father stuttered and stammered at the other end of the line. He only did that when he was upset.

'There was no other information, other than he'd gone down in the sea,' he said quickly. He heard his daughter's sobs at the other end. He tried to use calm words. 'There's not much information my dear.' Then he added quietly – 'Apparently, his effects and last wishes will come to you to sort out. Cherry stopped crying. 'Mother's not very happy about that,' he added.

'What? I bet she isn't.'

That made sense, Bill never could cope with his mother's histrionics whenever things went wrong. She decided to contact his CO as soon as she could.

She made her way back to her room in the Waafery she shared with her friends and told them the news. Her eyes were bright with fresh tears. How could her parents have waited to tell her about Bill? Why did they think her feelings didn't matter? And now her dear brother, who had been her hero, was gone.

'I can't believe he's gone. And for my family to not tell me for three weeks!'

'That's harsh.' They all agreed.

Several days passed, dry, sunny, balmy days. The hops were brought in the fields near her parents' house and the crops were harvested, but still, there was no more news of her brother, whether he'd been found or if he was dead. The family had to make do with 'Missing Presumed Dead' as an explanation, like many other families.

Hitler had turned his attention to London and German bombers were blitzing London, night after night. Fires were rampant and families were getting killed.

A telephone call to Eddie confirmed that no one had seen Bill bail out. Her heart felt heavy. What was she to do without big brother? He was the one person she could rely on in the family.

'Let's get together for a drink when you go home,' Eddie said. 'Let's toast Bill.'

'I'll ask for time off as soon as I can, we're in the middle of tests at the moment. It couldn't hurt, she thought, seeing him just as a friend. It would be nice to see a pilot's blue uniform again. He told her he would pick her up on the first Saturday afternoon in November and take her out for a drink.

Cherry completed her training and passed her tests with high marks. The women were allowed the weekend off but had to return back to the hospital and continue training until December. By the time November 1st came around she had almost forgotten she was supposed to meet up with Eddie on the first Saturday in November. She had been so absorbed in learning new skills that her mind was full of it when she caught the train home to Portsmouth on Friday evening. On Saturday morning she awoke and remembered she was meeting Eddie that afternoon. He was waiting outside their gate and he drove them to a pub in the countryside closer to London.

'I'm glad you didn't come into the house,' she said. 'My mother wouldn't let you go and we'd never get out. Especially seeing you in the RAF uniform, it would remind her of Bill.'

The pub was busy but full of civilians. It was late afternoon, and while most people were waiting for opening time around six o'clock on a Saturday evening, Eddie seemed to have found the only pub that was open all afternoon.

'I know how to get away from our lot,' Eddie said grinning. 'Sometimes it's just nice to get away from uniform.'

'Even though we're both wearing uniform.' She laughed and took a swig of her watery beer. 'You must know lots of pubs.'

'I do, it's what I'm good at,' he agreed and grinned. He'd managed to get some chairs outside just as the sun was getting low in the sky. He downed two pints of beer in quick succession. People were looking at them, but it wasn't her they were looking at in her grey-blue WAAF uniform, it was Eddie. He looked dashing. Looking at him across the small table he looked like Bill in his RAF cap and uniform. She swallowed, a lump in her throat.

'Are you all right m'dear?' Eddie asked, watching her face.

'Yes, thank you. You just remind me of Bill sitting there in your uniform.'

She tried to be more cheerful. Eddie had a tough enough job and she didn't want him to see her upset. They talked about where she might be sent when she'd finished her training. The time went surprisingly quickly. Eddie was interesting to talk to. He told her where the squadron had been flying and how they had the latest Supermarine Spitfires. They had a larger petrol tank, which let them fly further over France. They were fast and had more armaments, he was very confident that they were now stopping the invaders.

'But are they enough to stop the 109?' she sighed.

'I have to hand it to your brother, he taught you well – not just learning about the British planes but the German ones too.'

'I was more than interested. And I always want to learn more. He had patience with me.' She looked downcast remembering how Bill had taught her about the different aircraft he knew so that she could identify them in the sky.

'Cheer up ol' girl, don't look so depressed. I'm sure we'll stop the Hun from invading British shores.'

She tried to smile but the recent loss of her brother gave her a heavy heart. Eddie was sensitive to how she was feeling, which surprised her.

The bell sounded for last orders. They got up reluctantly and he said he had to report back to RAF Tangmere that night. As they went outside, they walked over to his car.

'I managed to stop the thieving British Army from pinching my Speedster.' He showed with pride the Ford model with a wave of his arms. 'But the bastards commandeered my father's Rolls!'

Cherry wasn't sure if he was joking and laughed.

'Are you driving back tonight?'

'Lovely evening. Full moon. It'll sober me up!'

Only Eddie would have a careless attitude about driving on narrow roads in the dark. There were no street lights and most of the countryside signposts had been removed in case German spies landed and were looking for directions.

'Keep your window down, so you don't fall asleep. And it's a good job it's not freezing yet,' she said and frowned at him. 'Should you really be driving?'

He laughed and planted a big sloppy kiss on her lips before she could turn her head. When they arrived back at her gate, he parked at the end of the drive.

'I won't take you to the front door,' he said, 'I want to talk to you.'

'No need, the walk will do me good,' she said relieved that they had got back from the pub without mishap. 'But you should be careful on the road back to Tangmere.'

'My dear girl, that's the least of my worries. I might get shot down tomorrow.' He laughed, then said more seriously. 'I really like you, Cherry. Let's do this again. I'll see if I can get a weekend pass soon, and we'll go up to London.'

'It must be about two hours to get back to base in the dark.'

'As long as I'm back for daybreak!' he laughed and got in his car, he revved the engine, and with a wave, he shot off with his red rear lights already fading in the distance. Cherry shook her head. He's mad, she thought. He's lucky to get petrol vouchers let alone a weekend pass. Going out with Eddie was like a whirlwind, it was a relief when he had left. She couldn't take a lot of his company. He was all right in short bursts. She sighed, she wished she had Bill to talk to. She walked slowly down the drive to her front door, glad of the peace of the mild evening. She stood outside and looked up at the stars, she didn't really want to go inside to talk to her parents, they would be asking her all sorts of questions about Eddie. So she went in quietly before they realised she had gone upstairs.

About a week later the Wing Commander at Tangmere wrote to Cherry asking her to come and collect Bill's personal effects. It was time. It was what Bill had wanted. Even so, she still hadn't expected it yet. Half of Bill's squadron had been killed in just a few days. She told her friends that it was the worst time in her life.

Cherry waited day after day hoping to hear that Bill had miraculously returned, after being rescued by a trawler, but no such thing happened. And as the days wore on, she resigned herself to the fact that her brother wasn't coming back. She wondered about Sidney, he was still away with the Navy but her parents hadn't heard from him either. But then Sid never wrote letters. In fact, her mother had only ever had one letter from him in the year he'd been away. She wondered if Sid had received her parents' letter about Bill missing in action.

Cherry had written to Rosie because she had promised and even though she had been busy studying, she was still waiting for a reply. She didn't know what her friend did in the WRNS, but she knew it was confidential, so she didn't ask. They had signed The Official Secrets Act on joining the RAF and she knew it was wrong to talk about others' work in the military.

When she came to pick up Bill's personal effects, she borrowed her father's car and parked outside the main gate. As she walked past the bombed-out WAAF building on her right, she remembered the base had been in a raid the previous week. Men were hauling up a temporary demountable to replace the damaged building. She hadn't realised the Waafery had been hit and worried if anyone had been hurt. It wasn't just the pilots and ground crew who were in danger from enemy aircraft around Britain. It was the women in uniform too.

When she knocked on the door, she expected the Wing Commander to be older, but he was surprisingly younger than she anticipated and he probably wasn't much older than Bill. But then young men didn't live very long these days, she thought. He had been brought in from another group, he said, as there'd been no one with experience to take over in the squadron. No, he hadn't known Bill. He handed over Bill's personal effects in a box, it was sealed with a band. She would return it to mother once she was able to go home, she'd try next weekend, she said. Her heart was heavy. She didn't know what to say next. A sob caught in her throat. She tried to pull herself together, as she fingered his spare cap badge and his special ink pen with which he always wrote his letters. And there were some letters to the family. Her bottom lip trembled. She didn't want to cry in front of this Wing Commander who was telling her how her brother was admired and looked up to by his comrades. He looked at her sympathetically, which she hated, it made her feel sad all the more. He left her for a few moments in his outer office where thankfully no one was present, and he drew her attention to a letter specifically for her. Cherry knew she had to read it.

Seeing his handwriting brought back memories and she tried not to cry.

'Dear Cherry, you will be reading this because I've copped it - my luck ran out. I've given instructions for you to be the person to deal with my things. It's up to you what you do with them. Why? Because you've always been so sensitive about people's feelings and I know you will be sensible. Give Mother my bible it's signed by me. Papa my cigarette holder (I never had time to use it) and cufflinks. Sid can have my spare boots and if there's any posthumous medals going for me...you can have them.

Oh, by the way, do NOT marry Eddie Trenchard. He's keen on you, and I've told him to leave you alone. Of course, he'll do exactly as he likes, he always has. Don't grieve Sis, live your life, and don't let Mother tell you what to do. In fact, don't let anybody tell you what to do!

Love always, your brother, Bill

How typical of Bill, flippant but to the point. It gave her lots to think about.

Coming out of the office Cherry looked across the field towards Dispersal where Bill and his crew had waited day after day during the relentless hot days of summer waiting for the call to scramble. It was autumnal weather now, but still warm during the day. RAF airfields all over Britain were a lot quieter, because the Luftwaffe had changed their minds about bombing RAF stations and had directed their planes over the capital, and now a 'Blitz' was happening night after night.

Cherry was in two minds about going over to see Eddie, after what Bill had written about him. But she heard Eddie's voice before she saw him. She looked over to where he was talking to a mechanic. He was walking with his back to her towards Dispersal, she thought she'd better go and say hello. He turned and saw her walking over to him. He waved. 'Been to see the Wing Commander?' He seemed to know all that was going on. She nodded.

'Where is everyone?' she asked. He kissed her on the cheek, she felt guilty as if everyone on the field were watching them, so she turned away, embarrassed.

'Gone to the hereafter or moved on.' He waved his hands in the air. 'Dicky has been diverted to some remote place in Yorkshire to be put in charge of a squadron!'

'Gosh, why's that?'

'Didn't want to take over here, nor do I. So no one with any experience is in charge. And the CO had copped it like ours did. Sorry.' He then said realising he'd mentioned her brother.

Cherry's heart missed a beat. 'Oh.'

'I've missed you, Bill's sister.' He led her over to seats under the big oak tree. 'I think it's going to rain soon.' The clouds were building up overhead, and some of the men went inside Dispersal.

'Yesterday it pissed it down,' he said. 'Oops sorry.' But then carried on. 'We managed to get up once, even though it was for training. The weather's not our friend this month.'

Eddie kicked out a fresh-faced recruit from the seat next to him, and one of the young pilots jumped up next to him and offered her his seat. The chairs were weathered and sagging, a bit like the tired pilots who sat in them. It was very different to when they had sat in the same place last time she was here. That was before she'd started her basic training. Cherry gasped, the boy looked about eighteen years old. Eddie took her hand to help her into the sagging seat. She slipped her hand out of his, feeling self-conscious. Typical

Eddie, he was putting on a show for the others. But she couldn't help feeling fond of him and sad all at the same time. She knew that all the boys were on borrowed time. He smiled as some of the new recruits gawped at her as she sat down carefully on the rickety seat.

'This is Cherry, our belated boss's sister.' He introduced her.

Cherry's cheeks went pink. But although they smiled and murmured hellos, the mood was nostalgic, and she remembered it wasn't that long ago she had been waiting for Bill's Spitfire to land.

'Pity that coin didn't protect him,' she muttered to Eddie, as only he would understand.

'Pity,' he agreed, lighting his pipe.

'I didn't know you smoked a pipe.'

'I don't think cigarettes are good for you. I hear they shorten your life,' he said quite loudly so that the others could hear. There were some muffled guffaws from amongst the men.

'Only a man smokes a pipe.' He winked at Cherry. Looking around at the new squadron Cherry was shocked by the young fresh faces of the new recruits. She looked around and didn't recognise anyone.

'Most of them look a lot younger than their predecessors,' she spoke softly to him so she wasn't overheard.

'That's because they are younger. No more than babes in arms,' he said quietly between puffing on his pipe. The smell of pipe smoke will always remind me of this moment, she thought to herself. I wonder how many more of these young men will be killed before I see Eddie again.

They sat next to each other under the oak tree's canopy while Cherry observed the new pilots. He followed her eyes as she looked at the recruits.

'That's Ted. He's only had five hours experience.' Eddie pointed to where he was playing Draughts with another young man under a canopy.

'My goodness Eddie, they don't look much older than me!'

'They're twenty, I think. I feel like an old man and I'm only twenty-five.'

Cherry scanned the men's faces. 'Sam?'

'Shot down. Missing...'

'Robert?'

'Drafted to another squadron. The squadrons about Britain are in short supply for experienced pilots.'

'Tim?'

'Went down in a ball of flames last week.'

'Oh my God.'

'Sandy bailed out last week, but we haven't seen him since. We assume he's lost at sea.'

'Missing in Action. Like Bill.'

He puffed on his pipe, thoughtfully. When she had first known him, over a year ago, he appeared to have a careless attitude to life, but Cherry thought he looked haggard and tired, now she knew him better, it was a front he put on to protect himself from the pain of losing friends and comrades.

'Lots of new faces.'

'Certainly are. Most don't have enough experience or flying hours.'

'Good grief.'

'Precisely.'

'It's very quiet.'

'We must be grateful for small mercies.'

'What do *you* think's happening over the other side of the Channel Eddie?'

'Well, we think Hitler is giving up on his invasion of Britain and is appearing to turn his attention to the East.'

'But they're bombing London now.'

'They're trying to break the British spirit.'

'Well, that won't happen!' she said indignantly. 'When our backs are against the wall we fight back!'

'Trouble is,' he said, 'we're on our own. The Krauts had us by the short and curlies until recently. Pardon my expression.' He said looking at her embarrassed face. 'At least we're able to draw breath and get some recruits in some flying hours. We have new Spits turning up. The Hurries are dead on their feet. They've really done the majority of the defences.'

Just as he said that two Spitfires landed clumsily on the tarmac one after the other.

'They're practising circuits and bumps,' he explained.

'I know. I've seen them practice before.' She nodded. 'I would love to fly a Spitfire,' she told him.

'So would the Luftwaffe,' he responded drily. 'Their Messerschmidts are too lumpy. And they've withdrawn the Stukas for nighttime flights. I'm assuming that Goering is none too happy with his famous Luftwaffe. They don't seem to have come up to scratch.'

Cherry nodded. As usual, Eddie had put it succinctly.

'Are you staying for tea?'

'That would be nice.'

'Well, we'll have to make a night of it at the Crown and Anchor then, won't we?' And he winked at her.

'I'm not sure I can stay that long. I borrowed transport and I'll be in trouble if I don't get it back by nightfall.

'That's not until ten. Anyway, I want to ask you something.'

The light started to fade and everyone left the field, flying was done for the day. When they were ensconced in the pub she sat waiting patiently, almost sure he was going to ask her to get engaged. Her brother had warned her off him, hadn't he? She liked him a lot. But enough to marry him? Pilots were here one day and gone the next.

Sitting opposite her at the small table he plonked a pint of beer in front of her.

'Goodness, I can't drink all that Eddie, I'll be sozzled!'

Eddie smiled. 'That's the idea. I want you to marry me,' he said matter of factly as he sat down. His smile did not fade as she stared at him, he had come straight out and asked her. Well, Bill had warned her but she hadn't taken him seriously.

'I suppose I guessed you were going to ask that. But do we really feel enough for each other?' she asked with sad eyes. 'I need to be in love to marry someone.'

'I'm mad for you,' he countered, taking her hand and kissing her knuckles. 'I could be dead tomorrow.'

'That's what I mean. What's the point of getting married when tomorrow I could be a widow.'

'If there's one thing I've learned,' he said taking a swig of beer, with his left hand, but still holding her right. 'You have to live for today.'

'I don't know. What if you get killed?'

Eddie stared at the top of her head as if realising for the first time it could be a possibility.

'Well, you would have all my worldly goods. My family's not short of a bob or two.'

'That's not really the point, is it?' She said slightly frustrated. How typical of Eddie, only thinking of himself. 'I don't fancy being a widow at nineteen. Anyway, I always wanted to join up, and now I have, I don't want to give up my independent life.'

'Why would you want to continue?'

'I knew you'd say that. The upper echelons in the RAF will want us WAAFs to give up our jobs and keep the home fires burning when the men want their jobs back. I would be encouraged to leave. Marriage and the armed forces don't mix. That's what my Papa told me.'

'That's old fashioned.'

'Maybe. But it's what people think.'

Eddie looked at her as if seeing her anew. His face held a small series of shocks in her defiance of refusing him. She could tell he hadn't expected it.

'I expected you to refuse at first. Isn't that what all young ladies do?' He said, smiling again. ''I won't take no for an answer.'

'You don't give up, do you?' Cherry was getting exasperated. 'I don't want to get married. I'm too young.'

'Live life for today. For tomorrow we die.' he grinned not a bit perturbed by her refusal.

'Look, Eddie, I'm sorry. But I don't want to tie myself down.'

'That's what I *used* to say to your brother!'

'What's he got to do with it?'

'I said I was going to ask you. Hell! I'll probably be dead next week. Who's going to mourn me?'

'Your parents? And of course, I will,' she said hastily. But that seemed to fall on deaf ears. He continued. 'He said you'd say no.'

'He was right. Anyway, when did you talk to Bill about me?' She held her breath.

'The morning of his last flight. Yes, that's it. We were discussing you that morning before the balloon went up.'

She frowned, she didn't like that Eddie casually talked about her to her brother. Especially as she knew he had tried to put her off him. Eddie was selfish and had usually got what he wanted, she thought.

'Why did you talk to Bill about me?' her eyes were sparkling now with the mention of Bill.

Eddie lit his pipe and puffed until a cloud of smoke filled the void between them.

'Oh, I thought I'd run it past him, see if he thought it was a good idea.'

'And I'm betting he didn't.'

'Absolutely he didn't.'

'And you decided to go ahead and ask me anyway?'

'Of course! It was the decider. Especially as he disapproved!' And a grin spread across his face as he looked at her across the table. She couldn't help smiling back. He is really annoying, she thought, as she tried to remain calm. Eddie was like a child. And like her mother, he had decided not to take her seriously.

'No thanks, Eddie. Friends, yes. But not marriage.'

Eddie shrugged his shoulders, 'Oh well, I had to ask.'

'Not really Eddie.'

'You might go and marry the first chap who you fancy.'

'Hardly. Anyway, I've only just joined the WAAF. I don't want my life to end when it's only just beginning.'

'Some women's object in life is to get married, have children and look after her man when he's back from war. I would have thought you were like that.'

'Really? I'm not sure whether to laugh or act insulted.'

'Why would you be?'

'It's not everyone's wish to be married. Certainly not mine.'

'Why ever not?'

'Oh, really Eddie, why would I want to give up my exciting life, it's only just beginning now I've joined the WAAF.'

'Well, I don't see what's wrong with that. You'd have a nice life. Rearing our children while I'm flying Spits.'

She looked at his face to see if he was joking. His face was straight and deadly serious. But she couldn't tell. There was a little quirk at the corner of his mouth. Some lines crinkled at the corner of his eyes. She was so annoyed with him. She didn't know what to say. He had been teasing her. His face broke into smiles. Her eyes went to the ceiling. Really, men!

CHAPTER 8 -Christmas 1940

The Supermarine factory in Southampton was manufacturing Spitfires and churning out forty a month. Unfortunately, the Luftwaffe found out about it and it was targeted several times and heavily bombed on September 24th and 26th. The firestorm flames were seen as far as Cherbourg in Northern France. Portsmouth close to Southampton was also a strategic bombing target for the Luftwaffe as it contained both busy docks and factories. As a large port off the south coast, it was within easy reach of German airfields in France. During the day the RAF tried to intercept the Luftwaffe from targeting the major cities and ports but when night fell England was vulnerable to attack. Britain had no long-range bombers to counterattack Berlin. The RAF was unable to fly at night and Britain was virtually helpless.

At the beginning of the Blitz in September 1940 British anti-aircraft gunners were unable to prevent the Blitz. Thousands lost their lives. But radar improved and ground defences and radar stations, which were bombed by the Luftwaffe were fixed within 24 hours.

In November and December Southampton and Portsmouth were suffering their own Blitz. The ARP warden's main tasks were to protect people during air raids when enemy planes dropped bombs on the city. Mr Caldwell and his team were kept busy rescuing people from bombed houses night after night, and helping to put out homes that were on fire. He directed people to underground shelters that had been built recently, but mostly people sheltered in their own Anderson shelter in the garden.

The raids at the end of November and the beginning of December 1940 were by far the worst. They started at night and ran through until the next evening. Hundreds were killed and injured. The raid ruined the city's water supply and many of the fires had to be left to burn themselves out.

Winston Churchill kept the country motivated and he would hear no talk of peace with Hitler. 'He will have to break us to win the war,' he told the British nation. The British spirit was indomitable - they weren't giving in to Hitler without a fight.

Mr Caldwell wrote to Cherry to cheer her up and keep her motivated after Bill's death. There were days when he wasn't feeling the best, he wished he had his daughter home to help him.

'Mrs Proud's daughter came home from training before she was sent to her first station in

Southampton. She is in the WRNS and she came around and showed us her uniform yesterday. I told her you had joined the WAAF and she was most impressed. At last, women are allowed to do their bit for our country. I couldn't agree more. I'm so pleased that you decided to join up. It wouldn't be much fun for you to continue to live here. Even though I do miss you and especially your help during the air raids.

It looks like the government is making it compulsory for single women to join one of the women's services, or they have to go to work in a factory. Meanwhile, your mother has told me she's writing to you to get you to change your mind and come home. I have tried to tell her - you have signed The Official Secrets Act and cannot come home. You have to do your duty. She is adamant she will write to you to come home. What I would say, my dear, is take no notice....'

Oh dear, Papa, she thought, if you'd stood your ground first of all, we wouldn't be talking about this now. It was too late for her dear Papa, he just wanted an easier life. His job is traumatic enough as a warden, she thought, no wonder he stays out all night to keep away from mother.

Out of the ten girls on her medical training, she alone was drafted to RAF Finsham. She was sad to leave her new friends but hoped they'd meet up again. Finsham was a new RAF station in the middle of the flat countryside of Norfolk. She was allowed leave to go home to Portsmouth for three days over Christmas. She had three days to get home and see her parents then after Christmas she was to get herself to RAF Finsham on the train.

Cherry didn't expect to hear from Eddie again, but he wrote to her telling her they were being sent to RAF Wittering to be rested back for the winter.

'The Luftwaffe seemed to have taken time off for a holiday because they haven't been around for ages. Meanwhile, London gets bombed to bits night after night...

She wrote back to him. *'I'm glad we can still be friends. I'll keep writing to you if you like...'*

He wrote back two weeks later asking her to get engaged again.

She wrote back and refused.

'What do I have to do to convince you to marry me?' he wrote in big letters across the page.

She didn't write back. That was it. Let sleeping dogs lie, she thought. Two weeks later another letter arrived for her.

'Bill would've wanted us to get engaged,' he wrote.

No, he wouldn't. She thought. How little he understands me, and how soon he forgets.

On Christmas Eve, Cherry arrived back home, and her father met her at the train station. It had been a frosty day, the condensation making the evening streets sizzle and shimmer in front of them. It was only four-thirty and it was already dark.

Cherry thought he looked tired. 'How are you, Papa? He picked up her bag and she took it off him. 'I can carry this. I'm used to it. You look tired. Are you still out in all weathers?' She hugged him. 'I've only got three days.'

'I'm all right,' he said. 'You look as if you've lost a bit of weight.'

'They feed us all right,' she told him. 'But if we're not training, we're on the parade ground, marching, marching, which is a bit of a pain. It was all right at first but now the novelty's worn off. And it's colder.' She grimaced. Mr Caldwell laughed, 'Is the shine of the RAF getting a bit dull now?'

'Absolutely not. I'm having a great time. I mean I'm making lots of friends, and because we're all in this together, the camaraderie is really good. We all help each other. There's no reason for Hitler to win this war now.'

'That's my girl,' he chuckled as they walked up the driveway to the house. 'Fighting spirit!' He had a torch to show the way up the path because there were no street lights. She had forgotten how dark the houses were at night here, with all the blackout curtains and boarded-up windows. It looked depressing. The houses at the end of her parent's street were a mound of rubble.

'Oh no, did the people get out?'

'Yes. They were in their Anderson shelter. The house the other side of the street though, the Andrews family...that was a different story.'

'Oh no. They had two small children, didn't they?'

'Eight and ten. I dug their bodies out.'

'Oh Papa,' she put an arm around his shoulders as they stood on the doorstep. 'How awful for you.' She alone knew how terrible it was to bring the dead bodies of people you knew, from out of the rubble.

She braced herself. 'Well here goes. I've gotten used to nice people. It'll take some guts to not answer back to mother.'

'Do your best,' he said. They went inside quickly and shut the door. A light was coming from the dining room.

'I've got to travel up to RAF Finsham the day after Boxing Day.'

'It's not on the map. Perhaps you can show me where it is, after dinner.'

'Well, Finsham won't be. It's new by all accounts. One of these newly built RAF stations to put their new aircraft in. It's a shorter route from Norfolk to Germany from that airfield,' she said. 'So, I expect I'll see lots of Spitfires and bombers.'

'We've had no bombers over since the bad weather set in. But you can bet Jerry is waiting to hit us just as soon as they've finished with London's East End.'

As it happened the Germans hadn't finished with Southampton and enemy bombers came over on Christmas Day. She went out with her father at midday after the air raid sirens sounded but the Luftwaffe flew over and missed Portsmouth completely, dropping their bombs on Southampton in the distance. They heard the bombing and went back home.

'That's given you a reprieve Papa.'

'Yes, they must have decided to give me a day off,' he smiled. 'Although the day's not yet over,' Mrs Caldwell called from the kitchen. 'We've said that before, haven't we?'

Cherry could hear her mother tutting in the kitchen. They went in and stood in the doorway. Mrs Caldwell ignored Cherry as she stood there in her WAAF uniform. She was cooking meat and making anxious noises.

'Anything we can help you with dear?' her father called.

'Can I help mother?' Cherry asked.

'Too late,' came the reply from the kitchen.

It was midday on Saturday and Cherry was explaining what her badges meant on her uniform to Tommy, as they sat in the living room waiting for dinner. She looked for her father, he was setting the table in the dining room for four people.

'You don't need to set the table in there,' Mrs Caldwell called to him from the kitchen. 'We'll eat at the kitchen table. It's only Cherry,' she added.

'No. I'm setting the table in here. Just because we *have* our daughter home with us.' And her father winked at her as he said it.

Cherry raised her eyebrows. Goodness! Her father was contradicting her mother. That was a first!

There followed a lot of puffing and panting as her mother went back and forth to the kitchen bringing in the food.

'I'll help you, Mother,' she said. And her father also went to help her.

'No need,' she snapped. 'I've done it now.' Mrs Caldwell plonked herself down with a huff. Cherry immediately felt guilty because she'd been having a nice tete-a-tete with her father. But remembering what Bill had written in his letter about her being sensitive, she decided to ignore the noises her mother was making.

The meal proceeded in silence. Until Tommy sitting opposite Cherry blurted out.

'Have you shot any Germans yet?'

'No, I haven't Tommy. Germans don't tend to parachute onto enemy airfields. Anyway, if any had come down by parachute they would have been forked by the farmers in the field.'

'That happened to us, over there!' He pointed in the direction where their garden met the fields.

They were looking out of the window. Her father had removed the shutters and pulled back the curtains to let the light in and lift the mood. Cherry talked cheerily about her training and the friends she'd made. Her mother sat despondent eating her dinner slowly. Even her father made a comment to his wife. 'Come on dear, it's Christmas Day and we have a lot to be thankful for.'

By one o'clock Cherry was thoroughly fed up. The plates lay empty in the kitchen. She and Papa had brought the plates in to wash up. The afternoon sky was pale and misty, the sun tried to peep through the clouds. The forecast was set to rain on Christmas Day. The air was cold and the trees dripped with condensation. Behind were green misty fields as far as the eye could see but beyond those fields was Southampton, and Cherry sat in thoughtful contemplation of how many times they had watched enemy aircraft fly over ready to drop bombs.

'Last week,' her father added. 'We saw a German parachute from his aircraft when it was shot up. The police were on him within minutes. We watched the parachute come slowly down and we were ready for him when he landed, he was terrified...' he didn't get any further.

'I was gonna shoot him. I was!' Tommy shouted excitedly.

'He was Czech, Tommy. He was on our side!' Father reminded him. 'He might sound like a German, but he isn't.'

Tommy looked out of the window and pointed. 'Right out there it was!'

Cherry looked at both of them. It wasn't like her father to snap at his children, he looked pale and tired.

Cherry followed her mother into the kitchen.

'Is Papa all right? He looks very tired.'

'We all are Cherry. We all are.' Her mother said. 'Oh, there's a letter for you from Rosie.'

'How do you know it's Rosie?' Cherry asked.

'I can tell her writing.' Her mother answered quickly.

'Have you opened it?' Cherry demanded.

'Of course not. Anyway, you shouldn't be keeping secrets from your mother. It's not ladylike.'

'What utter tosh Mother. You just want to nose into my business. It has nothing to do with you what Rosie tells me.'

'Cherry!' her father reminded her. 'Don't answer back to your mother.'

'Oh, for goodness' sake. Really? I'm not ten years old anymore. I'm a grown woman, I have to make life and death decisions daily.'

Cherry caught a sideways glance from her mother, as she turned away to get the letter. It was on the shelf behind two other envelopes.

'How was I supposed to see that if you hid it behind them?' she asked irritably.

Her mother shrugged her shoulders. It was obvious someone had tried to steam the letter open and then ripped it and stuck it down. Cherry was fuming inside but trying to keep calm for the sake of peace. Her father was looking confused.

'There are some tinned peaches, we've saved as a special treat for Christmas, would you like some?' He asked. She nodded.

'I helped to revive an injured crewman last week,' she said in between mouthfuls. 'After two enemy planes strafed the parade ground. It was a shock when they zoomed in low, and narrowly missed the aircraft that were outside the hangar.'

'I expect you have to be careful at all times out in the open. You just don't know when the enemy is going to fly under the radar,' her father said with a frown. 'You'd better be careful Cherry, until we've got rid of the Luftwaffe from our doorstep.'

Mrs Caldwell scoffed. 'Ha, when will that be?'

Her father stopped his spoon halfway to his mouth and frowned as if picturing it. 'No need to be sarcastic Cora, we need to nip that kind of negativity in the bud. It doesn't do our servicemen and women any good.'

Cherry's eyebrows shot up and she stared at her mother and father for a moment. She hadn't ever heard her father admonish her mother. She was stuck for words.

'Were they shot to bits?' Tommy shouted excitedly making her jump. 'Did you see lots of blood?'

'Tommy!' shouted Mrs Caldwell at him. 'Now look what you've done,' she turned on Cherry. 'He's never going to let this go.'

Mr Caldwell frowned looking at his wife. 'That's Tommy being silly. Tommy don't be so bloodthirsty. War is not a game. People get killed.'

Tommy looked at his father with surprise. Mr Caldwell tried to change the subject.

'I heard the dockyards took another hit, another ship in the harbour bought it - not sure which one,' he said to Cherry.

'How is Sid?' Cherry asked, putting her letter in her pocket. She had forgotten Tommy's ability to dramatize everything. He really needed a dose of reality to calm him down. But the next minute she felt guilty, he was still only a child. It wouldn't be long before war was not the exciting adventure he thought it was.

'We haven't heard from him. We don't know where he is.' Mr Caldwell shrugged his shoulders. Sidney had only ever written one letter to his mother whilst in training. Meanwhile, she had written several to him. Cherry had written to him but she knew how lazy Sid was, she didn't expect anything from him. Sid was different to Bill. Sid was in the Royal Navy, but they weren't sure where and in which ocean, but she knew he wasn't allowed to tell them.

'God knows where Sidney is!' Mrs Caldwell threw up her hands dramatically as if it was the last straw.

'Now dear, I'm sure Sidney is all right,' said Mr Caldwell. 'No news is good news.'

His wife glowered at him, pinning her hair back up into a bun.

'Papa's right. Sid was never one for writing letters.'

'I told him to write,' her mother started to get emotional. 'Now Bill's gone...' and she got up quickly into the kitchen sniffling into a handkerchief.

Her father scratched his head. He had tried to keep a pleasant atmosphere, but his wife had deteriorated into tears again. Cherry had tried her best not to be drawn into an argument with her mother, and she realised seeing her in uniform may have brought back memories of Bill. But it was hard for Cherry, she had really only come home to see her Papa, she had missed him.

She spoke to her father to distract him from her mother crying in the kitchen. He looked anxious as if he should go to her.

'Good job you kept up your allotment Papa. You still have plenty of greens to feed the family?' she said loudly to drown her mother crying in the kitchen. She tried to ignore her, it had happened so many times before.

'Yes. At the moment not much. Just some cabbage left. Enough to keep the family in greens until the frosts,' he said, glad to have a diversion and tried to speak louder above the noise in the kitchen.

Tommy groaned, 'I hate cabbage!' he shrivelled up his nose and stuck his tongue out.

'There's not much fresh food to be had these days. Or meat. Food's in short supply. Our ships being bombed by U-boats don't help.' he grimaced. 'How is it where you are?' he asked her tentatively. Families weren't supposed to ask questions because people were worried there were spies everywhere. 'I would imagine the RAF feeds you well.'

'It's all right. It's not like home cooking though,' she added trying to be diplomatic, as her mother came back into the dining room, and wiped her eyes on her handkerchief. She sat down at the table, not looking at either of them.

'What do you do?' Tommy asked her.

'I'm a medical orderly.' She started to tell him what her job involved, but within seconds he'd lost interest and went to play with his toy soldiers.

'But a woman's job is not as important as a man's job, is it? Like Bill's job as a pilot? Stopping the enemy from dropping bombs. His commander said he had done a fierce job. He may get a medal.' She said proudly.

There was a silence.

'A posthumous medal,' she added and sniffed so loudly, that Cherry found her jaws aching from gritting her teeth.

'Do you still see Eddie?' her father asked her.

'Sometimes. His squadron got 'pulled back' to rest at RAF Wittering.'

Her Papa would always be sympathetic.

'Goodness knows they need a rest.'

'Eddie?' her mother picked up the name immediately. 'Wasn't that the young man Bill brought back last summer?'

'Yes.'

'Well, I wouldn't have thought it's a good idea seeing someone whose life is on the line daily. He may not....'

'Cora!' her husband interrupted. And she did not finish her sentence.

Tommy's face shot up from his food. He didn't want to miss any row starting off. 'I'm going into the army!' he said, using his knife as a gun. 'I'm going to shoot all the Nazis dead!'

'No, you're not!' said Mrs Caldwell to him, giving him a slap across the head. 'And eat your dinner. That meat cost me two weeks' rations.'

Her father raised his eyes to the ceiling so that only his daughter could see.

‘The Hun have turned their attention from the airfields to blitzing the cities. We’ve had several raids since you were last here,’ he said.

‘How are things with you, Papa? You look tired.’

‘Oh, I’m fine. I have to be, don’t I? He grimaced. A stab of doubt crossed her mind as she looked at him concerned. His eyes had dark circles around them.

‘You’re doing too much again, aren’t you? You don’t look well.’

‘Oh, I’m all right. Same as everybody else. We all have to keep going, don’t we?’ And he got up and helped his wife clear the table, she suspected it was to divert her attention from talking about his health.

Tommy pretended his spoon was a gun and made suitable bombing and splashing noises. Cherry made an excuse to pop upstairs after helping to wash and dry up, she went to her old bedroom to read her letter. Rosie wrote her letters like she talked, very quickly.

Dear Cherry, I came home in September for a weekend and came to your house to ask your mother where you’re stationed. I knew you’d gone training somewhere, but I lost your letter. You know what an empty head I am!

She didn’t know where you were. I knew it was somewhere in England! Because as I was leaving an RAF chappie came up your garden path. He had a lovely American drawl. He said he was in Eagle Squadron and looking for you. I told him you had joined the WAAFs and had gone away to training. I couldn't tell him where in England you were.

I must admit it seemed strange. My mother knows where I work but not exactly what I do. We have signed the Official Secrets Act after all. Pity your Papa wasn't there. He would have known. I know your mother doesn't like Americans, but she really did treat him like a leper! I felt so sorry for him, his face was crestfallen. He'd come a long way. He is moving around England a fair bit and is unable to leave a telephone number. Anyway, he's been at RAF Kirton in Lindsay in Yorkshire and is now, by the time you get this letter, somewhere in Lincolnshire. Church something.....

I walked with him up the street. He said he'd rung twice and tried to ask your mother where you are. It sounds like your mother didn't want him to find out. And she didn't sound convincing. He gave up, poor thing. So I told him to write to me and I would find out your address –I remember now...that's it Church Fenton! RAF Church Fenton because he's in with the RAF. He was not sure for how long. Surely if you put Eagle Squadron and RAF Church Fenton it'll get to him?

Cherry couldn't believe what she was reading. That Joe had been trying to contact her and her mother turned him away? Her cheeks turned pink. She felt the anger rising in her chest.

Anyway, he took me out for a meal and was jolly glad I think to have someone to go out with. He wasn't very happy that he'd wasted his time again, trying to get in touch. We went out into London yesterday and had a great time. You owe me one kiddo! I had to placate him and show him Portsmouth of course, he was quite angry with your mother.

It went on for another page but she didn't read it. Slamming down the letter on the bed. She stormed downstairs. She was furious.

'Mother!' Her mother was sitting in the lounge where Cherry and Joe had sat. She didn't look up from her book. This made Cherry even more angry because she knew her mother had hung onto this letter as long as she could, it was obvious to everyone she didn't like Americans.

'Why did you send Joe packing? How rude of you to tell him you didn't know where I was and why didn't you give him my address? Why?'

Her father put the newspaper down he was reading and looked at his wife from the sofa. His ears were going pink.

'I don't know why you're making so much fuss. No good would come of you chasing an American.'

'And you Papa! How could you encourage her to do this?'

'I don't know what hap....'

'Don't give me that excuse every time. You're just as responsible for sending him away even if you ignored what went on. You certainly didn't help!'

She turned back to her mother.

'It makes my blood boil to see you interfering in my life, you had no right to send him away without telling him where I was! And no, I'm not engaged. For your information Bill told me not to accept him, Eddie's a philanderer for one thing...'

Her father made a noise from the sofa. 'Well Cora, if I knew Bill had said that, of course I would...'

But Cherry didn't let her father finish.

'I can't believe you both went against him just because he's an American! He's over here to help us fight Hitler, and the Luftwaffe. I can't believe you're both so mean-spirited!' By now Cherry's face was red, Mr Caldwell looked remorseful. Mrs Caldwell didn't move. But Cherry still wasn't finished.

'And, he helped put the fires out the first night he was here. And Bill asked him to come by and introduce himself! So much for handing an olive branch to our American cousins!'

At the mention of Bill's name, Mrs Caldwell looked up.

'If you'd told me about Eddie in the first place, I would know what was happening in your life wouldn't I? You didn't tell me you liked Joe otherwise I might not have sent him away.'

'I told Papa about Eddie because I know he can keep a secret. Although he obviously can't because he told you. And I'm not engaged to him. And never will be. You shouldn't have sent Joe away. You call yourself a Christian, how is that being a Christian?' Her mother blushed showing the first sign of guilt.

'You never tell us what you're doing...'

'That's because I don't trust you, and quite rightly! Look how you hide my letters and open them and seal them up again. I don't trust either of you!' She was so angry she didn't know what to do. She burst into tears, turned on her heel, and ran back upstairs, leaving her parents to look at each other.

When she'd calmed down a bit she wondered where she could start to rectify the awful hole she felt in her stomach. So, Joe had tried to contact her again, and her mother wouldn't even tell him where she was. It wasn't as if it was a state secret. And as for Rosie, well, she turned out to be no special friend at all. But then she had only met Joe once so it wasn't as if she was engaged to him. She realised the thought of him trying to find her again made her happy, it sounded like he was still keen. She decided to write to him at RAF Church Fenton and see what happened.

Cherry sat up in bed, she hadn't taken off her stockings. She was still so angry at her mother and father that she left her parents on their own that evening. She decided to pack her bag and leave early tomorrow.

Later, Cherry came downstairs with her bag ready to leave. Her mother was on her own in the living room. She stood awkwardly at the door not sure what to say.

Mrs Caldwell was bent over the settee her head in her hands looking up at the telegram that was on the mantlepiece in the dining room. It was the one that informed her that Bill was missing. Cherry rubbed her palms together and was about to come into the room when Mrs Caldwell dried her eyes on her pinafore and swung round to see Cherry in the doorway. She gasped as if seeing her was a shock.

'I don't know what you're gawping at!' Mrs Caldwell exclaimed. 'It's not all about you, you know.'

Cherry blurted out; 'For goodness' sake Mother, can't you for once think about how others are feeling instead of yourself?'

'You always think it's about you, don't you?' her mother said nastily. 'Even your father talks about you more often than Sidney. Why do people always want to know about *you*?' she exclaimed tearfully. 'Especially when you were responsible for your sister's accident,' she added and turned her back on her daughter. But Cherry had heard her comments.

'So that's what this is about?' Cherry answered calmly. 'Well, I'm sorry you don't like it. It's a shame you blame me for Cecily's accident. And yes, it was an accident, and neither of us could swim. But where were you and Papa? We were only small, I just don't remember how we got to the river.'

Her mother turned and stared out of the window, her mouth turned down at the edges. She resolutely decided not to say anything.

'You can't blame me for all your woes. And I won't accept that I'm to blame for my sister's death, because you and Papa should have been looking after us. You can't keep blaming me all the time for Cecily's accident.'

Her mother remained silent and continued to stare out into the garden. It was a gloomy afternoon, and the fog seemed to be slowly returning. Cherry hated dismal afternoons like this. But she wasn't going to leave without saying how she felt. No more tears and ringing of hands. Events recently had been teaching her to speak her mind, life was too short to beat around the bush.

'Nothing will bring her back and you can't blame me for the rest of your life. You have to think about the people remaining, it's a shame you don't appreciate the family you do have.'

Cherry had waited a long time to say this, they had not spoken about her sister's drowning from the day it happened, but her mother had made her feel it had been all her fault.

'A lot of people have lost their sons, fathers and brothers,' Cherry continued. 'People are suffering all around you. They're in their own bit of misery. Another day, another loved one being taken away from them, it happens every day.' She was fed up with being the scapegoat. 'This blaming me, it has to stop. Otherwise, you'll push me away and I won't come back.'

Her mother remained silent, she slowly turned away from the window and looked blankly at her daughter. She was wrapped up in her own misery.

'I think you use it as an example to treat me badly. I used to think all mothers were like you.'

Mrs Caldwell looked away unable to look Cherry in the face.

'But then I found out they weren't. Thank goodness. You never ask me how I was after Bill was killed. I've felt his loss keenly just as much as you and Papa. It grieves me to see you acting like this, making life harder for Papa and Tommy.'

The sound of bombing in the distance made her mother move suddenly and she quickly put the black curtain up against the window again.

In the kitchen, her father was reading the newspaper. It was obvious he had heard everything. He avoided looking at his daughter, but she could tell he was sad.

'Can you walk with me to the station please, Papa?' she asked.

'Of course,' he got up quickly.

At the train station, the reverberation of bombs could be heard in the distance.

'They've started early this time,' she said as her father looked in the direction of the docks.

'I bet that's the docks again,' he said. 'I better get back Cherry. It sounds like it's kicking off earlier today. I'll be needed.'

'Be careful dad. Love you.' And she hugged him tightly. A slightly embarrassed Mr Caldwell hugged her quickly. It wasn't the 'done' thing in some British families to display your emotions in public, even though his upbringing had been in France. She climbed into a carriage with her kitbag and tucking her identity tags in her coat around her neck, she looked at him out of the window. She opened it as the steam hissed from under the wheels.

'Be careful,' he called and waved as the whistle went, and the train started moving slowly away from the platform with big trails of coal smoke coming out of the funnel. She shut the window quickly to shut out the smoke and waved to him.

He suddenly shouted; 'Don't make any rash decisions!'

‘What?’ she strained to hear as the train chugged away.

‘Promise me you won’t make any rash decisions!’ he shouted to her.

‘All right.’ She waved, and as the train pulled away from the station, she realised she missed him already and that she felt desperately lonely.

CHAPTER 9- January 1941-RAF Finsham

The flat lands stretched out for miles in either direction. A layer of white was covering everything. Cherry looked out the back of the truck that was bringing her and four other WAAFs to their new billet at RAF Finsham in Norfolk. She closed the tarpaulin, it was cold, dank and grey in a countryside she had never seen before. It made her feel depressed, at least there were four others with her who'd been picked up from the train station and were new too. They all looked like they had Christmas hangovers. Not many smiled back, only one of them when she smiled at them. She was a tall, slim girl with short wavy hair, and did return Cherry's smile.

'My name's Cherry. Nice to meet you.' They shook hands and Cherry had a chance to look at her. She had blue eyes and reminded Cherry of Lana Turner, only younger. Lana was one of the most popular Hollywood stars on the silver screen.

Still smiling, Sally pulled the tarpaulin back.

'Where on earth have we come to? I'm Sally, by the way, I'm an engineer.'

'Have we arrived in hell?' said Cherry. 'Only it must've frozen over.'

The other three girls introduced themselves. Ivy, also a medical orderly, Nancy and Enid were telephonists. They had been telephonists in civilian life.

The truck pulled up and the girls lifted the tarpaulin again to get a better view. On one side was an array of grey hangers protected on the far side by deciduous trees. The trees were bare as it was winter, but when the trees were in full bloom, they would give some camouflage to half the buildings in the summer. The rest of the surrounding area was flat with farmer's fields as far as the eye could see. And all Cherry could see on her side of the road were fields and fields of green she thought must be vegetables. The next field looked like rows and rows of frozen brussel sprouts.

It was cold and damp, and Cherry thought it looked dismal. She had caught the train at the crack of dawn. She was still excited to be here and to be able to do something she had longed to do for such a long time – to learn how to save lives.

The runway and aeroplanes were hidden from anyone turning up at the main gate, the buildings hiding what they really were. There were some petrol bowsers in the bulk aviation fuel area not far from a huge grey hangar which seemed to be full of people. She knew what they were because she had identified them at Tangmere. Noises emanated from the hangar, people talking, people walking across the parade ground. This is what I'm used to, she thought. She felt less lonely. No doubt they would find out more when they were shown around. Some sentries with rifles slung over their shoulders were talking to a Sergeant who stepped up and pulled the tarp back completely.

'All right ladies. You can jump down.' He said as he dropped the tailgate. 'I'm Sergeant Beck from administration, I do all the paperwork,' he said looking at all five women. There was no hiding, his eyes took them all in from top to toe.

'You call me Sergeant Beck. I call you by your surnames. And I have a nice titbit to impart. You'll be glad to know you're the first women on this base.' His grin was so wide, that Cherry wondered how big his mouth was. The girls all looked at each other nervously.

'I'll take you to the places you'll be working.' He pointed over to some buildings. 'That's the new telephone exchange, medical quarters, or sick bay as you may know it. And that's hangar one, that's where you'll meet your commanding officers.'

There was almost a complete city built up from the ground on this bleak airfield in the middle of nowhere. Technical buildings, personnel blocks, the operations tower – standing erect out of the grey landscape. It was one of those new satellite stations that had sprung up out of the mud like her Papa told her it would be.

They stood staring around them.

'Don't we have a WAAF officer in charge of us?' Sally asked.

'She arrives tomorrow. You're a day early.'

They all looked at each other in surprise.

'You came a day early,' he emphasised.

'But we were told to arrive today.'

'I know. Someone else's mistake,' he said. 'It wasn't me. Not my doing.' He said again, shrugging his shoulders.

A trio of young airmen walked towards them coming from the hanger. One of them whistled at the girls, and the men laughed, one of them nudging his oppo and commenting and pointing at Sally. The girls guessed they had insinuated something ungentlemanly at Sally's expense, who seemed not to notice. Enid and Ivy looked embarrassed, and Cherry commented. 'How rude.'

'You'll have to get used to that,' the Sergeant said. 'They're not used to seeing young ladies on this base. Come on, follow me.' And the girls struggled behind him with their kit bags.

'You don't have to put up with that,' said Sally aside to Cherry. 'I did at first, in training. But I learned a thing or two. We'll see the CO tomorrow. And have a talk with her.'

'Leave them there, someone will come and take them to your billet,' the Sergeant told them.

'I'm not leaving mine,' said Cherry scathingly, 'For some erk to come and pick it up and rifle through my private things.'

The other girls followed suit and picked up their bags, following Cherry, they heaved their heavy kit bags trying to keep in step with the Sergeant.

'Wait, Sergeant!' Called Sally. 'Take us to our billet first so we don't have to struggle with these all morning.'

The Sergeant pretended not to hear them and walked on. Cherry began to feel her hackles rising. If this was the way they were going to be treated, things would have to change, like Sally said. She plonked her kitbag on the ground and surprising herself she remained steadfast and unmoving.

'If you insist on being very unhelpful Sergeant, I will have to follow this up with our CO. We're doing you a favour by carrying our bags to our billet. Now kindly show us the way. If you don't, we'll choose our own billet.'

The rest of the girls looked on in surprise, the Sergeant stood in his tracks and sighed. Turning around 180 degrees he marched back the way they had come to a new Nissen hut they could see a few yards from them.

'I have better things to do than play your games, Caldwell,' he said. Sally winked at Cherry.

One Brownie point to them. They followed him. Already Cherry had decided she didn't like him. But with Sally's support, she found she could stick up for herself. As a Sergeant he could have put her on report, that wouldn't have looked good for him or her on their first day.

'Better things to do than help a new group of WAAFs who are here to serve their country?' said Sally. She was determined to tell their new CO tomorrow what they had experienced on arrival. 'We never had any trouble during training. Mind you we were all women.'

The girls nodded in agreement and for a few minutes, the Sergeant kept his mouth shut. The WAAF hut was empty, and very cold. There were three others in a line next to it behind the hangar. All empty.

'Are you expecting many more crew?' she asked him.

'Oh yes,' he grinned - as if sharing a private joke. 'You're the greenhorns. You'll be our experimental recruits.' The WAAFs looked worried.

'He's trying to wind you up,' said Sally to them. 'Take no notice. I'm getting used to this joker.'

The Sergeant looked her up and down. 'Not only a looker but she has spirit as well!' he exclaimed to them all.

‘Not only am I a looker, I’m also not going to take any flak from cheeky men like you either,’ Sally responded. ‘And I shall be reporting any disreputable comments about women to my CO when she arrives. We don’t have to put up with this kind of thing.’

‘Yes,’ chimed in Cherry, standing next to her and trying to stand tall, she was glad her new friend was sticking up for them all.

‘We’re here to help the RAF. You may not like it. But you’ll have to put up with it.’

‘If you get on the wrong side of me, I can make your life difficult,’ said the Sergeant. ‘Likewise, Sergeant,’ said Sally pulling herself up to her full five feet ten inches and towering a good four inches above him.

‘I’ve known erks act more gentlemanly than you,’ she glared at him.

It went quiet. Cherry groaned inwardly, this isn’t a good start, she thought to herself, had Sally gone too far? But the Sergeant seemed to think it was amusing.

‘We’re going to have fun with you lot,’ he half laughed and took a step back. Cherry felt Sally was going to say more. She tried to get Sally’s attention and gave her a warning look. It wouldn’t be good to push this Sergeant until he lost his sense of humour. They could easily be put on a charge for insubordination.

Their hut was drafty. Her father had warned her about these new Nissen huts springing up on new bases all over Britain. It was a quick and easy solution to housing a lot of people, but in the winter, they were hard to keep warm. They heaped their kitbags on the floor, and at a shout from the Sergeant fell in line behind him. He wasn't happy about stopping. The camp was brand new. The buildings had only just been erected, there were men still building huts next to the airfield.

The aircraft pens looked empty from this distance. Although she could hear the sounds of aircraft engines practising circuits and bumps in the distance. Ah that's better, she thought, that's the familiar sound I'm used to, whether they were fighter aircraft she couldn't tell.

They visited the new telephone exchange with one civilian woman working on a busy wire. She looked relieved to see them.

'I'll drop WAAFs Waller and Simpson here for you Mildred, so you can show them the ropes. You three come with me.' He beckoned for Cherry, Sally, and Ivy to follow him.

They followed him quickly to keep up with his long strides.

'There aren't many RAF personnel around,' said Cherry.

'That's 'cause we're still setting up,' Sergeant Beck quipped. 'This place is only six months old.

Once the planes come back from their sorties it'll be busy.'

He was right. The Naafi was packed with RAF crew later on.

The Sergeant took them from the Naafi to the administration block.

'What bombers do you have here, medium or heavy?' Sally asked him.

'An assortment,' he said and pointed to the second hanger being built where the engineers were putting the roof on. 'We have mostly Halifax, we're building up the Wellingtons,' he said. 'A few more Wellingtons are being delivered tomorrow, along with the crews. So there'll be a lot more personnel on the base then. And you're our first female fitter.' He said to her. 'Let's see how you handle the fitters,' he smirked.

'I'm more bothered about working out in the cold,' she said.

'I hope the fitters are more polite than that clown,' Cherry said to Sally under her breath. 'He seems to take delight in trying to pull us down a peg or two.'

''I suppose that's his job in life. It makes some men feel more important,' whispered Ivy. She was shorter than Cherry, and she seemed to be the quiet and shy sort, but she did join in with the banter.

'Don't worry about him,' said Ivy shaking her head. 'I've come across worse than that. It's the men who feel inferior next to a smart woman. They don't like to be shown up. You just have to develop a smart retort and get on with the job. In medicine, men are more used to seeing women.'

'You won't get the needling as much as me,' said Sally. 'Mostly because I work in a male-dominated job.'

'Do you get nasty comments?' asked Ivy.

'Not since the training. The trainers there nipped it in the bud when I trained with the men, there were only three women. I think they realised they needed us females and didn't want to put us off. It's old salts like our Sergeant here who say they don't like women doing a man's job. Some men don't like it and will let you know that.'

Cherry grimaced. 'We have our work cut out. But I admire your attitude Sally, I shall endeavour to copy your positivity and determination,' she said, her head held high.

'Good girl. Don't put up with any rubbish. Whatever rank they are.'

Sally won't put up with any rudeness, Cherry thought to herself, but I'm not sure how far I'd stick up for myself, I'd be worried I'd get into trouble.

At Hanger One they observed young men in overalls working on several aircraft. They were busy working on a Wellington bomber, a Halifax and two Hurricanes. The girls watched with interest.

'Pity you won't get paid the same as the men,' the Sergeant continued sarcastically as if trying to stir things up again. Sally's eyebrows shot up.

'I can't understand why,' she said. 'We're doing the same job as the men.'

Sergeant Beck muttered something under his breath about women taking men's jobs, and they watched him turn on his heel and march off.

'I assume that's an *au revoir*,' said Sally.

'So he isn't going to tell us where to go next?' said Cherry.

'Perhaps we're allowed to find the Naafi canteen for ourselves,' said Ivy. 'In which case it's over here.' They followed her towards a low building, they could see it had large windows in it and the lights shone from inside.

'You don't mind working outside then?' Cherry asked her as they got a cup of tea and some cake from the servers. She thought Sally was an interesting young woman. Someone she'd like to call a friend and get to know better.

'It's not too bad if you're used to it. I was brought up on a farm and I was out helping dad in all weathers. Fortunately, I like working outdoors. And I'm allowed to wear trousers the same as the men.'

'Well, that's handy,' said Cherry. 'I wish I could. Especially in this weather, they'd keep your legs warm.

'Anyway, they need fitters badly, they told us in training, that's why they're encouraging women with an engineer's brain.'

'Where are you from, Sally?' asked Ivy.

'Kent. And I had four brothers so I know how to stick up for myself.'

Ivy and Cherry smiled at each other, Sally wasn't going to take any nonsense from anyone.

'You're the first WAAF I've met who's been trained to work on aeroplanes,' said Cherry.

'Hopefully, not the last,' Sally answered.

Sally bent her head to the girls. 'This station is going to get bigger to accommodate heavy bombers. That's the reason they're building here. It's only an hour to the rest of Europe.'

They met up back in their hut with the rest of the new girls. Enid and Nancy had already obtained blankets, sheets and pillows from the bedding store and had made their beds. They told Sally and Cherry where to go and the rest of the girls went to get theirs.

No one groaned out loud but Cherry felt it was stone cold, just as her father had predicted, theirs was a drafty, dark Nissen hut, with cardboard at the windows and one electric light bulb in the middle of the room.

'Christ! What an awful place to arrive in winter!' said Sally rubbing her hands together.

'I'm sure it's nice in summer though,' said Nancy.

'At least you girls will be inside. I'm outside working on the planes, in all weathers.'

'Don't you work in the dry, inside a hangar?' Enid asked her.

'Yes, but the wind whips through them in the cold weather, that's usually autumn, winter, and spring. Even summer, sometimes.'

The girls looked at her in amazement. 'You're very brave working outside,' said Ivy. She looked tiny standing next to Sally.

'My father told me the wind blows across the Fens and in the winter it's cold and damp,' she said. 'I bet it gets darned cold in here when the wind blows. At least we have a stove. They haven't left us much coal though, I don't think that'll last all night.'

Cherry chose the empty bed near the centre of the room and closest to the pot belly stove that was in the middle of the room, her papa had told her this was the warmest place to be during the winter. She was glad to see a bucket of coke and some lumps of coal next to the stove. Rationing affected everybody, even in the forces.

The WAAFs sat on their beds, some re-arranging their clothes and tidying, Ivy was writing a letter.

'I remember my father telling me they had gone foraging for the fire to keep it stoked up during the night time to keep warm,' Cherry told them. 'I don't think a few pieces of coal they give us a day will keep us warm enough.' She stood up and looked through the window that had cardboard stuck to the window in place of curtains, one piece was hanging down. She pointed to a copse in the distance. 'We should go foraging for bits of twigs and branches in the local wood over there. Anything to keep the fire going that bit longer.'

The rest of the girls nodded, it was a good idea. Nobody wanted to freeze. They decided whoever had some time, would go and collect the wood. Cherry lit the stove with some matches next to it, crumpling up newspaper to get the coal heated up.

There was no one else in the hut, just the five of them. There were twelve beds in the room - arranged along the two sides with only one and a half feet between each bed. That was the regulation. Not much privacy then, Cherry thought to herself. Not very good if the person next to you is a snorer. The storage space was small, there were a few pegs for uniform and a small shelf above the bed. An orange box was present at the bed nearest to the door and acted as a bedside table and chair. Two rows of jointed mattresses stood up like drunken dummies in the middle of each bed. These were called 'biscuits' by the WAAFs and they knew they were lucky to have sheets. The men didn't. The girls had blankets to be folded up and put as a layer at the head of each girl's bed. Not knowing when they would be allowed on leave to go home, they had taken as many clothes as they could. Most of the windows were covered in cardboard and already had been fixed to the window. There were no curtains and it looked bare. This was the blackout. No frivolous curtains allowed for them.

The night was freezing cold, and the next morning there were no flights. They met their Commanding Officer whose name was Station Officer Hewitt. Sally, Ivy, and Cherry told her about their initial reception from the men, particularly Sergeant Beck. Although she was sympathetic, the girls could tell their SO had other things on her mind, because she kept looking at her watch. Sally looked at Cherry who shrugged her shoulders, when the SO had given them their orders and where they were to work, they were shown outside.

'So this is who we're relying on?' said Cherry

'She looks no older than my younger sister. When she said do the rounds of the camp, I felt like asking her if she wanted me to show her around!'

There were lots of young airmen about the base. They went to Pay, Accounts, the Orderly Room was used for administration, and then they went to the Gas section to pick up their new gas masks. At last, ending up at the Naafi to get a cup of tea with bread and jam. Cherry was famished.

After reporting for duty at Sick Bay with Ivy the girls were shown around by another officer. Later they met Sally in the canteen at four o'clock just before three returning Wellingtons landed on the tarmac. It was getting dark already. They hurried to the front just as the hordes of crew came in and formed a huge queue behind them.

'I'm guessing this lot were out flying sorties today,' said Sally. 'Am I glad we came now, or we would have been at the end of the queue.'

The sun tried to peek through the clouds as the girls sat in the Naafi after the airmen had gone, looking tired and deflated. No one said very much.

'I'm thankful we all started today,' said Sally. 'If I'd been on my own, I would have probably turned round and gone home.

'Yes, me too!' said Nancy.

Cherry returned with another cup of tea.

'Well, at least the sun's trying to come through,' she said trying to sound cheery.

She was only dimly aware of lumbering aircraft in and out of the station. But she noticed a Wellington bomber parked up inside on the edge of another hanger behind the Naafi.

'Is that a woman working on one of those?' asked Enid.

'I think it is, it's probably a civvie,' said Sally. 'Sometimes civvies are brought in to help out. And I thought I was the only girl in this hangar. Well, that's amazing!'

They watched the young woman go inside the aeroplane then come out and slide under it. Before they knew what Sally was doing, she had left the canteen and hurried over to the young woman under the Wellington. Cherry ran after her, intrigued, while the others watched with interest out of the window.

The young woman was doing something under the aeroplane, Cherry couldn't work out what it was. When the young woman in overalls saw two feet appear next to her, she rolled out on a board to see who it was. She was flat on her back and pushed the board out by her feet, which was running on small wheels.

Sally was surprised to see how young the civilian was. She was in greasy overalls, her hair tied back with a red headscarf. Sally helped her up.

'Hello,' said Sally. 'My friends and I were intrigued to see a female working on a Wellington.' She pointed to the rest of the girls watching her through the window of the Naafi

'What's your name?' asked Cherry.

'Jessie.'

'How long have you been working here?'

'About a week.'

'Nice to meet you,' Sally said. 'I work on planes too. I'm a WAAF fitter. They shook hands. 'How did you come to work here?'

'I'm a civilian. When they asked some of us from the village to work for them, I jumped at the chance. There's not much work in this village for a girl anyway.'

'How many of you?'

'Just me for now. Although there's another three coming soon they said.'

'I guess they need all the help they can get with the men away fighting. Even if that means women.'

'Especially for women,' she said. 'They have to get used to it,' answered Jessie. 'They don't have enough men to do the job.'

She was no taller than five feet three inches. Sally at five feet ten inches seemed to tower over her.

'What are you doing? Is it a difficult job?' she asked.

'Stinky.' The woman pointed to the bucket of brown squelchy liquid causing a heady smell to the side of her. She rubbed her back as she pushed herself up from the trolley. 'I get to patch up the Wellingtons when they come in damaged, then paint the torn fabric with this stuff. But it's a hellish job. Hurts your back up and down on this trolley all the time.'

'I bet it does.' said Sally. 'I guess I'll be seeing more of you because I'll be working in this hangar too,' Sally smiled at her.

Cherry heard a male voice call to them from the other side of the hangar. But the echo muffled the sound. Jessie sat back on her trolley.

'We'll have to get together with you girls,' Sally said hurriedly. 'There aren't that many of us, and we all need as much support as we can get.'

'I'm glad you're here because there's no one to talk to.'

'Aye up,' said Sally under her breath to Cherry.

'Oi!' a male voice shouted to them from across the hanger. Heavy boots clattered on the concrete echoing across the hangar, marching towards them.

'I think the men here are so surprised to see a woman under a Wellington,' said Jessie.

'*I'm* surprised to see a woman under a Wellington,' said Cherry.

'Better go. Sergeant's keeping tabs on me.' With that Jessie lay back down on the trolley and pulled herself back under the belly of the Wellington.

'What're you doing?' a voice boomed at them. A tall Sergeant with his cap at an angle reached them in seconds. His face was brown and lined, he was large and intimidating. The rest of the girls watched them from the Naafi window, their faces pressed to the glass trying to hear what was said.

Cherry turned with a sweet smile up at the Sergeant. 'Just talking to this young woman,

Sergeant. Giving her a bit of support. She's on her own.'

But the smile was lost on the Sergeant. 'No, she's not. She has *me* to keep her company. And you - leave her alone, she can do her job without you slowing her down. So don't stop her. She has to keep her mind on the job.' He looked at the girls' uniforms. 'You new?'

'Yes, Sergeant.'

'Where should you be?' he demanded.

'In the Naafi, Sergeant.' And the girls turned and hurried away before he could say anything else.

January was cold and bleak, and a week later the girls saw three new civilian recruits working in the hangar with Jessie. Sally, Cherry, and Ivy invited them into the Naafi when they had a lunch break. Following that day, the civilians met up with the other WAAFs in the canteen. Jessie said she was thankful she had made more friends, and the girls planned to meet up regularly during the winter to warm up before they started work in the hangar.

February brought chill winds across the Fens. Every day new crew were joining Finsham, and Cherry saw different faces every week in the Naafi. The number of workers was growing and they were still erecting more buildings.

On her return from the Naafi the first week of February she received some sad news that took her by surprise. There was a letter waiting for her that looked official. She ripped it open too worried to open it properly. The letter was from Eddie's CO at Tangmere telling her that Eddie had been shot down – 'killed in the line of duty.' Inside was a letter was from Eddie's mother. The CO had enclosed it because Eddie's mother didn't know Cherry's address.

He must've told his mother about me after all. Cherry thought. And I didn't think he was serious. As she read the embossed-headed letter a sense of guilt came over her.

'I'm sorry my dear, I have sad news. 'Eddie was killed over the Channel. He was shot down in December. I've only just written to you now because I've had a lot to do - sorting out his funeral. I'm afraid his father is not very good at organising. I didn't know where you were stationed, otherwise I would have asked you to come to the funeral. I know he thought a lot of you, Cherry. He didn't get a chance to bail out. They retrieved his body from the English Channel and his funeral was yesterday.

Cherry was so shocked she had to sit down. She hadn't anticipated Eddie getting killed, even though he had joked about being the next one to go. He'd always had a laissez-faire attitude to death, and it shocked her that she wouldn't see him again. She felt as if she'd been dealt a blow.

My apologies for not writing sooner. The letter continued. *I hadn't realised that Eddie had a serious girlfriend, I didn't realise until your letter arrived the other day for Eddie.* She realised it was the last letter she'd written to him telling him that they could still be friends. But his mother didn't mention it. She sat on the edge of the bed - her throat was sore. An immense wave of guilt swept over her. She wasn't sure if it was the cold weather or because of her sadness for her friend. She sighed and looked at the letters in her hand lost in thought. His poor mother, she thought, it was kind of her to write to me, I'll write back straight away. If she had accepted him, perhaps he would still be alive. Then again, maybe he wouldn't, you could never tell whether he was serious.

There were more WAAFs joining their hut every week and by March it was full. Spring arrived about the same time and bomber flights increased across the airfield. A new Lancaster bomber flew in and stayed for a while, the news was that it was a test aeroplane for the new design due to arrive next year, which was due to be stationed at Finsham. It looked like the RAF were bringing more squadrons in. A squadron of Wellingtons and Blenheims stayed, while another squadron of

Spitfires stayed a while then left, there was constant movement among the stations.

Twice some low-flying enemy aircraft flew in under the radar and strafed the parade ground. Cherry didn't see the Stukas but she heard them. This time no one was seriously hurt, apart from a young fitter who was walking across the parade ground. It was easy to get lackadaisical and they had regular practice emergency drills, where the medical orderlies took turns having mock injuries. But personnel were still being killed on British airfields. The ground crew supporting the pilots were not immune to the Luftwaffe bombers.

Apart from some anti-aircraft guns scattered around the perimeter, there was little in the way of security. Sorties had commenced now the weather was milder and two hangars were up. There were some cold clear days and in April a group of Spitfires arrived and stayed for a few weeks then disappeared. Then some Hurricanes appeared next to the airfield and each morning the squadron disappeared for a few hours and then came back in the afternoons. Where they had been, the girls were never told, and they didn't ask. Cherry suspected they were doing sorties over France and Belgium. They didn't have far to fly into enemy-occupied territory. Secrecy was all important.

The mornings were crisp and the days sunny, and the frost had gone by Easter and they had no rain for two weeks. Things were starting to get warmer, especially in their hut.

Cherry and some of her friends were in the habit of gleaning the local wood and coppice for bits of bark and dry wood to feed their pot belly stove. Their hut was at the end of a line of huts, and the line had grown over the past two weeks. When the wind hit the end of their hut - they felt like they were in the Antarctic. But the girls were in the habit of keeping the stove lit during the night, so it kept warm until the morning. They often had parade training when it wasn't pouring with rain. It was so cold early in the mornings they would rush to the canteen afterwards and join the throng of RAF personnel for a hot breakfast.

Each week there were more and more men and women joining Finsham. Sometimes they would get the transport into the nearest big town which was Cambridge. So far they were lucky they had not suffered bombings like they had in the south. But on Sunday 13th of April, it all changed.

Cherry was walking from the medical quarters at the end of her shift towards the Naafi and she was looking forward to a nice evening. She was going for a walk with some of the other WAAFs. They had found a footpath that ran along the sides of the dykes which ran for miles. On this day it was a sunny, warm evening and it wasn't dark until seven-thirty. The girls had decided to investigate and see how far the footpath went.

It was a day Cherry would not forget. To everyone's surprise, a group of enemy aircraft flew under the radar and before she knew it as she was leaving the medical bay, a group of Focke-Wulf 190's strafed the parade ground. She ducked as everyone else did and looked up to see the Nazi insignia on the tail of the last one. Some men were crossing the parade ground and also dived for cover, as three Stukas appeared from out the sky. Like birds of prey, they dived from a great height. The scream from the nose of the Stukas sent shivers down her spine. She ducked and ran towards the trees. But then a barrier fence appeared before her, it wasn't there before, and panicking she turned back towards the building she'd just come from. The Stukas flew round and let out terrifying shrieks again as they dived towards the parade ground. Flat on the ground, she looked up to see what was happening, at the same time the thundering of German bombers followed overhead.

Someone shouted out to the WAAFs across the parade ground.

'Take cover! Look sharp! It's a raid!'

Some of the girls ran screaming to the nearest women's trench as one-thousand-pound bombs hit the airfield. The noise was deafening. A smoky fog descended on the airfield which gave it a ghostly hue. The Stukas shot low over the airfield, aiming at people who were trying to get out of the way. There was confusion, shouting and screaming as personnel tried to take shelter but the screaming of the Stukas drowned everything out. Bombs hit the ground all around her and ripped up the airfield. The initial shock was taken over by innate preservation and she got her limbs moving and ran to the nearest shelter. It was one of the men's shelters because she didn't have time to run to the women's. As she dived into the shelter the hanger to her left exploded. There had been planes filled with fuel inside, Sally had re-fuelled them yesterday. Her eyes were wide with horror as she watched the carnage developing around her. The ground shook as one of the hangars and the admin block next to it took direct hits behind the trench she was in. The ground shook and trembled as the bombs fell.

Mud and dirt clumps flew in the air leaving big gaping holes in the ground. To Cherry's right at the edge of the airfield, two Spitfires were trying to take off to avoid being blown up. They bumped along the ground swerving around holes and gaining speed. They passed two Bristol Blenheim's and took off just as the Blenheim's were blown to pieces. Cherry remained hidden underground but had a grandstand view of her surroundings through the open vents in the bunker. People had dived into the shelter after her and they watched the carnage unfold in front of them, she'd never felt more helpless. A man and a woman were hit by shrapnel in front of her. She watched in horror through the slit in the trench. She tried to recognise the people who'd been hit. Other bodies were lying on the ground at eye level. The people in the trench who had been lucky enough to dive in out of harm's way, stood in silence looking out at the carnage in front of them. A man in uniform screamed as he tried to put out fire on his arm. Someone tried to get him down on the ground to stop the flames. She froze. She couldn't move, it would've been suicide to even try to get outside to help.

The raid was completely unanticipated, two orderlies watched with her looking out of the slits in the shelter. A truck careering past burst into flames, it was out of control, and the people on board burned alive.

Cherry was stuck in a trance, she couldn't believe the horror developing in front of her. She had never seen anything like it. It was different to the practice emergencies they'd done. This was real. People were getting killed. It was different from when she had been a warden too – this time, there had been no warning.

The sounds of the aircraft had already gone. It had been a quick in and out by the Luftwaffe causing complete devastation. She came out of the trench with everyone cautiously, in shock, she tried to think what to do. This was real - this was no practice.

Lying next to the trench was a WAAF and the twisted body of a young airman. The bodies were both bloodied. She didn't recognise their faces. The faces looked peaceful although their bodies were twisted into awkward shapes.

An ambulance ringing its shrill bell went racing past. The Sergeant Major shouted at them as he ran past.

'It's too late for them. Follow me!'

She wasn't sure how she put one foot in front of the other, but she did. Looking up in the sky and left to right, in case of more surprise attacks, she followed the others.

Medical personnel jumped out of the ambulance in front of her and checked the people on the floor. One of the WAAFs came up to her. It was Ivy.

'Are you all right?' she asked, a concerned look on her face. Cherry opened her mouth to speak but no sound came out. She shook her head, it ached and her ears were ringing. She thought she said something, but couldn't hear her words.

'It's the bombs - the noise makes you deaf,' Ivy said. Her hand touched the side of Cherry's face, as Ivy looked at her and mouthed the words, again, then led her to the ambulance.

Cherry pulled her arm away from her and pointed at a WAAF on the ground. She was covered in blood. Cherry started to shake.

'It's alright. Let's get you in the ambulance first. Then I can help bring these people in.'

Cherry had survived bomb blasts before in her street, but they were her friends' bodies this time.

'No, I'll help you,' Cherry insisted. And bent down and tried to feel for a pulse. But her hands were shaking.

'I'm afraid she didn't survive,' said Ivy. 'This one takes priority,' she pointed at a young fitter who was bleeding from his arm, and his arm was bent awkwardly. He was in a lot of pain, gritting his teeth. Cherry shook her head trying to get rid of the crackling in her ears. She did a thumbs up to Ivy and between them they helped the young man into the ambulance.

'Wait, I'll come back and help you,' Cherry said anxiously.

'You need help yourself.'

'No, my ears are clearing, I know what to do.'

'All right. Stay here, see what you can do for the others until an ambulance comes back. I'll be back soon.'

There were people on two stretchers and three people sitting. Some new USAAF crew who had turned up last week put injured people on their jeeps and sped off towards the medical centre.

The blood, the smells, the whistling in her ears made her dizzy and she crouched down suddenly and vomited in the middle of the airfield. She tried to get up quickly but someone helped her to sit on a chair next to the flattened and smoking hanger.

She turned and looked behind her and someone had put a blanket over the WAAF who'd been killed. Cherry couldn't seem to get her jumbled brain clear. She knew she was in shock and she had seen death before. It was awful that she couldn't remember the young WAAFs name, she had looked like she was asleep. Cherry caught her breath and a sob got stuck in her throat. There were people scattered around the field who were covered in blankets, with just their feet sticking out. She felt the enormity of the raid suddenly and she stared at the number of feet sticking out from under the blankets. The blankets weren't long enough to cover their feet. She tried to swallow. Her throat was bone dry. Now was not the time to lose her nerve.

I've seen dead bodies before, she thought. The woman and her baby back home. But it still affected her. She somehow managed to keep her feet and arms moving and helped check the names of the WAAFs who had been killed. Some of the deceased were new recruits. She helped a

Corporal check the names of the dead from a sheet.

'These are mostly fitters!' He exclaimed. 'What a terrible loss.'

A jeep came back and two airmen jumped out and put the WAAF who had died on a gurney. A WAAF orderly returned and stuck Cherry next to her on the transport, they zoomed off across the field in an ambulance, swerving around the potholes. The pounding of the bombs had finished but the pounding in her head had just started. She didn't know if the WAAF had spoken to her because all she could hear was a hissing-like noise in her ears.

The scene inside the medical quarters was chaotic, with the injured filling the ward. The beds were full. In the corridor people were squashed together, leaning against the wall, or leaning on someone else. Two were sharing a chair. The nursing staff were dealing with the most urgent first. While those who were not urgent were left to sit on the floor.

Cherry's legs were wobbly. Her medical orderly friend made her sit on a chair and she watched her hurrying around helping with the sick and wounded. She tried to get up and help but her knees gave way, and her friend made her sit down. Cherry looked into her face and Ivy indicated with her hands that she should sit down until the ringing stopped. Cherry sighed heavily and put a thumbs up, she could lip-read. After a while the pounding eased and she felt less like being sick. She got the attention of a WAAF orderly.

'What can I do to help?' she heard herself say. She stayed with the injured and monitored them after they had been seen by a doctor until some of them were shipped off to a bigger hospital at the new RAF hospital in Ely. She reassured the injured who were conscious trying to act self-assured, even though she still couldn't hear anything. She pretended to hear what the patients were saying and comforted them. When Ivy saw that she was talking to the patients leaning against the walls she got her to clean some of the wounds and bandage them up.

Sally and Cherry helped to clear up the mess the bombs had left the airfield and parade ground in.

That evening Cherry lay on her bed scratched and bruised, her ears hurt and she had a headache. Sally came in through the hut door with a plate of food for her.

'You didn't come to the Naafi for tea so I've brought you some sandwiches,' Sally said cheerfully.

'Thank you. But it's the last thing I need right now,' Cherry said. 'I think it's the after-effects of the bombing, I feel so silly. My training has made me aware of it, but I still can't get myself better.'

Sally sat on the end of her bed. 'You probably should have stayed in Sick Bay for a while. Come on, sit up. I know you feel horrible. But you must have something to eat, it'll make you feel better. Honestly.'

'I feel so awful. I didn't expect the after-effects to last this long.'

'You probably should have taken it easy instead of moving rubble.'

'We all had to help out.'

'Sit up. Have some water to drink. You will feel better. Come on.' And with a lot of chivying she encouraged Cherry to drink.

'If you don't eat half of this sandwich, I'm going to tell the doctor that you aren't better and you should spend time in Sick Bay.'

'You wouldn't....'

Sally grinned. 'I might. Now sit up and take a bite.'

Cherry did as she was told. She did feel better after taking a couple of bites of the sandwich. Sally sat next to her on the bed and watched Cherry eat her sandwich.

'Are you making sure I eat?' she asked Sally.

'Yes, come on,' Sally said, smiling. Cherry was amazed at how her friend always managed to stay cheerful. Cherry swallowed her sandwich and drank the tea she brought her.

'I am lucky to have a friend like you,' she tried to smile back at Sally, but her head hurt.

Sally was popular with everyone, airmen and WAAFs alike. Her personality seemed to shine even in the dark aftermath of the bombing. Her face shone with a smile. How did she manage to remain positive all the time? How could you be sad with a friend like that? I should try to be more positive, like Sally, she thought.

Over the next few days, Cherry drove back and forth to the hospital with Ivy to bring back the servicemen and women who had recovered from their wounds. The Luftwaffe had certainly won this time, the RAF had to halt flying for the next few days until the buildings and the runway were operational again.

CHAPTER 10 - Church Fenton

Pilot Officer Joe Taylor looked down on the scene below him. The Spitfire hummed loudly and vibrated gently between his hands. It was thick fog below him. Not a good thing to fly back into after a morning spent flying over France and the English Channel.

'Damn! I can't see a thing!'

His instruments had gone haywire in this new Spitfire. An update on his Mk II from the beginning of the year. And before that, he'd flown a Hurricane. It was disappointing. He had high hopes for this plane. He flicked the mike switch on his mask and tried to keep the worry and irritation out of his voice.

'Hello Church Fenton, this is Red Leader two, I can't see a thing and my instruments have gone haywire. Tell me where to put down.'

A voice crackled over the short-wave radio. 'Welcome home. Another five miles then lower your wheels, and come in gently. There is no fog below 1000 feet.'

'Thank God for that,' he muttered to himself. 'Roger. Out.'

He came in gingerly. Better safe than sorry. He shivered whether through cold or fear. He didn't like these foggy evenings. He had taken off in the sun. But a short while later the cold had come down like a blanket and if you weren't back before dark, it was dangerous. It was easy to get disorientated. A layer of chilled air spread threateningly as he lowered his undercarriage, he felt it seep through his padded trousers and leather flying jacket. He had never known such cold since Texas.

At one thousand feet the fog started to clear and as he lowered his flaps, the sky miraculously cleared and he could see around him to land.

Suddenly an enemy aircraft flew past him at speed. Joe swore under his breath and shouted over the comm to control.

'What in hell's name?... Where did that come from?' That should never have happened if people were vigilant and doing their jobs he thought. He was furious when he jumped down from his aircraft, telling his RAF mechanic about it.

Joe went to see his squadron leader to inform him of the incident before he did anything else. He was shaken up.

'I can't understand how they got through our defences!' said his CO. 'We've Bofors guns and anti-aircraft positions around the airfield. We've a lot more than other airfields. At my last place, there were only a few pillboxes and some rifle pits. But we didn't get any surprise attacks.'

Even though they wore the same uniform, some of the British were cold towards the Americans. His squadron leader though was not one of them, and he was already trying to find out how the enemy aircraft had slipped through their defences.

On the way back to the canteen his friend appeared from behind and slapped him on the back.

'Close call eh Joe?'

'Hank, did you see the plane from the ground?'

'Sure did. Good job you didn't run into it.'

'Almost,' Joe said, wiping his hand across his brow.

'You joining the crew tonight, Joe?'

'Maybe.'

'Just maybe?'

'I have something to do first.'

'Well, see you at The Crown and Anchor. You're not visiting that lovely Wren again, are you?'

'Oh no, she was just a one-off.'

'I thought I saw you twice with her!'

'Oh, well twice then. But she's been getting a bit too keen.'

'Joe, one day you'll fall hook, line, and sinker!'

They walked into the mess to pick up the mail.

'There's a letter for you Biff. Lucky you.'

Biff sniffed it. 'Yep, smells like her perfume. I'll read that in my room.'

'That from your wife?'

'Well unless I have a secret admirer, a bit like you Joe,' he grinned. 'You get more letters than me! No, I recognise Jody's hand on the letter.'

'You know the spies have had their grubby hands all over it, don't you?' Joe said.

'Is that from the Wren?' Mack pointed at Joe's letter he had taken from his pigeonhole.

'I don't think so.' Joe studied the handwriting. 'It's one I don't recognise. It might be from my younger sister. She doesn't write often.'

'Well, you should know your redhead's writing by now, she's written several letters hasn't she?'

'Three.'

'Must be keen.'

'I'm not. I wrote her and said I'd a girlfriend at home.'

Joe wasn't going to tell his buddy that it was her friend that he was thinking of. Only he was having no luck at all with her. He looked at the writing again. Then on the back. It wasn't his sister. His hopes rose. It looked as if there were a few sheets to read. That's good, he thought, a decent letter. He only got them from his sisters.

He wasn't much of a letter writer but knew they would be anxious for news although there was little he was allowed to tell them. They were anxious for news of dances, of the local nightlife, of the girls. They didn't understand about black-outs and surviving on rations although the military had decent food compared to the civilians.

He knew the sensor sometimes opened letters. The ones from Rosie hadn't been opened by the sensor. She wrote a one-page letter asking to meet up with him again. She told him not to forget to bring nylons or candy.

Joe read the short note from Rosie;

'*Why are you not replying to me? I thought we had a good time in London? I am going home the weekend after next. Why don't you pick me up and we'll go home for the weekend together?*'

He had a funny taste in his mouth. He didn't like the way this was going. He had tried twice to find Cherry, and where she was stationed, but her family had told him nothing, they didn't like him. But that wouldn't put him off. He ripped up Rosie's letter and threw it in the bin.

He'd try again, a third time. He felt their connection had been genuine and he had felt different since meeting her, he couldn't get her out of his mind. He had tried hard to find out where she was. Meeting up with Rosie was a coincidence, twice she turned up when he had arrived at the Caldwell's house to enquire after Cherry. He had told Rosie he was going back to Portsmouth to find Cherry. It didn't put her off though, far from it. It wasn't Rosie the Wren he thought of, it was the pale brunette with the silky hair that he couldn't forget. She had made him completely enamoured. It was worth trying to communicate again, but how? She hadn't answered any of his letters. Something was wrong, he'd try one more time.

He opened the letter slowly then looked at the end of the letter, it was signed Cherry. Well, wonders would never cease! He eagerly read the letter bumping into the door before he sat down to read it.

Dear Joe, I hope this letter finds you eventually...you move around England so much. And I hope it finds you well? And that flying is all you thought it would be and you're not wounded. My friend, Rosie, you met in Portsmouth, told me where you were stationed.

I found out from her - that you had been back to our house and my mother had been her usual painful self and refused to give you my address. I'm sorry you have been to my home and I wasn't there. I am at RAF Finsham, Norfolk, and learning to be a medical orderly.

When I saw you in August, you said you'd call the next day, so when you didn't – well, I thought you had changed your mind. I went into town and signed up for the WAAFs.

Since then, a lot has happened. Sadly, my brother Bill has been lost, MIA over the Channel. I guess it has happened to your friends too. Are you flying? I shouldn't ask those things, should I? The sensor will delete it. But I long to hear all about it, and how you are doing.

There are some bomber crews here, they're so young. It's frightening when I think they have such a big responsibility. I see some of the aircraft come limping home and some are badly shot up. I think of you often and wonder if you are still ok and if you would like to renew the friendship? If I don't get a reply, I will know what the answer is. Yours truly, Cherry.

A flurry of emotions went over him all at once. He was glad and guilty all at the same time. He wrote back immediately.

Dear Cherry, it was just great to hear from you I thought you probably had forgotten all about me once the clear light of day dawned. Your mother doesn't like Americans! Well, I don't care, she'll have to get used to us. There's a lot more coming over the water.

We are busy flying over Europe and there's talk of the squadron moving again. But I won't upset the sensor I will call you once I find out your telephone number. I'm not sure where Finsham is. I'll find out and see if I can get over to you.

At the beginning of the year, we had orders to move to Suffolk which is miles from Portsmouth. I managed to get a 48-hour-pass and I came to see you before we got shipped up here. I thought one last try before I left but I bumped into your best friend Rosie! She's a swell gal, isn't she? She explained about your parents. I'll be in touch soon. Write me. Yours, Joe

Cherry was so pleased when she received his letter two weeks later. She was so glad the letter had caught up with him, so many went missing. Yes, I would certainly plan for time off and she wrote back saying she would be happy to meet up with him. But at the back of her mind was something gnawing away at her, it was the fact that Rosie had become his friend.

A few days later Cherry got a letter from Rosie.

Hi there! I thought I'd better come clean and write to let you know that I actually went on a date with Joe. And thought it best to let you know that he has a girlfriend at home...there he was stringing me along, and completely cuts me off when I write to him...there you go! I knew nothing about it! I expect you don't either. I thought I'd better give you fore warning so you don't get hurt. These Yanks think they can do as they please over here!

Yes, I've gone out with him and have slept with him. But it didn't mean anything, honestly all those darling Americans. They bought me nylons and candy, why would I stay with just one?

The letter lay where she dropped it, open on the page staring up at her.

Cherry could feel the blood pumping in her ears. She realised she was holding her breath. At that instant, Sally came into the hut and saw the picture on her face. She knew something had happened.

'What's the matter? It looks like you've seen a ghost!'

'My friend has slept with my boyfriend.'

CHAPTER 11 – The truth will out

Cherry lay on her bed, hoping to wake up from an awful dream. She lay on her bed like someone who is bleeding and terrified to move. She had the sensation that her heart had dropped heavily to her stomach and she could not move. She felt her heart pounding. The last time she remembered feeling like this was when her younger sister had been ripped away from her in the river when she was little.

In the early hours of the morning, she penned a reply, then ripped it up. The next morning, she told Sally she'd written a letter to Rosie.

'Don't be too hasty, perhaps think on it for a day before you send it. You might regret it.'

'What, regret telling that tart what I think of her?'

'She's your friend.'

'Was. Not anymore. She's a selfish girl. I've told her she can have him.'

'What? I thought you loved him.'

'It takes two Sally. It takes two. Rosie isn't the only one to blame.'

'To be fair, you missed each other by miles most of the time. Well, we'll just have to see what she does now. If she wants him, she'll take him. Of course, he may not want her, it may be just a fling.'

'But then would I want someone like that?'

A myriad of confused thoughts went through her mind. No, she didn't want anything to do with any boy like that - who so easily went off with her friend. And to own up to having a girlfriend at home? She was confused and upset. Why would he be trying to see her those times when he had a girlfriend at home? She had a sneaking suspicion some of that was to do with Rosie. She knew Rosie of old. She had always wanted things that her friends had in school. She saw the irony of it all. Rosie had told her to stick up for herself before she had left to join the WAAFs, and her friend had taken off her the only person she wanted.

She was suddenly aware of Sally sitting on the end of her bed. With a question on her face.

'What are you going to do?' she asked.

'I'll write to him and if he replies. That's fine. If he doesn't, he doesn't.'

'So, you're going to give him the benefit of the doubt? Over your friend whom you've known since primary school.'

'It really is Mother's fault for causing this situation. Not Rosie's.'

'Oh Cherry! You're exasperating. Your best friend has slept with your boyfriend. Don't excuse her...You must talk to her and him to get a better picture of what's happening,' she said.

'I couldn't bear to,' she said at last.

'Somebody must. Does she know you're in love with this man?'

'Who said anything about...?'

Sally interrupted with exasperation. 'Of course you are, it's written all over you. Why else are you in this state? I'm sure it's been a terrible shock. But Cherry-think! You must see it's not really Joe's fault. He didn't know how you felt about him, and your mother sent him away. He didn't know where you were or how you felt about him. He probably gave up when Rosie threw herself at him.'

As usual, Sally's no-nonsense attitude made sense and Cherry started to think about it.

'Do most girls do it? You know...it.'

'I know some girls want to keep their boyfriends and in order to keep them they sleep with them. They're afraid of losing them.'

'But the boys will probably get killed next week.'

'That's probably why they do it.'

CHAPTER 12 – Facing Rosie

That weekend Cherry got a pass to go home. She'd called on the telephone to Rosie's mother to let her know she'd be calling on Rosie at the weekend when she was home. If Joe wanted to see her, he could go to her house. But she needed to speak to Rosie first. Rosie's mother said that she expected her home; they only lived a few minutes' walk from the Caldwell's house.

The weekend arrived and Cherry wandered down the lane towards Rosie's house, rather nervous. Rosie's house was a charming Edwardian cottage overlooking the village green. It had a small front garden and a rickety wooden fence covered in ivy.

Cherry took a deep breath determined not to get upset as she knocked on the big knocker. Rosie opened the door quickly with a big smile on her face. But it changed when she realised why Cherry had come.

'You slept with my boyfriend!' Cherry blurted out, her tears grabbing at her throat.

'Who's that? Oh Joe,' Rosie said casually, leaning against the door in her WRNS uniform looking all at once smart but unconcerned. She flicked her blonde hair behind her ear. Cherry smoothed her hands down her grey uniform, feeling inferior, but then pulled her shoulders back.

'It wasn't my fault about Joe Taylor,' she said in a sulky voice. 'You have to admit that. You never breathed a word that you knew anyone in the Eagles. He turned up one evening looking for you. I didn't know he was anybody special. He just said you were a swell girl, and you met on the big bombing night. He hung about, and I gave him what was left of the sherry. Then he asked if I'd like to go for a drive, he'd got hold of a car and some petrol. So off we went. We drove to the country and had supper in a pub.' She shrugged. 'You know how it is.'

'No, Rosie. I don't.'

Rosie looked heavenward. It annoyed her that Cherry was acting so pious and Victorian. All her friends had sex.

'Oh Lord, are you shocked? Are you upset? Honestly, Cherry, it isn't important. Lots of girls nowadays do it.'

Cherry turned away from her, she couldn't bear to seem so old-fashioned in the eyes of her friend. Or even jealous.

'You're so out of date,' Rosie flung at her.

'So, I'm out of date. I don't care.' And as she stormed off, she began to think about what Rosie had said. Rosie was going up to London and having casual sex with men, and having a high old time. She had nylons and new dresses. While Cherry, didn't. She was struggling to keep awake most watches, living from week to week not knowing if they were going to be bombed in their beds. She felt worn out from lack of sleep and worry. She really didn't want to face her mother at the moment.

It was spring now, the daylight clear and pale. She was sad and subdued as she walked towards home. Looking over a gate near her parent's house, the roof had been blasted off, and no family was living there anymore. The house had a high wall with a gate. Children had played among the shrubs, and there had been a swing under the pear tree. Now the garden was growing wild and branches were interlacing. By summer it would be a jungle. On the unkempt lawn, she saw a patch of late yellow daffodils. It looked like they were struggling to survive amongst the overgrown green of the lawn. She trailed through the open gate of her parent's house. A figure in Air Force blue was sitting on the front steps. It was Joe.

CHAPTER 13 – Joe

Joe stood up and gave a mocking salute, his cap at a rakish angle. Cherry felt dizzy as if she imagined him there. But it was him. He ran forward and squeezed her hands.

'Good to see you! I wasn't sure if I would find you. But your father told me you had gone to visit a friend.'

She had no time to recover but managed to mutter something about being surprised. He walked up the steps with her to the front door. Still talking, he accompanied her into the hall.

'You look swell in your WAAF uniform,' he continued, hardly taking a breath. She felt overwhelmed, he looked exactly when she last saw him only his uniform was more lived in.

'I've gotten a forty-eight-hour pass, I wasn't expecting it, on my honour, that's why I didn't call you first. How've you been? Ages since I saw you.'

'August.'

'As long as that? I suppose it must be. A lot has happened since then. We've moved to RAF Martlesham, not sure how long for, I figure you need to know where I am. We're not supposed to tell all about that, but I know you won't say anything.'

He squeezed her arm. 'You got my letter?'

She didn't answer, the consequences of Rosie's letter made her feel sick.

They went into the drawing room. With her mother out all day, the dust had settled thick on the furniture, with no one to clean it had returned to its wartime state. Some flowers in a vase were weeks old, roses in a bone-dry vase. Their heads had dropped off.

'Sit down, Joe. I'll see if I can find anything to drink.'

'How about English tea?'

He leaned comfortably back against the sofa cushions.

Escaping into the kitchen, Cherry put on the kettle, thinking desperately – I wish he'd go. Why does he continue with this farce? As if nothing has happened. Perhaps she should have it out with him.

The American voice called, 'Can I help?'

When she returned carrying the tray, the tea things rattling, he sprang up and claimed she should not wait on him, it was not the way things should be. Back home his sister would be shocked to her soul. He took the tray and put it carefully down in front of her.

She poured tea and he talked about the squadron's operations since they'd last seen each other. They were at Martlesham Heath. Did she know? Wasn't it wizard? They were fighting the Germans over their own territory now. He'd been flying over France, Belgium, as far as Germany on the new Spits. They were wonderful planes. He was getting lots of experience since he'd last seen her. He'd been lucky to stay alive the last scramble. Last month one of his friends was killed by a Messerschmidt.

'The sky became filthy grey in a few moments the clouds came up so thick!' His friend, he said, had tried to avoid the Messerschmidt and gone into a steep dive from 20,000 feet. Joe had followed him, shouting over the radio transmitter, telling him to pull out.

'He couldn't. Perhaps he fainted or his oxygen failed. We saw him crash. Later we found out what had happened. His plane had gone into coarse pitch.'

'What does that mean?'

'The engine's out of control. You can't get her back again.'

She nodded. She wondered if that was what had happened to her. My heart's in coarse pitch, she thought.

He changed their conversation, and told her that now the squadron was on ops, all the letters from home were full of heroes.

'How we hate it. Did you know Hollywood is making a movie called *Eagle Squadron*? Can you beat it?'

He continued in that vein, telling her that his squadron were proud of their RAF eagle badges, but they would have to transfer to the USAAF soon. He didn't know where they'd make them go after Martlesham.

He gulped down his tea.

He's a little nervous, she thought. But he hides it well.

'You look very beautiful. But very pale, honey. Your skin's honey-coloured. It's got just the same golden look of the blossom honey we eat at home. Blossom honey. That's you.'

She put down her cup and it rattled in the saucer.

'Joe. I must say something. Don't interrupt, please, just let me get it over with.'

He raised his eyebrows and made a comic face. But Cherry did not look at him.

'I know about you and Rosie.'

He started.

'Please don't say anything yet. I know it's no business of mine. We've not had a good start, have we? Especially since my mother's interference –'

'How in hell –'

'Rosie admitted bumping into you coming out of my parent's house. She used to be my best friend in school,' she sighed. 'But I can't pretend that it hasn't made me feel different. I can't be your friend anymore.'

He was horrified. He stood up and went over to the window, standing with his back to her. She wondered with dull curiosity what he would say next. She thought how beautiful his figure was silhouetted against the spring light. She imagined what it would feel like to stand close behind him and wind her arms around his waist. She'd spent a few sleepless nights worrying about what she would say to him if she met him again. The trouble was she had wanted to see him again. She was still in love with him. Now she told him how she felt, she felt better.

He turned.

'What did she say about me?'

Cherry blushed and burst out, 'What did you expect her to say? That you're marvellous in bed? I can't bear any more of this. What do I care if you made love to her? It's nothing, nothing, nothing to do with me except that I won't see you anymore. I suppose you're in love with her like everybody else. I just don't want anything to do with it.'

She began to run out of the room but he followed her, caught hold of her and pulled her roughly into his arms. Kissing her. She pushed him off her as hard as she could.

'Don't, don't! You don't care for me, it's horrible of you –' she gasped and tried to push him off. 'Leave me alone. You're hateful. Hateful.'

She only managed to escape because he suddenly let go of her.

'Rosie meant nothing. I got carried away with the moment. I was just glad to find a friendly face coming out of your mother's house. She took me dancing in London because I had a car.'

'So, you had it offered on a plate!'

'Your mother told me you were engaged to a pilot. I thought you'd forgotten all about me.'

She rushed out of the room, leaving the door open. He heard her running up the stairs.

He shouted up the stairs after her. 'I didn't get any of your letters!'

He heard a door slam.

He remained in the empty room, breathing fast. Then, with a fierce grimace, he picked up his cap and left the house.

After a sleepless night of tossing and turning, she wished she had stayed to hear him out. She did not know what to make of her feelings. He wanted her still, despite Rosie. She wondered about him all next day. Wondering if he had gone after Rosie to see if she was home again, he had her address. Nothing was stopping him from going to see her. If she believed him. He had a forty-eight-hour pass after all.

She thought she must have shocked him yesterday, he certainly looked upset. She was staying one more night with her parents.

She saw Tommy coming down the street towards her kicking something in the gutter. He hadn't seen her and she didn't want to engage with him, she needed to talk to someone. Her friends were working in the factories or away in the services. After a few minutes she decided there was only one person she could rely on to be honest and succinct, so she walked to find her father, towards the sea. She needed fresh air and to think about things. She caught her father walking back to the house carrying a black bucket and spade. When he caught sight of her walking towards him, he seemed delighted.

'Cherry! Is your mother home?'

'Yes. I thought I'd come and find you. I needed someone to talk to.'

He looked at her then slowed his pace to hers and they walked slowly towards his allotment.

'My American came back. He went off with my friend Rosie when I was in training.'

Her father's eyebrows went up.

'I thought I saw him with Rosie the day they both came to call for you. I wouldn't put it past your mother to tell him you already had a boyfriend, just to put him off.'

'Oh, for goodness' sake pa. That's exactly what she told him. That I was engaged! Why didn't you tell him the truth?'

'I was in the back garden. I heard them talking on the doorstep. I don't like to get involved. Your mother seemed to be telling him lots although she wouldn't admit it to me. You know she doesn't like Yanks.'

Cherry rubbed her hands over her eyes in desperation. She tried to think. She was annoyed with her father for not having enough backbone to intervene.

'Why didn't you say something? Anything!'

'Why would I? I don't know what you think...'

Cherry held her breath. She couldn't think of a better reason why he went off with Rosie. And her father was right. She hadn't told anyone what she thought of Joe, and that she had fallen in love with him. Hell, she hadn't known herself.

Her father, as usual sounded reasonable. If Joe had been told she had someone else, she shouldn't blame him for going off with someone else too. She felt guilty that she had gone off the wall a bit with him now. He hadn't received her letters. He didn't know how she felt. He'd tried to get in touch twice, and each time had met Rosie. Strange that.

She stood for a minute and reflected. What with Rosie and her mother both trying in their own ways to stop Joe from communicating with her. It was obvious he was still interested, that's why they had got together yesterday. She made a decision then and there. She decided if he did come back, she would change her tune. If she wanted to keep Joe, and he was still interested she would do whatever it took to keep him. But after yesterday he might have changed his mind. She decided to give in to her stubborn righteousness and try and contact him.

They sat in Papa's hut and he brewed some tea.

'It's a long time since we've done this,' he smiled at her. 'I don't get a chance to see you these days. None of my children...Well, apart from Tommy.'

'Have you heard from Sidney?'

'You know your brother. He's not a letter writer. We wrote and told him about Bill. But he may be....' Her father looked away suddenly emotional. 'We just don't know where he is.'

'He's probably fine Papa, just lazy with writing. And having too much of a good time.'

'No doubt he's busy with his new ship.'

'Not so new now Papa. He's been with the Royal Navy for two years. I've been in the WAAFs a year!'

'Sacre Bleu, really? Time flies.'

'All right. I've made a decision. I'm going to try and contact him again.'

'You must do what you think is right for you. Not for anyone else. I think you're finally growing up my dear, aren't you?'

He watched her go. As she walked down the lane, she thought how ironic it was that what Papa had told her he didn't do for himself.

Cherry decided to do the running this time. She was going to try and contact him before he moved again. He may have decided to spend the forty-eight hours in London. She hoped so. He'd come back before, hopefully, he would come back again.

CHAPTER 14 – It's only love that sets us free

Cherry did not know what to make of her own feelings. He had tried to kiss her against her will. But although she felt revulsion at his brutal treatment, a part of her was excited by it. He wanted her still, in spite of the infinitely more desirable Rosie.

Mrs Caldwell was washing up in the kitchen. Before she left, Cherry was going to give her a piece of her mind.

'Thanks a lot, Mother,' she said sarcastically.

'What for?' Mrs Caldwell poised halfway between cutlery and drawer.

'For completely ruining any future I might have had with the man I love.'

There you are I said it, she thought. Leaving her mother standing with her mouth open. She opened the door and slammed it behind her without a backward turn. She felt better for venting her feelings, that wouldn't have happened a year ago.

She didn't know how to get in touch with Joe. She telephoned the American Serviceman's club in London but they did not have a Joe Taylor staying there. Should she go back tonight to

Finsham, a day early? She'd had a weekend pass, she didn't want to ruin it. They were like gold dust.

To have to talk to her mother whom she disliked more than anyone at this moment, was abhorrent to her. But then if Joe came back and she was gone...she dared not think of that happening. Her mother wouldn't think twice about sending him away again, and she thought he definitely wouldn't return after a third rebuff.

After a walk to clear her head, she returned home. The house was empty. Her mother had gone to the W.I. She sighed with relief. Should she go back to Finsham or stay?

There was a knock at the door. She stood up and through the opaque glass saw a blue RAF uniform figure on the other side. She held her breath and opened it to see Joe standing there.

'I want to talk to you,' he said harshly.

She moved aside to let him in.

Nobody had been in the drawing room since they had left it the previous day. The cushions were still squashed where Joe had sat. There was a cigarette end in the ashtray.

They stood facing each other.

'What do you want to say?'

'Listen, Cherry,' he sat down and lay back too far as if trying to seem relaxed. But his olive-skinned face was nothing of the kind. He looked unfamiliar because he did not look easy but drawn and tired.

'Listen, Cherry. And if you hate me after what I'm going to say, okay then you do and I'll have to put up with it. You said yesterday that I must be in love with your friend. I am not and never could be. Sure, she's glamorous and there isn't a guy in the country who wouldn't be proud to take her around. She's fun. And she's fun in bed too,' he added, staring at her fixedly. 'I can't say she isn't, though I wish in hell you hadn't found out. Do you know who I'm afraid of starting to love? You, for God's sake. You said no to me when we first met, remember? I wanted us to make love but you didn't want me, something like that. I thought – hell, I'm not hanging around if there's nothing doing there. I daresay that sounds filthy but it's the truth. Guys feel like that. My sort, anyway. But then I wanted to see you again and when I rang the next day your mother answered and was vague about where you were...'

'She didn't know I'd gone to sign up with the WAAFs.'

'I came round here, and I found Rosie. Can you blame me? I was shocked and unhappy, I guess, and she was good to be with. We got on fine. What we did that night was fine too for both of us, but no more than that. You don't understand any of it, do you?'

'No.'

'I didn't think you would. I don't blame you. But will you see me again? The Rosie thing is over. We went out twice, and that was twice I'd come looking for you and you weren't here.'

'You wrote to Rosie and told her you had a girlfriend.'

'I don't have a girlfriend at home, it was to put her off. See me again, Cherry.'

'I want to. But I know I shouldn't,' she said and began to cry.

He stood up and looked at her in tired silence at her face. He did not touch or go near her.

'I'll call you,' he said and leaned down and pushed the hair off her face and wiped her wet tears away with his hand. Then he walked out without looking back.

She did not go to the window or hear the door close. She sat down on the cushions as if taking possession of his warmth and his body. Leaning back, she closed her eyes. What should she do? What would he do? She decided to leave tomorrow.

The next day was one of the worst barrages on the Portsmouth and Southampton area by enemy aircraft. She helped her father on fire watch on the local church roof.

The sky was crimson in the distance. The south of England was really copping it. It was late evening and the whole heavens seemed to roar with aircraft. Cherry ran into the garden to watch the waves of raiders coming over. Guns were roaring and as she stared up for a glimpse of English fighter planes, she suddenly saw what appeared to be four enormous German bombers diving straight for the house. She fled indoors and down to the basement with her mother. She sat with her mother in silence while they heard the bombs falling but it was a mile away.

She felt she couldn't go under their shelter in the living room because it reminded her of Joe. There was no phone call from him that day, and the next day she had to return to Norfolk. With a heavy heart, she returned to Finsham, and told Sally that night that she feared she had lost him.

Two days later Cherry was in Sick Bay and a telephone call came through. Usually, the officer in charge answered it. But it was an unspoken rule that she answered it if there was no one around.

'Someone for you at the main gate,' said a voice at the end of the telephone.

Cherry looked at the telephone. Who on earth could it be? She hurried to the main gate. And standing there in his RAF uniform was Joe. A jeep was parked at the side of the security office next to the main gate where they had been dropped off the first day. She was so pleased and so surprised, that she ran into his arms. And he kissed her.

'I keep turning up,' he said when he let her go.

'How lovely,' she smiled up at him. Still in his arms. She looked over at the guard room. Two guards were leaning against the wall, their gazes fixed on the two of them in each other's arms. A few months ago she would have been embarrassed by their presence. But today she was just so happy to see Joe that she just stood there smiling, gripping both sides of his shoulders.

'What are you doing here?' she asked him.

'Just passing through, so Ike here dropped me off. Have to be back in an hour. Can you get off for an hour?'

She gave a sharp intake of breath. She could get into trouble. But what could they do? What the heck? She didn't care. He wouldn't be allowed on the base. But they could go somewhere.

'Will you get into trouble?'

'Let's just go. Somewhere. I don't think they'll get rid of me. They need as many of us as they can get.'

They climbed into the jeep behind the driver. Joe introduced her to Ike, his driver.

'There's a very old public house we passed in the village. Ike knows where it is. Let's go Ike!'

They sped off into the village. Coming to an abrupt halt outside the King's Head. Their eyes squinting to adjust to the dark interior, which smelled of last night's beer. Joe had to duck his head under the beams.

'Wow, they were small in the sixteenth century.'

'Isn't Ike coming?'

'No, he's minding the jeep.' He winked at her. 'I've had to commandeer the jeep because we need urgent medical supplies from Finsham.'

There were only two men at a small table in the middle of the room. Cherry and Joe sat in a corner, close together. She wanted to touch him.

'Oh?' then she realised he was kidding and she laughed, then grimaced, when she sipped the watery beer.

'You only have an hour? There's so much to say.' She sipped thirstily. Wondering how to tell him how she felt, but not sure how.

'Then say it now. We have ops tomorrow and I'd rather go with a clear head knowing how the land lies, than having to guess whether you're going to see me again. I wish,' he said, 'you wouldn't look that way.'

'I wasn't aware of looking any particular way.'

'You have a way of making your eyes larger when I look at you, you look like a deer caught in headlights.'

She screwed up her eyes and made a face. But went a bit pink.

'I love you,' he said. 'I want to kiss you in here. But I don't think the landlord will allow it.'

Her heart did a little leap. The burly landlord with a short moustache was eyeing them from the corner of the bar. He looked a bit like Hitler from where she sat.

'He thinks we're spies the way he's looking at us,' she said. They both laughed.

'I think he's thinking what a lot of British guys think, he's over here to take our women.'

She felt guilty but excited at the thought of him coming to find her, and no one at RAF Finsham would know they were here.

'How did you find me?'

'Finsham isn't hard to find. It's only an hour from Martlesham.'

'I hope you don't get into trouble commandeering a jeep.'

'No need to worry. I'll try and get in touch next time we've started flying again. I don't know when I'll be free. Can I call you on that telephone number? How am I going to talk to you?'

'I'll find a more convenient telephone. The one you came through is for Sick Bay; our hospital. I'd like to be able to relax when I talk to you. So how about I find one and you call me at a certain time one day.'

They sat in silence so much going through her head. She looked at his profile in the dark trying to make out what he was thinking.

'All right, write to me quick at Martlesham and let me know the number to call you on.'

She had finished her drink before she realised. She'd been gripping the sides of the glass for dear life.

She took his hand. He looked at her as if he wanted to say something.

'I have to go back now,' she said. 'I'll be in trouble as it is.'

He left his beer, and they went outside in the bright sun. Ike was smoking under the trees and caught Joe's eye looking at his watch. Joe nodded. They walked towards the tree that Ike was under, he moved towards the jeep.

Joe suddenly took Cherry in his arms under the oak tree. Leaning against the tree he began to kiss her passionately but gently. Holding her against him so that every part of their bodies touched. Moving away after what seemed a long time.

'Do you still want me? Then the answer's yes,' she said in a broken voice. What is the use of virginity, she thought, I could keep it and Joe might die. Better, oh so much better, to love him now.

He did not answer but went on kissing her, breaking off to mutter indistinguishable words. After a while, he picked her up and carried her to the jeep where Ike was revving the engine. They sat in the back together holding hands. She leaned against him as they sped back to the base. Stopping a few feet from the sentry house. He held her close to him. He rubbed his cheek against hers so hard that his face scratched hers. Then he looked at his watch.

'Christ. I must go, or they'll charge me for stealing a jeep.' He turned to look at her. Holding her away from him a moment.

'Well…do you love me, then? I have a funny feeling that you do. What shall we do about it? I know what I want to do. Make love to you until we drop dead.'

'So do I.'

Her heart was pounding, was it love? Or it could've been the effects of the beer.

'Yeah, but we're not going to. What am I doing, feeling this way? I always thought falling in love was for the other guy. I know I slept with that friend of yours. Don't look so frightened, it meant nothing. But I'd come to find you, and you were off God knows where, and I hadn't heard a word.'

'But I wrote to you! I thought you didn't want to see me because you never answered.'

'I didn't get the letter. Hell. So what next? I don't have one-night stands with a girl like you. There's only one thing for it. We must get married.'

'I can't leave here though Joe. I'm needed, I'm doing something I love. I can't leave Finsham.'

'Then we'll have to think of something,' he said. 'You can still stay in the WAAFs and still be married. The nurses do that in the States. In fact, I think they're called the Flying Angels or something. I bet the RAF have something similar.'

She sighed. 'I only know you have to leave if you get married. They assume you want to start a family straight away. But I'll find out.'

Joe was quiet, digesting what she had told him. 'I've done so well with my training. I was top of my class. And I'm definitely going to become a nurse when the war's over.'

Cherry had begun to love the place with all her WAAF friends. She helped with the injuries for the boys coming back from bombing missions. Some of them were burnt from fire breaking out in their aircraft, some with shrapnel wounds, some with bits of body parts blown off. It was heart-wrenching but so vital for her to do what she did. She could never go back home to live, she felt she was needed here. She had lots of friends and enjoyed the camaraderie amongst the WAAFs. It was what kept her going, she knew she was making friendships that would last a lifetime. She knew what she was doing was worthwhile and helping to save lives.

Cherry wanted to marry him but she knew she couldn't leave the WAAFs. If he was the one. He would wait for her.

As she walked past the sentry box her thoughts were going round in her head.

A voice shouted, 'Oi!'

She spun round. It was the sentry.

'You didn't sign out or in! Next time...' he said and grinned and winked at her.

CHAPTER 15 – The engagement

It wasn't possible to meet up again for several weeks. There was a telephone box in the village, so she noted the number and wrote to him. Joe didn't receive her phone number in a letter for two weeks, and he rang once a few days later but Cherry hadn't been in the medical quarters and the officer had answered the telephone. He had not been pleased, and Joe didn't call again. It seemed strange seeing him after all those months, the passion they felt for each other, and she wondered if she had dreamt of his visit.

'Dear Joe, Did I dream that you came to visit? That we kissed? Was it a dream?'

Joe's squadron had moved to Martlesham Heath, and even though Joe was closer to Finsham, they found it difficult to see each other. The spring weather was good and the RAF flew daily so Joe was kept busy every day. Eventually, a letter arrived from Joe four weeks after he had asked her to marry him.

'I wrote as soon as I returned,' he wrote. *'I miss you like crazy. We fly daily. God knows how long this letter will get to you. So, shall we get engaged? Yes, I think we should, don't you? You can tell your*

folks and see what your mother says. We should face your mother together so that she can tell we're serious. I don't want you to face her alone.'

That's sweet, she thought, but there's no need, I can face up to her now, now I've spent a year away from home and she doesn't influence my actions.

Joe and Cherry finally met up six weeks later. At the first meeting, he told her of the sweeps into France and Belgium he had made. He was so happy they were fighting the Luftwaffe after all the training. Then he bought her a ring from a little jeweller's shop in Cambridge. They spent the day walking by the river in the sunshine. In a cosy café, they held hands and looked at each other over a pot of tea and scones between them. Cherry was too excited to eat. She just wanted to hold Joe's hand and gaze into his face.

'I've written to my parents to tell them I've just got engaged,' he said. 'My parents will be so excited to meet you. I have a photograph of my family I keep in my breast pocket. I want a photograph of you too, so I can keep it close to my heart.'

They were so happy sitting close to each other her arm through his, then he'd look at her and she'd blush.

'Is this what it's like to be in love?' she asked him. 'I suppose that's why it feels like an eternity since the last time we met.'

'I think about you all the time,' he said. 'Sometimes it's hard to concentrate on the job.' Then he laughed at her, 'Don't worry, it'll be all right. Once I'm in the pilot's seat, can focus on the task.'

They were completely immersed in each other overlooking the River Nene. They didn't even notice the daffodils had gone over and their heads and leaves were drooping now the weather was warmer. Summer was on its way.

It was a busy time with the Luftwaffe bombing cities and towns in Britain during the day and blitzing at night, destroying industrial areas but also decimating populated areas. Civilians were bombed out of their homes and being killed daily. The RAF fought fiercely to try and stop them taking control of the skies.

Cherry often watched the Vickers Wellingtons and Bristol Blenheim bombers fly out on early daylight raids little did she know they had been sent to target German warships hiding off the Scottish mainland and German airfields. But their bomber aircraft were easy targets for the faster Messerschmitts and British losses were heavy. Sally was sometimes gone all night working in the hangars, and when her shift finished in the morning, she fell into bed exhausted. The WAAFs in her hut got used to working different shifts passing each other as one went on watch, and another WAAF went off watch. Cherry often fell exhausted into her bed, she'd look around before she closed her eyes, to see many other beds were empty. Sally, in particular, would have to fix an aircraft before she went off watch, she very often did not return to the hut until late at night.

Cherry often passed by the hangars to see Jessie and her all-female civilian crew, patching up the damaged bombers that had returned. As soon as radar detected enemy bombers the air raid siren went up, the lights went out and they held their breaths for the enemy aircraft to pass over, often still sitting on top of or under a damaged Wellington bomber. They listened to the hum of the Heinkels passing overhead on their way to inflict more damage on the industrial areas of London, Coventry, Liverpool, and the big cities of England. Southampton and Portsmouth Naval ports were major targets and were being heavily bombed. She saw the newspapers and heard from the crew which cities had been damaged heavily the night before. She prayed that they would miss her parents' house and that her family stayed safe.

Thousands of civilians were killed or made homeless. Scotland too did not escape. The industrial areas of Clydeside suffered badly from the bombing at this time by the Luftwaffe. Moral was low but Churchill rallied the population with his speeches:

We shall fight in France, we shall fight on the seas and oceans, we shall fight on the beaches, we shall fight on the landing grounds, we shall never surrender'.

Cherry and Joe met up again as the summer turned into another hot one. Joe usually managed to get transport when he came to see her at Finsham. Picking her up in the jeep and taking her to the pub so they could sit and be together. One time the landlord even commented.

'A yank in an RAF uniform?'

'Yes,' said Cherry quickly. 'They're here to help defend us. Be thankful.' They walked away quickly from the men at the bar who looked like farm workers. She didn't like the look on their faces, they looked as if they were ready to start an argument.

'They don't trust us…Americans,' Joe said, 'I guess they think we're over here to steal their women.'

'They shouldn't treat you like criminals. People like that landlord mistrust everyone. Anyone who looks a bit different or out of the ordinary. Look at us!' She laughed.

Cherry felt she didn't have a care in the world. She wrote to her parents to tell them of the impending wedding plans .

'Don't worry Papa about the cost. We have enough to get married and we'll be married in uniform, we'll have to return to base as soon as we can. So no time for a honeymoon until next year or until after the war!'

Her mother replied almost apoplectic in her writing. *'Married in uniform? Not my daughter. If you must marry your American at least come home soon so we can organise your wedding and a dress!'*

But it was a while before she could return home. Cherry spent as much time as she could with Joe, who knew when they would see each other next?

The Luftwaffe chose to bomb cities all over Britain in an attempt to pulverise the British into submission. They still chose to fly under the radar and cause damage to the airfields in Norfolk. Since the last raid, the RAF had updated its defences. Finsham now had Bofors, large anti-aircraft guns, as well as pillboxes and mobile defence units all around the airfield. Nowadays it was less likely that enemy fighters would get as far as Finsham under the radar. Everyone was busy with repairs when the base was attacked by the Luftwaffe and when enemy aircraft offloaded its bombs before turning back to Germany.

Sally updated Cherry when a Wellington didn't return home. There were squadrons of Spitfires and Hurricanes coming and going during the summer months and Cherry tried to find out if it was anyone she knew, but usually they were young crews, who were inexperienced and with as little as five hours flying time.

Before she realised it there was another WAAF hut built because conscription in December made more single women join up between the ages of 20 and 30, their camp was filling up very quickly with WAAFs. Another hangar was built next to the remaining ones, they looked outside to see the huts being painted in camouflage paint.

'When did that happen?' She asked Sally one day.

'Oh, not long ago. Our numbers have quadrupled since last year. And anyway, you've been busy,' Sally said.

'I hardly see you now,' she said putting her arm through her friend's arm.

'I know, we're all so busy. And usually, I meet up with John after work.'

'Aha, I thought I saw you holding hands. Isn't that against regulations?' Cherry joked.

'I hope no one else saw us?' said Sally seriously. Although she didn't really mind who saw them. 'We were careful to watch who was about. We were only walking around the village.'

'Is John a fitter too?'

'Yes, he came to Finsham two months ago. We've just started courting.'

'Well, I want to meet him soon.'

'You will, and then I want to meet Joe.'

Cherry was kept busy in sick bay as the injuries to those flying over Europe became intense. Eventually Sick Bay grew into a small hospital, and the more seriously wounded were transported to local bigger hospitals for treatment. Some of the returning bombers had injured personnel inside. Their aircraft were shot by flak and bodies were burned. Recently she had had to extricate a young crewman from a damaged aircraft. He had tried to put out a fire but had received third-degree burns all over his body. Cherry and Ivy pulled the man out as quickly as they could and transferred him to the hospital. But he died in hospital later. She felt desolate at these times. She would quietly go back to her hut and try and sleep with the image of the burned man imprinted on her mind. Cherry would often hear a young WAAF crying in the middle of the night for some missing airmen who hadn't returned.

Every time she assisted a wounded airman, she thought of Joe scrambling to get out of a Spitfire cockpit which was on fire. She didn't see him for a month as his squadron was doing sweeps over Europe regularly. He didn't tell her what he was doing or where he'd been going, and she didn't ask. She knew she'd worry all the more.

As the weather turned cooler they had some rainy days in Norfolk. Flying was cancelled for the day and Joe usually managed to borrow the jeep to meet up with her. In September it rained for a week. And Joe picked her up in his jeep and they went for a walk after going to the pub. They found themselves in the church porch huddled together dripping wet. But Cherry didn't care about getting wet, she was warm with Joe's arm around her.

'Perhaps we stand a better chance of getting married in Finsham's church,' she said, as they looked in through the doors. It looked cold inside, but light shone through the stained-glass windows and highlighted the colourful saints that looked down over the altar below. They looked up the aisle from the font. Joe leaned against the font.

'I agree with your mother,' he said, you should get married in a white wedding dress. You'll regret it if you don't, it should be our greatest day.' They held hands looking up the aisle towards the altar. She looked at him in surprise.

'If you think so,' she said. 'In that case, I'll have to go home to see if it can be made in time for our wedding.'

'We should probably just say December, to keep it real. The weather's kinda unpredictable around then, so we don't fly as much. Plus, I'm more likely to get time off for my own wedding.'

The light filtered through the multi-coloured church windows. She looked sideways at him, disappointed that he agreed so readily.

'But I'll still take you home so I can meet your folks. So how about if we aim for a weekend in November for a forty-eight-hour pass?'

'Good idea,' she said thinking it would be tricky, but pleased he'd suggested it.

'Your supervisor may take pity on you as we've had no chance to get this wedding organised, have we? Mine will be more difficult to get. It all depends on the day.'

So much to organise. It was exciting. She hoped they could get the time off.

The Luftwaffe was blitzing London night after night. The anti-aircraft guns and barrage balloons did their best to bring down the Luftwaffe. But the sheer numbers overwhelmed the defence force and London was ablaze each night, especially the East End.

At Finsham, the Luftwaffe decided to fly under the radar once more and strafe the station. They were met with heavy machine guns in sandbagged emplacements around the airfield. This time no one was killed. Security was even tighter as more aircraft and personnel descended on the station the following month.

The weather turned cold and in November she was instructed to accompany three seriously wounded airmen to a special hospital near

London. A petrol bowser had exploded and the airmen were rushed to Queen Victoria Hospital, East Grinstead for emergency aftercare. They flew from Finsham to the RAF Hospital in Wroughton, where the airmen were left in the care of WAAF medical orderlies like herself. After transfer to a stretcher, they whisked them off in an ambulance to the hospital, it had taken an hour from Finsham to Wroughton which had probably saved the airmen's lives.

Cherry still hadn't managed to arrange time off for a weekend to Portsmouth. She was chosen to accompany injured airmen flying to hospitals around the country, and often didn't return until after the weekend. It was a new idea for medical orderlies to accompany sick airmen and before she realised it, she had become part of an air ambulance unit, which ferried the injured across RAF stations and hospitals around Britain. It was a busy time. She enjoyed flying to different parts of the country, passing the sick and injured into the hands of experts and flying back to Finsham. But it did mean she didn't see Joe some weekends.

On December 7th Cherry was shocked to learn of the bombing of Pearl Harbour in Hawaii. On the following day the United States Congress declared war on Japan. When Cherry spoke to Joe about the news, he was calm, and said he was resigned that the USAAF was now in the war.

'Now the Japs have blown up Pearl Harbour, Churchill and Roosevelt will have to get together and find a way of combining forces against Hitler.'

'Britain stands more of a chance of beating Hitler with you on our side,' said Cherry. 'Now Britain won't be on its own anymore. We stand a chance of winning with you Americans.'

It wasn't until Christmas time when Joe's squadron rested back at Martlesham Heath again, that they were able to go back to Portsmouth on Christmas Eve and Joe was finally able to meet Cherry's parents.

Joe spoke to her father in the sitting room over a glass of brandy. Even Tommy behaved himself interrupting Joe only twice, with Mr Caldwell asked him questions about his flying. Mr Caldwell was genial towards Joe and if he remembered Joe and Cherry straightening their clothes the first time he met Joe, he didn't mention it.

The new idea was to book the wedding for May or June when it was warmer and there were more flowers about, and her mother had had time to amend her wedding dress. Cherry had more training coming up and Joe was busy too. Cherry tried on her mother's old wedding dress upstairs in her old bedroom. She was surprised how excited her mother was now that it looked like the wedding was getting closer. Her mother said she would alter the dress to fit Cherry because wedding dress material was very hard to come by. The treatment of Joe previously seemed to have been forgotten, and Joe never mentioned it again. Cherry caught him looking at her when they were all together in the sitting room. Joe was sitting in the same place where they had been in July last year. Memories of their first encounter flitted through her mind and she looked at Joe and smiled. He seemed to be thinking the same thing and their eyes met and he gave her a conspiratorial wink. It was good her parents didn't see it, she thought, her mother would have been horrified.

Her father seemed jovial and her mother actually smiled at Joe. They decided to get married at the beginning of June. Mrs. Caldwell said she would organise things. Joe wanted to be married sooner. But Cherry wanted a sunny day if she was to be married in a white dress. She couldn't think of anything worse than getting married in the cold and wet. Joe was also due to go on special training in the Spring. Mrs Caldwell said she would organise the reading of the banns at the local church beforehand and alter the dress.

Cherry and Joe spent a pleasant three days with her parents which was only marred by the fact that her mother sighed every few minutes because she still had not heard from Sidney. After asking Joe a lot of questions about his family. Mrs

Caldwell cheered up very quickly when she found out that Joe's family lived in a large house with servants. And that Joe's father had a good job as an accountant and his mother and sisters did not work.

Joe had to go on ops training in January and Cherry had to fly up to a snowy Scotland with a special patient. The weather was so bad that the crew had to wait until the next day before the snow melted before they could fly back. There were no more flights for a few weeks after that. The snow covered most of Scotland and England and flights ground to a halt.

Joe's squadron was moving on and preparing for another operation. It would be happening in the next few weeks. There was no leave granted. But he managed to get to Finsham to see her before he went on training.

'Never mind honey, we're practicing for the biggest operation yet. The CO has promised we can have leave after the op, in the next few weeks, we can organise it for then.'

'You look tired,' she hugged him. 'At least America is properly in the war now.'

'They'll send planes and personnel to back us up, I guess. And Eagle squadron will have to disband and we'll have to join the USAAF. We may have to move on...will you come with me?' He looked at her earnestly.

'Let's wait and see.' She smiled ruefully, 'My wedding dress is ready and waiting.'

'Are you very disappointed?' he squeezed her hand.

'No. I know we'll get married when you return.'

Joe sighed. 'We're training daily for special ops. I've been promised leave after that.'

'It'll be better once summer comes, you'll see,' she said. 'Nothing can stand in the way of us getting married in August.' She said happily.

CHAPTER 16 – December 1941

The bombing of the south of England was now a daily occurrence, and in January Cherry received a letter from her father. It had been opened by the censor and had taken four weeks to get to her. But the south of England had been bombed by the Luftwaffe for 3 nights in a row. It was relentless and dozens of people had been killed. She hurried to the telephone box outside the shop in the village and called her parents. The telephone rang and rang... No one was at home.

The next day she tried to call her parents again. She called home on Saturday night from the telephone box again, the telephone rang and rang again but still no one answered it. She could stand it no longer - by now she knew something was wrong. She had to go home immediately. She managed to get an emergency pass and caught the train home. By the time she reached her local train station, it was dark. The lights were on as she walked up the drive to her parent's house, the kitchen curtains were open. She was surprised, her Papa had never allowed this to happen in the past. But when she opened the front door, she got the shock of her life. Her brother Sidney was sitting with her mother at the kitchen table.

'Sid!' she shouted. He stood up and she hurried over to him and wrapped her arms around him in a hug, she had forgotten that he looked so much like her brother Bill. Mrs Caldwell remained sitting looking down at the table.' It was when she looked up into Sid's face that she realised something was terribly wrong. 'It's Papa,' he said. 'He was killed last night in a bombing raid.'

Cherry was frozen to the spot. She hadn't expected that. She slowly sat down and stared at her mother at the table. Her mother had red eyes and had been crying.

'When did it happen?' She didn't know what to ask next. She tried to find the words, but they wouldn't come. 'How come you're here Sid, so quickly?'

'I arrived home this morning. They gave me leave when my ship docked last night. If they'd let me come home straight away... well, I might've been able to stop him going out somehow.' His eyes filled up with tears.

'It might not have made any difference. Your Papa would still have gone out to help others in the blitz,' his mother said. 'He always put others first.'

'Where is he?' Cherry asked quietly, envisioning his body being picked up and put in an ambulance, just like he had for others.

'At the hospital,' her brother answered for his mother. 'Did you get leave?'

'Yes, I couldn't get an answer from home although I rang and rang,' she looked at her mother. 'I thought something was up when you didn't answer so I just went to see the CO and caught the next train.' She wished Joe was here with her. Her throat was sore, she couldn't swallow and her heart was pounding. Her instincts had been right, it was her father who had been killed.

'The line's been down since last week. The outhouse caught a direct hit by an incendiary about two weeks ago where the line runs,' her mother said dully staring at the table.

Cherry looked at her brother's tanned face and contemplated what she should do.

'It's a good job you are home now Sid. You can help us.'

'Will you get leave for the funeral?'

'I'll have to call and get special leave from my CO.'

She looked at her mother again, the life seemed to have gone out of her. Everything seemed to slow down.

'Where was Papa when he was killed?'

'A few streets away near the docks.'

'Not far from me then,' said Sid quietly. 'We had to go in a bunker while the Krauts were bombing the harbour. The bombs missed our ship, but the Navy wouldn't let us leave until they'd passed over. Dad must've been killed in that raid.'

The funeral of Mr Caldwell was in her local church where Cherry had been confirmed and where she had hoped to marry Joe. Cherry and her mother cried during the funeral while Sidney looked sombre and Tommy looked confused and stared down at his feet during the service. The church was full because everyone had known the local warden, he had been a popular man. Sidney gave the eulogy. He was a friend and neighbour to many in the area and had rescued many from the bombings, and many people were tearful.

After the funeral Cherry went straight back to Finsham, she felt better back in the support of her friends. She was kept busy at work but felt desolate, and couldn't quite believe what had happened. Bill, now Papa gone. Who was next?

Sally tried to keep her friend cheerful when they went out for a walk in the surrounding countryside, the following weekend. They walked along a track alongside farmer's fields. There was nothing identifiable growing in the winter crops. The grass was wet and there'd been an air frost during the night. It was pleasant ambling along in the weak winter sunshine. Cherry felt as if her worries were lifting off her shoulders.

'Thanks for suggesting this walk,' she said to her friend. 'And for keeping me busy. I know you probably were meeting up with John today. And I've kept you from him.'

'No of course not,' Sally denied. But Cherry noticed a hesitation in her voice. 'It's good to catch up with you, we're ships that pass in the night at the moment.'

'It's early days for me and John,' said Sally.

'You're right to be hesitant. But from what I've seen of him he's besotted with you. And who wouldn't be? You're the best-looking WAAF on the camp. And the cleverest.'

Sally snorted and laughed.

'You are too! Everyone knows it. And John seems pretty wise for his age. You two will go along fine.'

'We have talked of him coming to meet my folks next month.'

'Gosh, it must be serious.'

'Just as a forty-eight pass, if we can both get leave. I haven't had leave in so long I forget what it's like.'

'Yes, it's difficult for Joe and I to catch a weekend together. Unless it's bad weather, but then I'm usually working these days anyway.' Cherry shrugged her shoulders.

'Keep trying. It was meant to be, after all those months of missing each other.'

'Joe's got something big coming up, he'll have leave when he returns.'

'We have some USAAF personnel coming into the camp now, have you noticed?'

'Can't say I have.'

'And there's talk of more. They're bringing their B17's here as well. The Sergeant said.'

'Wow, are they big planes?'

'As big as the Lancaster.'

They discussed the merits of which was the best bomber. Sally knew a lot about the new American bomber, but they agreed that the Lancaster was the better aircraft.

'I'm glad I can talk to you about these planes there's no one else in our hut who's remotely interested,' Sally said.

'Do the Nazis realise that Finsham has a large fleet of bombers ready to send over to Hitler?' Cherry asked her.

'Oh, I'm sure they do. There are loads of other USAAF stations springing up with just this capability. I wouldn't like to be on the receiving end when they get sent over to Germany.'

'That's why they're building up the security around this site,' said Cherry. 'I've seen more airmen with guns this week than I've seen the whole time I've been here!'

When they returned from their walk, Cherry felt happy that they had spent some time together. They didn't know when they'd have the time to do it again.

Although the medical bay had the capacity for minor surgery, more serious cases were sent to a private hospital in Cambridge. Those convalescing from surgery, injuries and illnesses were often sent to Thriplow House, a Victorian manor just two miles east of Duxford that had been requisitioned by the RAF after the outbreak of war.

When nearly 1,700 personnel of the US Army Air Force arrived in April 1942 the sick bay was moved to Thriplow House with building 10 remaining as the base's primary care centre. Working at Thriplow gave Cherry a more relaxed way of working instead of being at the medical centre next to the noisy airfield during the day and its noisy alarms going off at night.

Thriplow House was better for the patients as well. It was an old, quiet house and gave the patients a calmer atmosphere. It was responsible for treating injured fighter pilots returning from operations as well as the everyday medical needs of the squadrons. Working at Thriplow she was closer to Joe and they managed to get together at the weekends when it was cold and raining. But Spring was warming things up and soon the weekends were clearer and Joe was flying sorties again.

When she returned to her hut at Finsham, most of her WAAF friends were not around. Cherry went to the Naafi and was shocked to see a whole line of USAAF personnel lining up for tea. She decided to take her tea outside because there were no seats to be had. A huge B17 flew passed her as she made her way across the parade ground, and landed on the runway. It appeared to be the largest aeroplane she had ever seen. She was shocked. When had that happened? When had they all arrived? And she'd missed it.

A vehicle loaded with G.I.'s swept past her with the horn blaring and she nearly jumped out of her skin. They were armed to the teeth, with heavy machine guns mounted on a following trailer.

Sergeant Beck was walking towards her and observed her surprise. 'They're practising defence of the airfield,' he said.

'When did the US Army Air Force turn up?' she asked him.

'Last week. They've brought their B17's with them as well.' He pointed to a row of aircraft lined up in the distance on the other side of the airfield. A large group of airmen were busy in the distance.

'They're making the runways bigger - laying connecting steel planks to build another runway and making them longer, so we can accommodate the larger planes from now on.'

Cherry nodded, 'Ingenious.'

'Looks like we're gonna get busy.'

The Americans had arrived to help with daytime and nighttime bombing of Germany. Now they would win the war, the G.I's told them. They seemed confident and cock-sure but very young. Cherry felt ancient standing next to some of them. The girls often watched the huge B17's lumbering along the extended runway ready for take-off during the day. At night they heard the rumbling as they returned from their sorties.

Cherry was tearful when she thought of her Papa, and wished she had been to see him at Christmas before he was killed. Why was it always the good that died first?

One Friday evening in April the telephone rang in the medical centre. It was Joe, he had been put through by her friend Nancy, from the main switchboard.

'I've had a hell of a job trying to get through. We're moving to Debden tomorrow.'

'Oh, all right. I'll know to write you there then.'

'I hate not being able to see you. You keep me calm.'

'I'm on duty tonight,' she said. 'In my last letter I told you all about working here at Thriplow House.'

'I haven't had any letters from you for two weeks.' He sounded harassed and stressed.

'Sorry We have ops on and it's very busy in here tonight. You were lucky to be put through.'

'I realise that now. I said it was urgent.'

'Oh, Joe. How are you? You sound worried.'

'I wished I could've come home with you.'

'Yes, I wished you could. I miss you.'

'Just another month, then this ops thing will be over. We're moving on tomorrow, that's why I'm calling you now. I was thinking we would be married by June but it looks like we're building up to something big next month. They won't tell us where until the last moment. I've missed you like crazy. I'll ring you on Saturday before we leave.'

'All right. Yes, I've missed you too.' She said unable to leave the emotion out of her voice.

Cherry made sure she was outside the telephone box in the village on Saturday night for his call. If it was engaged and someone was in the box, she would look through the window and look pleadingly at the person willing them to hurry up and finish their call. She wasn't very good at waiting.

More American uniforms were turning up at the camp. There were more of their green uniforms than there were of the blue RAF uniforms. Another hangar had appeared almost overnight. Where had that come from?

With Cherry backwards and forwards to Thriplow House with injured airmen she saw the gradual building up of Finsham. Cherry missed seeing her friends, she and Ivy were at Thriplow House during the day working long days and just returning to sleep in the hut and out again early in the morning.

Cherry was walking towards sick bay and saw Sally one day coming across the parade ground. She waved to her. They looked up as a thundering Lancaster bomber passed overhead coming into land. They watched in awe as it circled in a huge arc and majestically came down on the extended runway. It landed with a faint bump of its wheels on the tarmac.

'That pilot knows what he's doing,' said Sally. 'I'd love to fly one of those.'

'When I joined up, I asked to fly an aeroplane,' Sally told her. 'The WAAF officer laughed at me.'

They stood watching as it taxied to a stop not far from a hanger where a group of fitters watched it admiringly. It was the first Lancaster that had landed at the base and every RAF personnel who was outside was watching in admiration as it glided to a stop.

'That Lancaster is about the same size as a B17 but seems more majestic somehow,' said Sally.

'I've never seen a B17,' said Cherry. 'How on earth do they get off the ground?'

'Goodness knows, but we'll find out soon. Because I heard we're going to get some soon, along with their American crews. So we'll be bursting at the seams here.'

They stared in amazement as the pilot got down from the aircraft and took off her helmet, as she shook her head free, shoulder-length blonde hair fell around her shoulders, she pushed her flying goggles up on her head and looked around her. The girls stood like everyone else, with their mouths open. Then Sally seemed to wake up and hurried over to where the woman in a dark blue uniform stood at the side of the plane.

'You seem to be able to talk, unlike those chaps over there,' the woman thumbed behind her to a group of fitters who stood staring at her.

'I've never seen a woman pilot before!' exclaimed Sally. 'I doubt they've seen one. Are you a WAAF?'

The woman showed her badge that said 'ATA' on her breast pocket. 'Good heavens no, they wouldn't let me join the WAAFs they said I wasn't allowed to fly! So we set up our own air transport.'

By now Cherry had run up behind her friend. 'Where can we take you? And how did you manage to fly a Lanc with no crew?'

'Training. And I'm a civilian. I'm Betsy, from the Air Transport Auxiliary. And we ferry new planes from factory to airbase, and sometimes the derelict ones to the Knackers yard!' She hoicked her parachute over her shoulder. 'Now tell me, ladies, point me in the direction of your Dispersal.'

Sally, who'd been hanging on her every word said with a smile, 'Even better. I'll take you!'

'Thanks, no one seems to have seen a female pilot before,' the woman said observing young erks watching her from the sidelines, astonishment evident on their faces. The girls marched alongside Sally, who was grinning from ear to ear.

'You're a sight for sore eyes, for sure,' she said. 'You just showed the RAF how to land a Lancaster!'

Cherry hurried behind them. 'I haven't seen one before, I mean one of you, ATA women, before. Or even a Lancaster close-up.' She stuttered, she wanted to ask so many questions. This woman was doing what she had always wanted to do – flying aeroplanes.

'Well, now you have.' The woman said. 'Women can fly anything. You just need the training.'

The girls were so pleased to speak to an actual female pilot. Sally pointed to a door, they had arrived at Dispersal. The female pilot smiled at them both and shook hands with them.

'What kind of planes do you fly?' Sally hung onto her hand, desperate not to let her go.

‘All sorts darling. I have to tell you, when I fly across this country delivering planes in all weathers and trying to keep away from enemy aircraft, it’s as dangerous as it gets for a girl!’ she said. ‘Now I must go and deliver the paperwork.’ And the pilot from the ATA disappeared into Dispersal.

‘I wish I could go in there and see their faces when they see it’s a woman pilot delivering a Lanc for them!’

‘That’d be a picture.’

‘Shall we wait for her to come out?’

‘I can’t, I’m on duty in five minutes,’ and she rushed off. Cherry made her way to the medical quarters, reluctant to leave, she wanted to catch the woman coming out of Dispersal, but knew she had to get back to sick bay.

The weather was warming up and more Americans were flying in with B17 Flying Fortresses. They were so big that the airfield thundered when they took off and landed. All the RAF personnel were in awe of them. Although thirty B17s took off most days in the spring of 1942 on special operations to Germany, many didn’t come back. The RAF watched them take off and counted them back on their return each time. It was becoming common for them to be attacked by enemy aircraft. One day they only counted fifteen returning - only half. The truth was that the lumbering aircraft were no match for the Luftwaffe who lay in wait for them and attacked them. The B17 was a tough plane able to withstand heavy damage and able to fly with only two engines. But it was slow and heavy and was unable to fully protect itself. As a result, Cherry and Ivy's work became a lot busier. There were many injured returning, some airmen had been shot by flak or died of their wounds when their plane caught fire.

After a few weeks some of the cheerful American faces, that the girls had gotten to know, were missing; the lifespan of the bomber crews was becoming notoriously short-lived. On the base, people were becoming disillusioned and depressed, with so many crews being killed.

When spring turned into summer, the Luftwaffe attacks on aircraft from Finsham became less and less. The USAAF introduced the B52 fighter plane. These aeroplanes were now accompanying the B17's and protecting them from the Luftwaffe. The B52 had a large enough fuel tank to accompany the monster aircraft to Germany and back. They would see off any German fighter plane that had an idea to pick on any lumbering aircraft that wasn't quick enough to fight back.

Dances were being organised in the town hall by the Americans regularly, and the WAAFs looked forward to dancing on a Saturday night. American flags hung across the ceiling from end to end of the hall. Cherry asked Joe to call her in the telephone kiosk on a Friday evening instead, so that she could go to the dances on Saturday. When Joe rang her, she thought it better not to tell him she had been dancing last Saturday with an American soldier dancing the 'jitterbug.' He had wanted to get to know her better, but she had said no, she was about to get married. The young man was disheartened, but she knew he would find someone else at the next dance.

Cherry wrote to her mother asking her to arrange the wedding for September at their local church. Her mother was very anxious. Sidney had gone back to sea and she was on her own with Tommy.

'Can't you come home anyway?' her mother sounded distraught. 'I'm on my own here, I need some help.'

'I'll try, I can't promise.' She told her mother.

Joe rang and told her it would be the last phone call for a while until they returned from special ops. He had written to her – *'so expect a letter...'* he said.

'That sounds ominous,' she said trying to sound light-hearted, he sounded so serious, and she was starting to worry.

'It must be something big if you can't talk about it,' she said when they spoke on the telephone. 'Will I see you soon?'

'Sure honey. You're right, it's big, so I can't say...but I wrote you a letter and it'll ease your worrying.'

But it didn't.

'I wished we had married in July now,' she said. 'We should've just gone and done it.' But in her heart of hearts, she knew it wouldn't have been a good idea, they wouldn't have had much of a chance to be together, with Joe away on training for ops all the time, and Cherry hardly getting any time off because ~~she was~~ they were so busy in sick bay. The number of injured airmen returning from their trips over Germany had tripled and the medical orderlies were kept busy working day and night, helping the injured and badly burned airmen out of the aircraft and rushing them to hospital to treat them.

CHAPTER 17 - August 1942, Dieppe

Joe didn't ring at all in August, but Cherry did receive a letter. It hadn't been opened by the sensor.

'My darling Cherry, they won't let us use the telephone from now on. Tomorrow, we go on special ops. By the time you get this in a week or two, I hope, it will all be over. I won't be able to get in touch until ops has finished which will be the end of August. And then we can be together - no more ops for a while then, so we can get married. I'll ring you as soon as I can. Yours forever, Joe.'

By mid-august, she hadn't received a telephone call from him. She started to feel an awful pain in her gut. On the base some of the crews were talking about an operation that had gone horribly wrong in France. Her worst fears were answered when she picked up a paper from the village shop and the sight brought a stab to her heart.

The newspapers were full of a raid on Dieppe. There were individual reports from reporters that it had been a disaster and thousands had been killed.

At first, after 19th August the media talked about the heroes of the Dieppe raid. But as the days went by the attitude in the newspapers changed; the operation had been a catastrophe. Cherry had bought a newspaper every day trying to glean as much information as she could. The Canadians and British had lost many men. But little else was mentioned. The British government was keeping tight wraps on what had happened and how many men had lost their lives. It was frustrating that she couldn't obtain any more information. But she knew in her heart of hearts that Joe would have contacted her by now if things were all right.

Cherry rang RAF Martlesham but the RAF wouldn't tell her anything. She needed confirmation, she needed to know what had happened. The not knowing drove her nearly mad. So, she wrote to Joe's commander, and two weeks later she had a reply. He had known about Joe's impending nuptials. But he said the situation was a mess, they didn't know who had been captured and who had died. Many of his men had been shot down. Some had returned. No, Joe hadn't been one of them. Her heart sank.

As she sat on her bed no tears fell, but her throat felt swollen and she felt that she couldn't breathe properly. She started coughing and felt hot and unwell, but she knew it was because she was stressed and couldn't sleep. Her CO asked her if she had a cold. But she quickly confirmed that she felt fine and that it was because her Joe had gone MIA.

Joe was recorded as 'Missing In Action.' But what on earth had happened to him? Not knowing knawed away in her stomach. There was no confirmation that he'd been captured, wounded or killed. She wrote and spoke of her anxiety to her mother, but no reply letter came back. Night after night she lay awake thinking about how he might have died. Visions of him on fire trying to get out of an aeroplane haunted her. Sally was the only person she could really tell her true fears to.

As the days went by, Cherry was back into the routine of working in sick bay, and she tried to keep up the pretence of not showing how upset she was. Sally told her she was being typically British and 'trying to keep a stiff upper lip.'

Work kept her busy, day after day, and her CO told her that if Joe had been captured or wounded she would have heard about it. He wasn't coming back, otherwise he would have found a way to get in touch. Sally was sympathetic and tried to keep things positive. What should she do now? Her whole future depended on Joe. There was a period where she wished she hadn't met up with him again. She wished she hadn't written to him. And then she wouldn't be feeling this big ache in her heart. All these negative thoughts kept circulating her head and she tried to get rid of them.

What did her friend Sally say? '*Better to have loved and lost than never to have loved at all.*' She wasn't sure about that. The ache in her heart was telling her that it was painful to miss someone, just like millions of other mothers, daughters, and fiancées. She wished she hadn't fallen in love at all. When Sally came into the mess and saw Cherry crying into the pillow, she tried to get her to go for a walk with her, thinking it would distract her. But Cherry didn't want to go. She didn't want to talk. She just wanted to mope around in the hut.

The fated Dieppe raid on 19th August was the only time the three Eagle Squadrons saw action operating together. On 29 September 1942, the three squadrons were officially transferred from the RAF to the Eight Air Force of the United States Air Force. The American pilots became officers in the USAAF. The Eagle pilots had earned 12 Distinguished Flying Crosses and one Distinguished Service Order – but only four of the 34 original Eagle pilots were still present when the squadrons joined the USAAF. About 100 Eagle pilots had been killed, were missing, or were prisoners.

Mrs. Caldwell wrote to Cherry and told her to come home, she was sad too. But it wasn't until the end of October that Cherry had the courage to go home and face her mother.

It was strange to think that her Papa would not be walking through the door at any moment. Only Mother and Tommy were there. Sidney had re-joined his ship and had left Portsmouth, not knowing where he was going. Cherry thought he was probably glad to leave because her mother could wear you down when she was depressed.

Mrs Caldwell greeted her daughter with little enthusiasm when she turned up at the door. She sat down heavily and looked as if she were about to cry.

Cherry tried to be cheerful, but the atmosphere was bleak. Her mother hardly spoke to her except to say it was a tragedy that she had lost Joe. Tommy was allowed out to play in the streets with his friends and Mrs Caldwell sat by her window looking out all day long, she no longer interested in the W.I.

'I feel like that too Mother. With Joe gone, I feel sad too.'

Her mother looked desolate and Cherry felt sorry for her.

'But,' she said, 'You're not the only one who's lost a loved one. And I've lost three. Papa, a brother and a fiancé.'

The leaves turned bronze and fell from the trees as she walked down the lane towards the field where Tommy was playing with his friends.

She stood under the big oak tree watching the boys racing across the field yelling to each other at the top of their voices.

A low-flying Wellington bomber was grinding its noisy way towards Cherry from the horizon and then passed overhead making a careful approach to the local aerodrome. She could see its bomb doors were stuck open. Tommy and his friends were yelling at it. It was high sport to be dare-devilling the aeroplanes to drop their bombs. The group of boys ran to the other end of the field. She watched them for a few minutes. The vibrations ground at her nerves. She shouted at the group of boys to stop. The noise of the engines was deafening. The engines reverberated as the bomber passed overhead slowly, they were going as slow as they could. They were probably trying to manually wind the doors up, but she couldn't tell. She burst into tears thinking of them. But in a few moments, it was out of view.

It was a dangerous feat to land a plane safely when this happened and she'd heard a plane explode at Finsham airfield once when their bomb doors had stuck. She could feel a palpable sense of panic and defeat for the crew. It was bad luck for the Wellington. She crossed her fingers. But she hadn't heard an explosion yet. She wished the crew good luck.

She still felt numb as if she was in a dream and any moment she'd wake up and Joe would have returned. But it hadn't happened and time was dragging on. How sad that daily young men and women were dying. She flinched a little when she heard an explosion in the distance. The crew had not survived. Her stomach felt empty, and she felt nauseous thinking about them. She thought of her loved ones who'd been killed. She hadn't really thought that Joe would be killed. He had seemed larger than life. He seemed to have gone away and forgotten to return. But there were no more telephone calls from him and no one to talk to, apart from Sally and some of the other WAAFs. The past few months had been blissful with him, and she had forgotten that he was flying daily and could be shot down at any time. The bomber flying over made it real somehow. She thought he would be indestructible. What on earth made her think like that? She was blinkered and in love, she had thought nothing could happen to either of them. How stupid she had been. Joe had told her he was indestructible. She had believed him. She sighed. The world was hateful. Joe gone, Papa gone, Bill and Eddie gone. Who was next?

CHAPTER 18 – The Air Ambulance Service

In November Cherry's CO called her into the office and told her that she was about to be shipped to RAF Hendon, to start special training for the Air Ambulance Service. Cherry had forgotten her CO had recommended her for training for the Service. She had had so much happen and so much on her mind with Joe gone. Every now and then she cried when her mood was low. She felt worn out like she'd been climbing a mountain, and she had no enthusiasm for anything. She decided to go and find Sally and talk to her.

'I'm leaving soon,' she told Sally. 'But. I'll come back and see you, I don't know when. Once we're in training, that's it!'

Her friend Sally had been a constant support and she wasn't surprised to hear Sally and John were getting married. Her friend would be leaving the hut. She was glad to be moving on herself. But would miss her friends so much.

'We'll meet up when this is over. I'll come and visit you. You'll be a housewife!' she said to Sally.

'Not for a while. I'm still going to serve in the WAAF until the end of the war. I can't just leave

John to fight them himself.' Sally smiled, and then she said seriously, 'I hope you meet someone soon Cherry,'

'Thanks, but it's unlikely,' Cherry shrugged. 'And I don't want to sabotage my chances of becoming a nurse. It'd probably be a good thing if I *don't* meet someone, I wouldn't want to have to give up my training as a nurse for a husband who wants me at home all the time, to bring up children. That's not me.'

She wondered if she would have given up nursing if Joe had wanted her to. Then she thought he wouldn't have wanted her to forgo something she was passionate about.

'Anyway, I don't feel ready to meet anyone, they'd have to measure up a lot to Joe. We'd been through such a lot and still stayed together,' she said sadly.

At Christmas time Cherry was allowed three days leave. Joe was constantly in her thoughts and her heart was heavy in the build-up to Christmas. Last Christmas they had gone home to Portsmouth and he'd got to know her family. It had been lovely. This year – well, she felt there wasn't much to celebrate. The streets were frozen, slippery, and empty after dark. Because there were no street lights it was dangerous to be out at night. Only when the sirens sounded did people hurry to the underground shelters.

It was a miserable Christmas without Joe and her father. She had sent Joe's mother in America a Christmas card that she had made herself. Mrs Caldwell had told Cherry that Joe's mother had sent her a box of presents that was waiting for her at home, which was a total surprise. Because rationing had bitten hard in Britain, and her family had no money, she hadn't expected much for Christmas presents. Cherry had received a bar of soap from her mother. She had knitted a pair of socks for her brother Sidney, and she made a Christmas pudding for her mother. So little and yet so much happiness from the receiver. In Cherry's parcel from Joe's mother, she had enclosed a small picture in a frame of her son when he had just received his RAF uniform - he had sent the photos home to his mother. With the Eagle Squadron flash on his shoulder, he was standing there looking proud in front of a Hawker Hurricane. She also received some stockings and some candy made in America.

'How did she know?' Cherry said to Sally. She was touched that Joe's mother was thinking of her enough to send her presents, and she was absolutely delighted with them.

At last, it was time to leave Finsham and take part in her Flying Ambulance medical training in Exeter, which was closer to her home in

Portsmouth. Her friends at Finsham said it wouldn't be the same without her. Sally wasn't due to leave until her wedding in June. But Cherry couldn't make the wedding, she already knew she would never get time off, The Air Ambulance were training for something special. The buzz was it was the impending invasion of France. But when and where would it be? The girls discussed this for a time waiting for the transport to the train station. Sally was staying with her fiancé and working over the Christmas period. Although the ground was frozen and flying had been suspended for a time - It hadn't stopped the Luftwaffe on dry days, from flying over and dropping their bombs on local towns. Nobody seemed to be able to get away from the Luftwaffe.

It was so cold when she went home at Christmas that it snowed and the snow didn't thaw for days. It was one of the coldest Christmases she ever remembered. Cherry walked to the stone in the village that her parents had erected in honour of her brother, Bill. Although his remains weren't there, it was his grave. She and Sidney had bought gravestones for her father and brother and put them next to each other in the churchyard. Her mother visited it regularly. At Christmas, they went to the church to look at the gravestones.

Her mother had transcribed simply on his tombstone: 'A dear son, William Caldwell, Killed in Action.'

Cherry pondered over Bill's headstone, then at her father's - a newer gravestone, one among many new ones at the far end of the graveyard. There were a lot of new graves here. More than last year, and the year before. The church was more than three hundred years old. The numerous new graves were of people killed locally, not just military but civilians who had been bombed.

It was a sad Christmas with just the three of them. Cherry, her mother and brother Tommy. They were all subdued that day over the small piece of Chicken that her mother had managed to buy. Cherry didn't feel hungry. Everywhere she looked in the house reminded her of her father and Bill. In the dining room the chair at the head of the table where her father used to sit, was empty. Her mother appeared to be numb, she seemed to have had her usual fighting spirit knocked out of her. Even Tommy seemed more subdued than usual. They felt the loss of her father and brother keenly.

Cherry was glad to leave after Christmas to start new training in Exeter. There were about twenty young women on the training course, and they weren't all WAAFs. Some were already nurses and not in the military. They were told they would learn about emergency field first aid in six weeks. Cherry had already learned a lot because of her experiences dealing with injured crew who came back from bombing raids over Germany.

Cherry studied keenly about new techniques and consolidated her learning. By the end of the six weeks, she had become a more competent and confident medical orderly. She felt she knew as much as some of the nurses. Some of them had not had the experiences that Cherry had had. She had kept injured airmen alive while having to deal with air sickness in the patients and herself, trying to keep them still while they were agitated and in a moving aeroplane. Some of the women left before the end of the course and eventually, there were only thirteen women left.

Cherry was able to travel back and forth on the train from Exeter to Portsmouth to see her mother. As time went on, Mrs Caldwell became calmer. Things were less fraught at home now Tommy was older and often out with friends. Her mother was constantly at home though, and Cherry tried to talk her mother into going back to the W.I. But her mother had a letter from Sidney that changed everything. He wrote to say he had been injured when his ship had been bombed at sea, and he was coming home in the next few days, and home to stay this time. He was to be invalided out of the Navy.

'I'll expect you to help me with your brother when he arrives,' Mrs Caldwell told Cherry.

'Sorry ma, I will be helping the RAF. They're sending me away on some secret mission,' she tried to make it sound important. There was no way she was staying at home with her mother, and to be told what to do - it would be like having her wings clipped. She was used to discipline in the Air Force but it was necessary for there to be order. She would not tell her mother where she was going, or what she'd be doing, just yet, because she couldn't fully trust her mother not to blab to her neighbour.

Cherry found out more information after Christmas. A letter arrived for her informing her as a new trainee nurse she was to be sent to serve under 46 Group Transport Command. Two hundred newly trained nurses would become part of the RAF's new Air Ambulance Unit. She was going to be based at one of three airfields: Down Ampney, in Gloucestershire, Blakehill Farm, in Wiltshire, and Broadwell, in Oxfordshire, which would be the areas the nurses would fly out from.

The letter said she was to be sent to Blakehill Farm in Wiltshire. She was glad because it wasn't far - only one county away from home. She wondered if they would be allowed to go home on leave before they were deployed. She found herself looking forward to starting her new job.

CHAPTER 19- RAF Blakehill Farm

In the middle of February 1944 Cherry arrived at RAF Blakehill Farm. She and a small group of newly trained Air Ambulance crew were deposited at the end of a muddy road on a cold and sunny day and their kit bags were dumped beside them.

Cherry gazed over the scene before her. She looked as the farmer's fields stretching to the south with rolling hills and pretty as a picture of small farms dotted about the countryside, with dozens of contented-looking sheep and cattle crunching on the wet, green grass.

Then she looked to the north, where they were supposed to go. They had been set down at the end of a muddy road and in front of them was a farm gate. But looking over the gate all familiarity of a farm stopped there. She scanned the surrounding countryside with a grim look on her face. In the field were rows upon rows of Nissen huts built for utility rather than comfort. It had been raining and the middle of the field was churning mud.

The place was already busting at the seams with military personnel, a service squadron with headquarters, ordnance, and quartermaster companies. The airfield was beyond the camp field which itself was full of administrative Nissen huts. In the fields beyond were a myriad of different aircraft. Douglas Dakotas, troop carriers, Flying Fortresses, and other aircraft she didn't recognise - all vying for position on the newly built runways. The noise of the roaring engines took her breath away, and the rows of aircraft in the fields next to them stretched as far as the eye could see. There were some attempts at camouflage over some of the inert aircraft, but it was obvious to those around they were grouped here for a purpose.

The airfield and camp were built on mud, and there was mud everywhere. The snow had melted and it had rained. The ground underneath her had a crusty feel of frosty mud first thing in the morning, but by the time midday came it was squelchy warm mud. A truck transported the group of women to the other side of the airfield, well away from the men and the goings-on of the newly built camp. The group of women watched the personnel fade into ants as they were dropped outside some more Nissen huts. There were three in a line. the small huts would be personnel quarters. The officers in one hut, the enlisted men in another not far away. And the women in another hut. The whole place looked dismal, busy, frenetic. Like a swarm of bees getting ready for...what? The buzz was that they were preparing for an invasion of France and that's why the aircraft were all congregating in this part of England. The hundreds of personnel were all very industrious and getting ready for the big 'off.'

Mrs Caldwell had become increasingly anxious as the time came for Cherry to catch the train to Wiltshire. There was even a tear or two as she waved goodbye. Sidney's ship was due to come in the following week. So her mother would be on her own with Tommy until then.

'I wish I could visit you,' her mother sounded genuinely sorry that Cherry was leaving. 'Are you sure you don't know where you'll end up? Or what you'll be doing?'

'I know what I'll be doing. Oh, it'll be a great adventure. I'm looking forward to it. Don't worry about me,' she said when she saw her mother's miserable face.

'I'm scared I'm going to lose another child. I've already lost one and a husband with this damn war!' Her mother shook her head.

'I'll be all right. Give Sidney my love and I'm sure it won't be long until I'll be home.' Although she hoped she wouldn't be home too soon.

Cherry wrote to her mother not long after she arrived.

'We have been sent to one of the new satellite airfields in Somerset. It's so green but cold. It is set up to cater to all the squadrons coming in from all

over the world. It has lots of runways, Dispersal areas for aircraft, administrative buildings, squadron offices, and various messes. It's huge! There are so many different nationalities here. Obviously, all working together towards a common goal. The weather is terrible though, and everywhere is muddy. The transport churns up the mud into a wallowing quagmire that hippopotami would be proud to wallow in.'

The excitement was building as different aircrews of all nationalities arrived.

By the way ma, she wrote in her letter, *don't go blabbing to the neighbours. Or you'll have me sent to prison.* Although she knew she shouldn't have written about the buildings and aircraft. She was excited to see the myriad of different nationalities and was caught up in the thrill of what was to come. She thought it was harmless to write this way. If the sensor was troubled by her letter, why he could just cross it out. It was kind of liberating in a way writing to her Mother. She felt she was sharing instead of keeping secrets. She hoped their relationship might change for the better now.

A week later she wrote another letter to her mother.

'The training started yesterday. What a surprise that was. We consolidate our training in a small Nissen hut on the other side of the airfield, well away from the men. Apart from the telephone

operators and nursing staff, we seem to be the only women here. Whether they think we need protecting from the men or whether we are sent over here so that we don't entice them away from their work we're unsure! The most exciting thing is that we are due to go up in a Dakota soon as part of our training.

We live in Nissen huts or what the Yanks call Quonset huts. They are cold and damp – no difference to Finsham really! There are a lot of American service personnel. The Americans are besotted with Betty Grable and her famous legs, the photos are everywhere where the men work. And of Lana Turner too!'

As the weeks went by, gradually more air crews arrived, things were hotting up towards the 'Big Event.' Nobody was allowed to talk about it publicly but everyone knew that they were being sent somewhere soon. The station seemed busy at all times of the day and night.

At last, she had the chance to fly in an RAF Dakota. She had done this before so wasn't worried, but some of her civilian friends were anxious that if they got air-sick they might not pass the course. The girls had been given lots of tips by their instructors to help their immersion into flying.

'When it's rough people get air sick. It's calm today so you're lucky,' the instructor told them.

'Tomorrow it will be rough weather. So, we'll find out who gets air sickness.'

Cherry had been in bumpy aircraft before when she had accompanied sick airmen in bad weather before so she knew what to expect. She was so looking forward to going up, she thought that she would be okay if there was bad weather.

That morning they were introduced to the pilots. Her pilot was called Ted, he was a cheerful Scot from Perthshire. Ted said he would take them up for their first training flight as they had calm weather at the moment. As a group of the women walked over to Ted's Dakota, another plane thundered past them coming into land. It startled some of them as it seemed so close.

Cherry noticed 'Lady Susan' painted on her nose cone when they climbed in. 'Why do you call her Lady Susan?' she asked Ted.

'After one of my relatives,' he said. 'She's been with me for a long time and she's as strong as an ox.' That seemed to placate some of the more nervous amongst the women. They were excited especially those on their first trip - for some of the nurses, it was their first flight ever.

The co-pilot was in the seat next to Ted and the others sat in the side seats of the fuselage. Ted explained to them all what to expect on their first trip. Usually, there was a crew of four, but as they were training there was just him and the co-pilot, who could be different each flight. As he taxied to the runway and spoke on his headset to the tower, Cherry relaxed, it was going to be a calm flight. She had confidence in Ted already.

It was a clear, crisp, and cold morning but when they took off at midday the sun came out. The girls were relaxed and there was hardly a cloud in the sky. As the Dakota climbed, Cherry looked down and below them, the landscape looked like miniature embroidery patches. One of the nurses was amazed by the landscape being so green. In some places where the sun had not yet reached the white frost glistened on the roofs - it was like a magical fairyland. They flew south, then out over the country of Hampshire, Sussex and over the sea. After a while turning back, the girls were quiet looking out of the windows.

'How did you like the trip?' Ted asked them.

'Amazing...Wonderful...' they answered. 'My first in a Dakota, the best,' some of them told Ted with enthusiasm.

'Of course, it won't always be as calm as today. You're lucky it's perfect weather for your first flight,' he told them.

'When it's rough some people get the flight sickness. With what you are going to do, you can't afford to get air sick, so we have to get used to some rough weather too. We should be getting that tomorrow, so we'll try again.'

'What are we going to be doing?' asked one of the girls.

'Don't you know?' he said. 'You're going to be the first women to fly into enemy territory and bring back the wounded!'

The girls looked at each other. The training they had been doing so hard and fast was making sense now.

The next day, the weather turned cloudier and there was a cold breeze. The same group of girls went up in the Dakota with a different pilot this time, called John. As time went on the flight was bumpier. Cherry felt fine, but half their group came back pale and were glad to land. Cherry was relieved the bad weather didn't affect her too much, and was rather enjoying being bounced about in a Dakota.

The next few weeks were spent going up in the aircraft with different pilots to get the girls used to different flying conditions.

It was springtime and things were hotting up towards the 'Big Event' - nobody was allowed to talk about the big event publicly, but everyone knew that they were being sent to somewhere soon. Different crews trained daily, day in and day out. The station seemed busy at all times of the day and night.

She wrote to her mother as often as she could and a lot more since her Papa and Bill had gone. She tried not to put too much information in her letters, but at the same time talked about how happy she was feeling and the fact that there was a good sense of camaderie between all the women.

'At RAF Blakehill the place is brimming with men. I have heard from Sally and she is getting married next Saturday. She wants me to go to their wedding in Lincoln. But I can't get away. They won't let us off the base now. Something is brewing but we don't know when. Papa would love it here. We're in the middle of hustle and bustle of all types of military equipment. Excitement is building, there's a feeling seeing all this that we can't lose against Hitler. Once we all leave this place though, it will be empty fields again of quagmire and mud. We don't even share the fields with the cows. Not that there are many cows left in the south after Hitler's bombs.

Cherry didn't hear from Sidney but assumed that any news from him her mother would let her know. She had changed since her son and her husband had died, well at least she has Tommy and Sidney she thought. Oh, and me, although I'm not sure she would prefer me to Bill being alive. Whenever she thought of her brother and Papa, she got a lump in her throat. And when she thought of Joe, she found it hard to breathe or swallow. Lots of wives, girlfriends, and mothers were going through the same thing. I must try not to dwell on things and concentrate on the work, she said to herself.

Her mother wrote back within a week and Cherry was surprised. She must be lonely, she thought. And she was right.

'I only have Tommy to talk to,' her mother wrote. *'Sidney's ship hasn't come in yet. Because he doesn't write I don't know when he'll return. I miss your Papa. I miss our conversations we used to have. Now I have no one to talk to.'* Cherry started to feel a little sorry for her mother. She wrote back and encouraged her to rejoin the WI or another organisation to keep her busy.

It was good to receive letters from friends and family. It was what kept her going. She wondered how Sidney was doing, and what injury he had. It was over a year now since Papa had been killed and she still hadn't received a letter from Sid.

'Dear Ma,' she wrote. *'All quiet on the southern front at the moment. Although we are building up for something big. Training daily –They work us hard every day. Training, training. It's very physical too. Although it gives you an appetite. There were 15 of us who started now there are only 9 left. The other girls who left found it really hard. They couldn't keep up. Some of them were from the rest of the armed forces, some were civilian nurses. It's not for everyone. I don't know what we're letting ourselves in for. We practice a lot of lifesaving skills in the swimming pool and learn what to do if our aircraft comes down in the sea. We practice how to*

inflate and get a huge rubber dinghy right side up in the water, how to climb in it, and how to pull wounded men into it. We are taught how to put the stretcher in the opening made for it in the plane. How to give oxygen and how to recognise the effects of lack of oxygen and judge when to give it. Once in the aircraft, keeping the patients alive is our responsibility. It's toughened us up. It's interesting and enjoyable, but so very hard! I have to develop strength in my upper muscles. Since pulling dummies (and each other) in and out of aeroplanes we have all developed our upper body strength!'

Cherry looked forward to the trips in the Dakota.

'How are they going to get injured servicemen in here?' she asked Ted.

'I'm sure the Air Force will work that out,' Ted answered. Anyway, you'll be flying nurses now.'

'But we can't officially be nurses Ted, because they'd have to pay officer wages and they're not going to do that!' she exclaimed.

'No, they won't pay women any more than they have to,' he agreed. 'Which is a shame. But perhaps things will change after the war.'

Ted had told her that he had returned the previous year from the Far East, where he had been flying Dakotas and dropping supplies and equipment behind enemy lines. He was an experienced pilot, telling her of his experiences and the scary situations he had been in, Cherry was very impressed.

On 22nd January the Allies landed in Anzio, Italy. And the siege of Leningrad finally ended on 27th January. In February a massive bombing campaign of Germany by the Allies commenced and the downfall of the Third Reich was assured. Everyone was starting to feel that it was the beginning of the end at last.

At the end of May it had become obvious the offensive was going to be soon. The weather had warmed up and the girls were going around without coats on. Everyone could feel the excitement building. Training began to come together and the news was passed by word of mouth from pilots to the Air Ambulance trainees, that they were indeed expected to bring back the seriously wounded from France. The Dakotas had been fitted with racks for the stretchers they were to use. They were in rows of three from top to bottom of the aircraft. With the pilot, assistant pilot, radio operator, and the air ambulance nurse that made four crew, and the total number of casualties would number no more than twenty-four.

Cherry and the other women continued to train daily, going up in the Dakota and going over again how to treat battle injuries. They would be expected to pick up from the field hospitals where the immediate battle injuries would be treated. It would be their job to get the patients back to the nearest hospitals in the south of England in one piece via the main RAF airports in the south.

Going out to France - the air ambulances would be full to the brim with rations, ammunition, and medical supplies for the field hospitals. Coming back, they would be full of patients - seriously wounded soldiers who needed urgent treatment. They couldn't have a red cross on the Dakota because it would be a beacon for every German anti-aircraft gun to shoot it down. And they wouldn't be allowed to use their parachutes on the return journey from France if the aeroplane was full of patients because they would be expected to put the lives of their patients first and foremost.

CHAPTER 20 – Time to go!

At last, the day arrived. Some of the nurses were told they were flying the next day – the Allies had landed on the beaches of Normandy five days before, which was now called D-Day. It was cloudy but calm after a windy night – Cherry had had a sleepless night, she was nervous - the time had come to put all her training into action.

Cherry and her section of the air ambulance pool were transported to a small aerodrome on the south coast near Southampton.

'My house is only a few minutes that way,' she told the others, pointing to the east. It was ironic that she would be flying over her house. If only her mother could see her now!

The girls spent the night in sick bay waiting for 'the off.' At breakfast, they were each given bacon and egg, but Cherry didn't have the appetite to eat it. Her nerves were like butterflies in her stomach. After breakfast, they collected their gear and were fitted with parachutes. They wore jackets and trousers, stout shoes, an RAF cap, and red cross badges on their sleeves.

A senior RAF officer with a lot of gold braid on his cap and broad ribbons of rank on his arm addressed the women of the Air Ambulance Unit. He wished them good luck and told them their mission was Northern France.

On 6th June the Allied Forces had battled across the English Channel in a storm and fought against the defending Germans on the beaches of Normandy. Some seriously injured were now waiting to be brought back to a hospital in Southern England. The air ambulance teams would fly through enemy flak and were told that they may get shot down and crash land into the sea, so were handed Mae West life jackets and told to put them on.

'Is this if we drop into the sea?' Cherry asked no one in particular. 'Surely we'd be killed on impact?

'Don't ask questions that they can't answer Cherry. We'll be all right,' Ted said with a grin and a wink, he had been waiting for this action for months, and he hurried over to their awaiting Dakota with Cherry hot on his heels. Her cap kept falling off, so she put it with her parachute. She stowed away the equipment and large flasks of hot tea for the wounded. The aircraft was already loaded with supplies of ammunition and weapons.

Ted and Cherry climbed into the Lady Susan. He smiled at her as they climbed through the hatch.

'Nervous?'

She nodded.

'You'll be fine. We'll be okay. Just think of those poor sods who are wounded. You'll soon get into the swing of things.' He climbed into the pilot's seat and started up the engine as the rest of the crew got into their positions in the Lady Susan.

Cherry sat on her own in the fuselage. She caught a sideways view of Ted's face as he spoke to the tower. He looked as if he was enjoying being back in the thick of it again. She kept her fingers crossed and hoped that they would get there safely and bring back the brave boys who had been injured in the fighting. She took a deep breath as they were given the green light to go by the control tower. She wondered what things would be like, although she had trained hard, what would it be like with a plane full of injured? Would they get through the flak coming back?

The Dakotas took off one by one, line by line. They all had different places in Normandy to fly to, to drop off the supplies, load the wounded, and fly straight back. It wouldn't take long, they said.

They were accompanied by fighter planes who flew alongside the Dakotas ready to protect them if they needed to. Cherry wondered if they had come from Tangmere, they looked like Spitfires, and she looked out of the windows trying to recognise the pilot, but she couldn't see their faces. Everything in the past few years had built up to this moment, and she thought of the loved ones who had given their lives for the same cause.

As they flew over the Channel, Ted alerted Cherry and pointed below them. She looked down at the sight below, which took her breath away. There were hundreds of ships below them; convoys of frigates, destroyers, and other ships of all shapes and sizes. There were barrage balloons protecting the convoys. As they came lower, she could just make out the landing craft on the beaches.

Ted brought the Dakota even lower so they could see the beaches clearer. The sight that met their eyes was one of total destruction. Cherry caught her breath. They could see clearly the shambles of wreckage below them. Tanks sunk up to their turrets in quicksand; she saw a wasteland pitted with thousands of shell holes and craters. She saw a concrete pillbox wrenched apart by the barrage of naval shells and bodies lying about their blackened entrances. The beaches were full of what she thought was rubbish, then with horror, she realised they were dead bodies. They were lined up ready to be removed onto an amphibious landing craft - to take them to the bigger ships waiting out at sea.

Past the beaches, the patchwork countryside spread out before her. They were still flying low over fields of corn. She thought it looked rather like England in some places. Eventually, Ted brought them down to land along a makeshift runway of honeycombed metal matting. As the plane drew to a halt, Cherry opened out the large Dakota door to the rear to take on the casualties. It was eerily quiet. She hadn't expected that. No birds were singing. Then suddenly she heard gunfire and shellfire not far away. She jumped down onto the cornfield and flung herself flat on her face.

'What are you doing down there?' laughed Ted. 'That's nowhere near us. It's probably miles away.'

Embarrassed she stood up. 'Where's the sun? My first time in France and it's cloudy and cold.'

'It's unusual for this time of the year. I feel sorry for the fellows who had to cross in the ships. It was pretty darn rough on the sixth, by all accounts.'

Another barrage of gunfire opened up in the opposite direction making her jump. 'Are they firing at each other? Are we caught in the middle?' she asked.

'They're still fighting nearby it seems they got as far as Bayeux but it'll get worse with the Panzer Divisions on the way.'

'How do you know this, Ted?'

'The pilots were told. They're still fighting the Germans down there - it's going to be tough for them. They're trying to take Caen and the

Cherbourg Peninsula. Our lads have the advantage of getting here first. But the Panzers take no prisoners and they've gotten to know the lanes and they camouflage themselves behind the dense hedges.'

'Oh no. It doesn't sound very good. I mean, it sounds like they don't stand a chance!' she said horrified at what she'd heard and now she'd seen the bodies on the beaches.

'Don't give up on our lads too soon! It's early days yet. Come on!' Ted beckoned her to keep with him.

From out of nowhere, soldiers tore up and started offloading ammunition as fast as they could. They appeared possessed as if they were to be bombed any minute and worked feverishly. The urgency of the situation came to her and she hurried over to where the men were waiting on lorries and ambulances to be unloaded. A gang of male medical orderlies appeared, carrying bloody, bandaged soldiers on stretchers. Even though she'd practised for months and had accompanied injured servicemen on aeroplanes, the real thing came as a shock to her. So much blood and so many young men. So many were seriously wounded. Some had faces missing, some had limbs missing. Some were groaning in pain, some were quiet. They had all been patched up for the return journey, and their lives depended on how quickly they got back across to the hospitals on the other side of the Channel. Cherry shook herself out of her stupor as one of the orderlies was asking her how the stretchers should be placed. She pointed and helped him. Within minutes they had crammed stretchers inside. Almost every bit of space was taken.

Ted spoke to some of the men while Cherry tried to organise herself seeing who needed help before they took off. She got the tea flask ready and the water. The orderlies pointed out to the crew where the hidden anti-aircraft guns were hidden amongst the bocage, they were camouflaged and were the infamous German 88mm guns. One hit to the Dakota and it would all be over. Ted could see them poking out of the corner of a field. There was one nearby that hadn't yet been captured by the Allies, and pilots had been warned to fly away to the left so that the enemy flak wouldn't shoot them down.

They had been no more than forty minutes on the ground when they were taking off once again. It wasn't good to hang around too long. Even though the field hospital was nearby, the Germans were dug into the hidden areas and were fighting back – they were desperate to keep their piece of land.

'Hold on!' Ted shouted to those in the back. 'Jerry is gonna do his best to cut us down!'

He cursed as the Dakota bumped and banged its way to take off, it struggled with its full load as they banked to port, and the Lady Susan climbed slowly with its loaded cargo. The wounded soldiers seemed to hold their breath. All Cherry could hear was the whine of the engines as the plane struggled to climb away from the *Boom! Boom!* of the huge guns following them in the sky. The Lady Susan climbed gradually into the sky, but within a few minutes they were out of reach and the sound of the guns got fainter and fainter. Once again, they flew over the Normandy beaches, only this time on the return journey. Cherry looked down at the two man-made harbours – the Mulberries, had been fixed in place and ships were queueing up to offload men and supplies. What an amazing sight, she thought, I'll probably never see the like of it again. There was no more flak and explosions following them, and then they were flying over the English Channel once again.

Cherry realised she'd been holding her breath and she started to breathe again, and then she picked her way over bodies on stretchers. At times she toppled and grabbed the stanchions for support as the Lady Susan banked climbing then started descending. The soldiers' uniforms could hardly be distinguished, their battledress was torn and soaked in blood. Some of the men lay twisted in odd attitudes, faces white and eyes shut. Some stared vacantly. They were dirty and worn out.

There was no seat for Cherry. But she was kept busy back and forth, giving water and tea for those who could drink it.

A young soldier who looked barely seventeen caught at Cherry's battledress trousers and opened his mouth to speak. She jumped at first, not used to being grabbed around the leg. But calming herself, answered him; 'What is it?'

His eyes stared, he plucked at her trousers, he mouthed words, but no sound came out. The young soldier's face twisted in pain his teeth clenched to keep back his screams. His legs looked like a tangled mess, his right arm soaked in blood and limp at his side. She hooked him up to oxygen and increased the flow. Then re-arranged his intravenous drip and made him more comfortable. The soldier relaxed slightly and closed his eyes. Cherry held his hand for a few moments and spoke to him. She wasn't really sure what she said, something about being home soon and in hospital and that everything would be all right. Eventually the young man went to sleep. Some of the men unable to speak, grabbed her legs as she went past them. One cried out. She touched their hands and spoke to them and told them they were nearly home.

It wasn't until they were coming into land that she checked on the young soldier again, and realised that he was dead. She touched his wrist, there was no pulse. Her throat constricted, and she tried to hold back the tears.

When they landed there were ambulances waiting for the wounded soldiers. The medical orderlies hurried to take off all the stretchers and whisked the men quickly away to the hospital.

Cherry stood on the tarmac taking deep breaths. Her chest hurt. She meant to let the medical orderlies know about the young soldier who had died, but she had forgotten and was still trying to make sense of it. Her first death in the air, and it had come as a terrible shock. Ted was there standing next to her.

'You all right Cherry?'

She told him of the young soldier.

'Aye,' he said. 'Your first one is always a death you can never forget. But there was nothing you could've done he was probably too badly injured to survive.'

She took some consolation in the fact that she had taken time to hold his hand and comfort him for a few moments before he died.

Later in her billet that night, Cherry lay awake thinking of the young soldier and that his mother probably didn't know yet that her son was dead. Her throat constricted and she tried not to cry, it brought back memories of loved ones she had lost. She knew she had to toughen up with all the things she had seen today. Her mother would be horrified that she had seen such things; men with half their face blown away, men with no mouths, men who had horrible burns all over their body due to tank flame throwers. It brought her back to Joe, and Bill, and how they might have died in fire. She had nightmares that night imagining they couldn't get out of their cockpits. She tried to get the pictures out of her mind, but her heart was pounding away with emotion and she didn't fall asleep until four in the morning.

Meanwhile the French Resistance groups had gone into action against the Germans. They cut telephone lines, blew bridgeheads, railway lines and ammunition dumps once they been alerted by the Allies to go into action. It had been a well-kept secret, and guerrilla targets had been taken by surprise. They had been unable to do an all-out attack before because the Germans had taken reprisals against the locals.

A few days after D-Day and troops and ammunition were streaming into Normandy over the Channel. The two Mulberry man-made harbours enabled a steady stream of men and machines across the causeways onto the beaches. The next time the Lady Susan flew over the Normandy beaches she saw rows of traffic coming off the ships and driving away up the roads and into the interior. From the crowded beaches endless columns of men and vehicles continuously moved inland. Rows of infantry plodded steadily up dusty French roads towards the front which was working its way inland as the days wore on.

The Allies had the French Resistance to help deter the Germans and they did their utmost to hinder the advancing Panzer divisions that Hitler had decided to send for a counter-offensive As it was, the 21st Panzer Division was the only German armoured division poised to launch any counterattack during the Allied landings on D-Day. They were instrumental in stopping the British hopes of reaching Caen during their first attack.

Germans in Bayeux had surrendered to the Allies on the second day. But elsewhere things were not going so easy. On the Cotentin Peninsula where the US paratroopers landed in gliders in the early hours of D-Day many were dropped with their heavy packs accidentally in the marshes and drowned.

Attacks by Mosquitoes, Bostons and Mitchells combined with bombers of the US Ninth Air Force and Bomber Command of the RAF, made devastating attacks on Germany's enemy lines and defensive positions. The German tanks tried to camouflage themselves and hide their military headquarters in the shade of the dense leafy woods.

The wounded from the front which had now moved on from the beaches were brought in from all around the local area to a nearby field hospital for the wounded. The doctors and nurses (from the RAF, WAAFs and Queen Alexander's Royal Naval Nursing Service) worked around the clock trying to save men's lives and patch up those who were injured.

The seriously injured were sent back to Britain by the air ambulance teams on the C47 Dakotas. Others not so seriously wounded were sent on ships back to England. On their return to England, the stretchers were carried off the aircraft at the three main airfields in England, which could each hold 300-400 casualties per day. They were situated close to hospitals and to railway stations where lower-priority casualties could be distributed.

One of the main hospitals that accepted the wounded was RAF Wroughton in Wiltshire. Here there were theatres in which ten operations could be performed by surgeons a day working around the clock, as the wounded were brought in dozens at a time. The surgeons worked in teams in a shift system.

The Movement Control Office kept in constant touch with airfields, with every ward in the casualty clearing station, and also with RAF station hospitals throughout the country, so that the surgical and medical staff were able to have up-to-the-minute information on the transfer of patients. This system worked very well and the seriously wounded were in hospital within hours rather than weeks.

CHAPTER 21 – D-Day plus nine

The Lady Susan's crew landed on a field strip nine days after D-Day. It was made especially for the air ambulance Dakotas, but it was a bumpy landing and the weather was deteriorating. Although the stormy weather had abated it was still very windy, which made landing dangerous. Low fronts continued to come across Normandy sooner than they all expected. Ted had veered off to come in from a different direction. They had flown through flak as they approached the airstrip. Cherry bumped up and down hanging onto the stanchions for dear life. 'Ouch!' No one could hear her as she was bumped between boxes of medical supplies.

She remembered the last time the Lady Susan had flown this way and looked out of the window to see the enemy's massive 88mm guns protruding through the shrubs below and was again trying to shoot them down between the coast and the field hospital.

'If they're in the middle, the poor field hospital will be at risk surely?' Cherry asked Ted when they landed.

'The front moves back and forth in any conflict,' he said. 'Very often they're behind enemy lines. Just like we are,' he pointed out.

'I hadn't thought of that.'

'Then don't think about it. Otherwise lassie, you wouldn't do what you're doing now.'

They jumped down from the Lady Susan. 'Gosh it's freezing,' she said, as they exited from the Dakota. 'I didn't expect this weather. And where's the wounded?'

'We better go find them, there may have been a hitch.'

As they went through an exit at the corner of a field which had once been pasture, they saw the camouflaged roof of the British Field Hospital in a field beyond. The high hedges between the fields helped disguise where it was situated. There were big craters in the field where the shelling had landed and they stepped around the huge holes carefully.

'I didn't recognise it from yesterday,' she said. 'Not sure why.'

'We came in at a different angle because of the anti-aircraft guns. And the high hedges help camouflage them.

'They're so high, and they look really old.'

'The area is called bocage. They're usually impossible to get through. They're ancient hedgerows from Roman times.'

'This is handy.' Cherry said as they went through a gap in the hedgerow which someone had cut with a machete, and they came out next to one of the hospital tents.

But the storm of the last three days had turned the ground to a sea of mud. There were duck boards on top of the mud so that people could walk in between the tents, Cherry felt like she was in danger of slipping into the mud. Her regulation stout shoes were covered in mud within minutes. They tried to stop slipping over the wet wooden boards.

They followed a medical orderly to the reception tent.

'We're looking for our wounded,' Ted told the Sister-in-charge.

'We're about to load them onto the transport,' she said red-faced and looking distressed. She gave orders to the medical orderly and then turned to face them. 'We've been attacked by enemy fighters, they flew over before you landed.'

'You'd think having a big red cross on the roof would stop them bombing it,' said Cherry.

'It doesn't work like that Cherry,' said Ted gravely. 'It's very often a red mark to a bull. They try to camouflage the hospitals as best they can.'

As if by magic the pounding of guns started up again. The noise of the gunfire and anti-aircraft fire was deafening. Shrapnel rained down on the tents and clanged against the trucks and ambulances.

'Is that ours or theirs?' demanded Ted.

'Probably ours,' the Sister answered, 'But who's to know these days, we're so close to enemy lines, we're behind enemy lines sometimes!'

She showed them through the field hospital as the men were preparing the transport. The tent where the patients were being prepared was a shock to Cherry. She tried not to move as she took in the scene before her. Blood was spattered all over the floor, and some had splashed up the inside of the canvas tent. Dozens of men were waiting to be put on the transport. Some men were unconscious, some gritting their teeth in pain, some crying out in agony.

A man grabbed her ankle and she jumped. He had a hole where his mouth should be. But his eyes were bright with intent. She had never seen anything like it, the carnage was appalling. There were wounds to the chest and abdomen from bullets and mortar fire. Some of the chest wounds had deep gaping holes. Men's faces were grey with fatigue and fear.

'Now you know you can't have a cigarette until you've seen the surgeon,' the Sister told a young man brusquely. She turned to Cherry and said under her breath.

'He wants a cigarette but that's not possible.'

'What if he wants a drink on the aircraft?' Cherry asked her quietly.

'It's not possible until the surgeons have fixed his mouth. He's on an intravenous drip so he's having fluids pumped into him.

How on earth will they fix his mouth? She thought to herself.

Ted lit a cigarette for a soldier who grabbed his hand as he walked past - instinctively knowing what he wanted without saying anything. The Sister also lit a cigarette for someone as she passed.

'I've lit so many cigarettes for people, I feel like I'm a smoker too,' she said.

Cherry watched Ted who was lighting cigarettes for people as he walked amongst the injured. Another wounded soldier lying on one side, who had been operated on, and had a bandaged arm to his side, called to Cherry.

''Ere nurse. I'm dying for a fag, light one for me will yer?'

Although she hated the smell of cigarette smoke, she saw that he was trying to reach his pocket with his good arm.

'I can't even get one out my trousers. Help me will yer?' he insisted impatiently and nodded down at his trouser pocket to the side of his injured arm. Cherry fumbled in his pockets and retrieved his cigarettes trying not to look at the bloody bandage under her. She lit a cigarette for him, and as she put it to his lips, she felt dizzy and wobbled slightly.

'You all right love?' the soldier asked taking a deep drag from his cigarette.

With the sight and smells of blood and sickness it was something Cherry knew she would never forget. She leaned against the tent trying to stop herself being sick.

'Yes. I will be when I've had something to eat, I think.'

Leaning against the tent she watched the nurses hurry around the patients, giving sedation, fluids, plasma, and reassurance. She watched them work non-stop to fix intravenous infusions, giving injections of morphia and penicillin, and adjusting the field dressings. One day I want to be one of them, she thought, and perhaps I'll become immune to the smell of sickness.

Some men brought into the ward being attended to by the doctors, were quiet and lay still, one man nearest the door was screaming with pain and fear. Some were groaning, and some calling for help. Patients who had T on their forehead denoted tourniquet, or H indicating haemorrhaging. M was for morphine, all marked with indelible pencil. Some young soldiers had half their faces blown away. Some bodies burned to a frazzle. Some lay quietly dying. But the man who made the most noise was screaming like a caught animal. His blood-curdling screams made

Cherry's blood run cold, and she could tell Ted was affected by it too. They walked quickly out of the ward back into fresh air. The sulphur smell of the distant guns reminded them that war was in the next field even though the German 88mmmm guns had stopped firing. Little did the medical staff know that the enemy guns were being overrun by Allied soldiers who permanently silenced them. It was a dull, grey day, but Cherry was glad the noise of the guns had stopped at last.

Sister followed them out of the tent. 'These soldiers are from a tank regiment,' she warned them. 'Their tanks have been hit by the German Panzer divisions, there's not much chance to get out if you're stuck in a burning tank. So many have burns all over their body.'

There was frenetic activity as the orderlies packed the wounded onto the truck.

'No doubt I'll be seeing you tomorrow,' she said as she turned away to someone calling out to her to help. 'I'll show you around properly then.'

They said goodbye to the Sister, and followed the truck as it made its bumpy and slow journey, so as not to cause too much pain to the patients across the pot-holed field to the Dakota.

'I'm not sure I want to see any more wards,' said Cherry quietly to Ted as they walked behind the truck.

'I've seen injuries on the battle field but when they're all packed in together it's awful. What with the sounds of screams, and the smells, I'm beginning to realise just how hard these medical staff work,' he said.

Cherry nodded still thinking of the sights she had just witnessed. 'You look white,' Ted said quietly to her.

'I'm fine,' she said. 'Did you see those doctors coming out the next tent covered in blood? It must be the operating tent. It must be awful for them trying to keep things sterile with all this mud and guts everywhere.'

'They probably didn't save everyone they wanted to.'

She thought about Ted's words as she walked back to the Lady Susan and when she arrived Cherry helped to arrange the stretchers, while Ted got the Dakota fired up and was talking on the radio. Within minutes she had shut the rear doors and they were taking off. Some men were hardly breathing and one man was making gurgling sounds. The physical wounds were bad enough, but what was most upsetting to Cherry was that the minds of some of the young men seemed to have gone completely with the trauma of what they had witnessed in battle. Men cringed as she went by to comfort them, some shouted out, panic-stricken, reliving the horror of their own battle a short time ago, and seeing their friends die in front of them. The crump of artillery shells and mortars exploding nearby as they took off made them all jump and re-live their battles all over again.

CHAPTER 22 - D-day plus ten – The move to Caen.

It was so blustery and cloudy the next day Ted was unsure they would fly. But eventually it cleared later in the morning and the air ambulance service was given the go-ahead and they took off for Normandy.

Ted and Cherry landed at the 51st Field Hospital again where they had been the day before. The Nursing Sister met them and showed them to the medical staff's sleeping areas. The grass had been a foot high and now because of the heavy rain pathways had become squelchy mud. Conditions were primitive and the low camp beds appeared to be floating on duckboards. Clothes were hung on hooks. Boxes were balancing one on top of the other to serve as shelves and cupboards.

'I only had two hours sleep last night in twenty-four,' she told them. 'What with the ack-ack guns cracking away in the fields next to us, and shrapnel falling through the tent roof when German bombers pass overhead, I have to sleep with my tin hat on most of the time!'

'I didn't know it was so hard here for you,' exclaimed Cherry. Her eyes were wide as Sister showed them the toilets.

'And snipers – you have to watch out for them too. We have to wash carefully in streams. Clean water is used for the patients. The toilets are shared by all, but we tend to go together and one acts as look-out.'

'It's like living in the jungle,' said Ted in amazement. They walked past a tent which was acting as an operating theatre, looking in they saw nurses sterilizing hypodermic syringes in fish kettles.

'I'm amazed at how you keep everything clean and sterile under the most basic conditions,' he told Sister.

A nurse was feeding a man through a tube up his nose, his face was burned and he had no proper mouth. As they moved on the Sister said that they had learned to adapt with the types of injuries they had to deal with.

'What will happen to the man who has a burned face?' asked Cherry.

'He'll be moved on to the Burns hospital in East Grinstead. And he'll be on your flight, because it's vital we work fast on the burns survivors. They'll be lucky to go to that hospital. They have some new and exciting methods for healing faces.'

'Incoming!' someone shouted at the top of their voice as a barrage of mortars and shells exploded around the tents. Everyone hit the floor as a cascade of burning metal fragments hit the top of the tent and holes appeared as they melted through.

'Imagine what that would do if it landed on your face?' Ted said under his breath to Cherry. 'I've seen enough. Shall we go?'

After a few minutes the barrage left off, and people resumed their work. Sister returned and told them that a squall was coming in, would they be taking off before it hit? Ted looked out of the tent quickly. A black cloud was above them and the wind had suddenly picked up. Cherry followed him.

'Oh no!' she said. It had started to rain suddenly very hard.

'Too late Sister! We'll have to wait 'til it passes over.'

They stepped inside the tent as huge drops landed on it, making it sound like gunfire on the fabric.

'I don't believe it. Hail!' Ted said with disgust. 'Well, this wasn't forecast!'

'What do we do now?' she asked him.

'We wait.'

Nearby a jeep with two civilians in was stuck in the mud, and the front wheel was whirring round and round. Ted went over to help out. He stuck a plank of wood underneath and he gave them a shove to get out of the rut. The driver called to Cherry waiting out of the rain.

'Hey, are you the famous Flying Nightingales the nurses are talking about?'

'Flying what?' she shouted above the din of the rain bouncing off the tent roof. The two men came under the tent to shelter.

'They're calling you *The Flying Nightingales* after Florence Nightingale. With what you're doing, saving lives, I'd say it's very accurate.'

'And very brave,' said his colleague. 'Do you get shot at?'

'Yes, we get shot at. And no, we're not brave. The nurses here are the ones who are brave. Living in this...' Cherry pointed to the squelching mud everywhere. At least I can go home every day.'

'We're waiting for the storm to pass so we can take off,' added Ted.

'Come with us!' said his colleague. 'We're war correspondents with the US military. 'We're going to the front where the action is!'

'That'd be great!' shouted Ted and he jumped into the jeep at the front without saying anything to Cherry.

'You're joking...' but she followed him into the jeep, and before she'd even sat down, they were revving to be off.

'We might not get another chance!' he tapped the dashboard.

The wind howled but the rain had eased and Cherry pulled the hood of her jacket over her head, as the jeep started up.

'Oh well...here goes nothing,' she said, and settled into the back of the jeep but then had to cling on as if her life depended on it. It sped off at breakneck speed bumping along a farm track and swerving around the puddles.

'I'm Jim,' shouted the driver above the engine's roar. 'And this is Toby with the camera, We've been reporting since D-Day.'

'Are we going towards Caen?' asked Ted. 'Aren't the Allies stuck in a battle with the Germans there?'

'Yes. That's where the action is. We've been waiting for the go-ahead to get some photographic evidence.'

Cherry swallowed and looked at Ted. He seemed to revel in the excitement – his eyes were wide and he had a fixed grin as they sped towards the action. She sighed and crossed her fingers and hoped they didn't get shot by snipers or even fall out of the jeep as Jim didn't slow down taking the corners at speed.

'Jim slow down! You're throwing us around like peas in a bucket!' Toby shouted to his friend.

'The Germans have been told to fight to the last man!' said Toby keeping a firm grip on his camera as Jim hurtled through the fields. They went flying over the bumps with Cherry holding on for dear life, while Ted was still grinning from ear to ear. At last Jim slowed down as he came to a road. There were bomb craters and the distended bodies of three cows. Ahead they could hear artillery shells exploding, then the acrid smell of gunpowder.

'The front doesn't sound that far away,' she shouted above the din. She was a bit scared, but surely it wouldn't be that dangerous if the journalists were going there. Jim drove carefully around craters in the road and then slowly down the road looking left and right for signs of soldiers.

She thought it ironic they'd slowed down at the road but had flown hell for leather bumping along a dirt track across the fields, but she didn't say anything. The jeep had a very hard suspension and she was trying to keep her hair under the hard hat she'd been given by Toby.

'We came down here yesterday,' said Toby. There was a trail of soldiers making their way from the beaches to the front. We don't know what happened after that. All we know is that Caen is an unplanned stall for the Allies. General Montgomery won't like it.'

'We've been in worse spots,' said Ted. 'Trying to dodge bullets and flak while we've tried to take off from dangerous airfields.'

Toby turned to Cherry. 'Why are you here? This isn't a place for a female.'

'I don't see the nurses in the field hospital complaining. What would the injured do without them?'

Toby nodded. 'True, we don't question why they do the job they do. I'm surprised to see women near the front lines. What is a young woman like you doing at the front lines anyway?'

'Behind enemy lines sometimes!' she laughed. 'The excitement I suppose, and doing my bit for the war. I'm with the RAF Air Ambulance support, I bring the patients back from the front in the Dakota and try and keep them alive on the way back across the Channel.'

'What kind of patients?'

'They're very seriously injured. We have to get them home as quickly as possible so that they can be saved. We have people who have been burned, lost limbs and lost lots of blood. The poor men have watched their friends being killed, and are traumatised.'

'Do you have family?' Toby asked her.

'Sidney. He's two years older than I am. He's on a ship somewhere.' He only just caught her last comment when she lowered her voice. 'My older brother was killed.'

The jeep had slowed down at Toby's request and Jim wound around the bomb craters in the road. Any cheerfulness they felt was soon dispelled by the sight that met their eyes. They arrived at a village. The houses had been flattened by the bombing, and the few that were still standing had roofs and side walls missing. Some looked like burnt-out shells. They were quiet as they passed a ditch with dead bodies in the hedgerows. Jim slowed down as Toby took pictures of the carnage. Just then the sun came out, and the flies gathered over the bodies.

As they turned a corner ahead of them was a line of wrecked British tanks, and other vehicles lay strewn about the French countryside. There were bodies in the hedgerows and dead cows in the fields bloated and stiff with death. The jeep sped along, approaching the sound of intense artillery bombardment which became louder as they advanced. Cherry was wondering when they would stop. Her throat was bone dry. The smell of burning and bombs was strong here. And as they turned another bend in the road, they saw more bloody, dirty bodies upturned to the flies and the sun. Bodies lay in ditches in twisted shapes. They hung from hedges. Jim stopped so that Toby could take a long shot of the carnage.

'Are you really going to put that on the front of a newspaper?' She asked.

'Why not?' said Toby. 'It's how it really is. Civilians in the States need to know what's happening over here. Hitler doesn't care how he kills us.'

Cherry was quiet and was thinking about what he'd said. 'There's no way of sugar-coating death, is there? I hope their mates come and bury them soon,' she said putting her hand over her mouth.

Jim sped up past the bodies and wrecks to the highest point on a hill. They craned their necks when they reached the top.

Sprawled out in front of them was the bombardment of Caen. They could see the artillery shells exploding in the distance. Smoke billowed from places around Caen, and in the centre of Caen. There were no civilians on the horizon. There was no movement at all.

'What's happening?' she asked, expecting to see lines of people trying to flee the city. 'Where are the civilians? Did they get out?'

'Not that I've heard. Caen's going to be a tough nut to crack by all accounts,' said Jim. 'If Monty thought they could invade Caen and get rid of the Germans overnight, he was so wrong. The Germans are digging in amongst the ruins, and probably hiding in the cellars.'

'What about the civilians?' she asked again, she felt sick because the civilians were suffering through no fault of their own. Ted made a grimace.

'Those that didn't manage to get out are probably hiding amongst the ruins. Trying to avoid the snipers and the rest of the German army!'

'The Allies have made mincemeat of the existing town,' said Jim, coming to a halt at the lookout. 'There's nothing else for it, but to smoke out the Nazis.'

'It's the main route to Paris for us,' said Toby. 'But we can't move on to Paris from here because the main roads need to transport the troops to Paris. Once we're there that's the beginning of the end for the Third Reich.'

Toby took more photos and they moved off slowly. Turning another corner, Jim had to drive even slower. Men in khaki uniforms were trudging along as if in a trance in which all their senses had been anaesthetized. They marched in single file along the narrow road, carrying heavy kits piled on their backs, and armed to the teeth. All traffic created billows of dust as it passed and covered them. They turned around with blank faces to see who was trying to get them off the road.

Suddenly somebody shouted 'Incoming!' and everyone dived for cover. The jeep swerved, Toby grabbed Cherry's wrist and pulled her out of the car and into the ditch. The bright flash hit their eyes long before the force of the explosion knocked them off of their feet. The shrapnel pinged everywhere, but the bomb missed them and immediately it had finished, everyone picked themselves up and continued on their way.

One man broke out of his daze and looked over to the jeep when he suddenly saw Cherry. He called to his mates.

'Blimey, a woman!'

They shouted and waved at her, calling 'Cooee!' Others looked over at the jeep, their faces aghast that there was a woman in their midst.

'Blimey, it must be all right if there's a woman round here!' She overheard someone say, and they continued to whistle and call to her. Toby took more photos, and they sped off in the jeep. Cherry was relieved they were moving on, but she was glad she had cheered them up.

'Can we go back to the hospital now please?' she asked. She was so scared that they would end up like the civilians. Jim and Toby seemed to fear nothing, and that worried her even more.

They passed a poppy-lined track and mounds with a simple stick and a British helmet on top. Someone had found the time to bury their mates, no matter how simple. At least the flies had not had a feast on them.

The jeep was driven within ear-splitting distance of the British gunners who were firing constantly at the enemy. They stopped at the end of a street and took photos for several minutes. The sun was out now, the storm had passed over, and there was a clear blue sky. It was hot and Cherry was sweating in her thick serge jacket.

Ted decided he'd had enough too. 'Can we go back?'

'Well, I think we have enough photos, but tomorrow we could get closer do ya' think Toby?' Asked Jim. And Toby nodded.

'Do ya wanna come?' Jim asked them.

'No thanks!' called Cherry.

At last, they returned to the airfield. Everyone was quiet. Contemplating what they had witnessed. Cherry was glad she was back. The Sister in Charge was organising the removal of the injured onto the trucks.

'We've reached saturation point here already. Another field hospital arrived yesterday and they're putting that one up in between Bayeux and Caen. We just don't have the space anymore,' she said. 'We're turning over six hundred patients every twelve hours. And they have to be in and out so quickly, that's the only way we can cope with them.'

Another Dakota was seen to land on the makeshift runway. Ted immediately knew who it was.

'It's my friend Bill! They've come to give us a hand!'

'Because of the weather delay, we have two hundred to send back to England. Most of them are for the Burns hospital,' said the Sister.

'We'd better get a move on then!' said Ted, and they hurried out to the Dakota.

As they approached the Lady Susan, they saw the rest of their crew and the medical orderlies who were piling in the casualties, suddenly hit the ground and cover their heads.

'Incoming!' they heard from a distance. The casualties on the stretchers could do nothing to protect themselves. Many didn't have hands able to cover their faces. A shrill whistling flew over their heads. And it landed in the next field with shrapnel and mounds of earth splattering the Dakota, all they heard next was crack, crack, ping, ping!

Within seconds the orderlies had jumped back up again and finished loading the few patients left. Cherry ran inside to close the doors the rest of the crew were in their seats and Ted started up the engines.

'Let's go!' he yelled to Cherry in the back. The Dakota roared as the aeroplane lunged forward. The Lady Susan shook and scrambled over the bumpy ground, some of the men became frightened, not sure what was happening. Some were groaning and another grabbed at her hand. But this time Cherry was more concerned with escaping the flak from enemy fire than worrying about the smells and sounds of the injured.

She cajoled one of the men as best she could. 'Let's get out of this flak first young soldier before

I'll pour you a cup of tea. It won't be long before we're home.'

'Hang on!' Ted shouted from the cockpit, as he took the Dakota into a steep climb. The flak pinged and clattered off the fuselage. The Lady Susan seeming to shrug off the bullets. The plane banked to port away from all the flak and mortar fire attacking the Lady Susan. Within minutes, they were in the grey clouds in an attempt to hide.

'Have we been hit?' Cherry called to Ted above the noise.

'Just hold onto the stanchions we're not out of the woods yet!' he shouted to her above the roar of the engines. The flak was still exploding below them. She didn't need to be told again. The aeroplane jumped and bucked like a horse as the flak exploded within inches of the fuselage. If anyone could get them away from enemy fire it would be Ted. Her heart was in her mouth and the patients were silent realising that the pilot was trying to get them out of danger. Cherry couldn't do anything but hold on and watch Ted out the corner of her eye struggling with the Lady Susan. The other eye she had on the patients. At last, he levelled off.

'Jerry doesn't like us in his back yard, does he?' Ted laughed a bit shakily from the cockpit.

'It's about time our lot overran those enemy gun positions,' said his co-pilot. 'What's going on?

Expecting us to get these injured lads home when the enemy's still taking pot shots at us!'

'Well said!' Ted laughed. The sense of relief was palpable in his voice now they were away from enemy fire.

'We've gone through the flak. Now we have the remains of the stormy weather to get through!'

'All right, I'm coming,' she said to one man who was in pain and trying to get rid of his oxygen mask.

'No tea in this stormy weather lads, sorry to say. But a few more minutes and we'll be flying over the white cliffs of Dover.'

She sounded confident even to herself, and out of one of the port holes she could see they had left the outskirts of Caen behind. She chivvied the patients along even though she felt sick herself. They could have easily ended up in the Channel below. She wiped the sweat from her brow, hoping the men didn't see how nervous she had been in the past few minutes. Some of the injured called out to her. 'Nurse! Nurse!'

'Now then, all's well, we're out of enemy fire. Just hold on. Yes, I'll get you some water.' She said to those who were able to ask her questions.

Staggering along amongst the stretchers she talked and calmed the injured, handing out water. A minute's lull and she pulled herself along on the stanchions until she reached Ted in the cockpit. They hadn't flown in such bad weather before.

'I want to put as much distance between us and that,' he thumbed behind him where the remains of Caen lay in ruins. 'It's not safe to fly near here, for us or the enemy. And the Allies are still bombing it.'

'And Jerry is still defending it!' said the co-pilot. 'Fight to the last man! I've seen the films of the crazy Fuhrer!'

The aircraft hit the end of stormy weather coming over the white cliffs of Dover and were tossed about again. Casualties were air sick, Cherry handed out sick bags to those who could hold them, as the Lady Susan bucked and tossed them around. She had to concentrate on the job in hand and try not to be sick herself.

Flying over the south of England Ted called her up to the cockpit. She recognised Southampton below them.

'Hey look at this!'

'My God! Is that a...?'

'Yes, I think it is.'

A black object swept past them at speed. 'Now it's gone,' he said. 'I wonder which poor sod is going to get that Doodlebug in his back garden?'

'My friend was killed in the East End last week by one of those things, said the co-pilot. 'You don't hear 'em coming. The engine cuts out before it gets to you, and it's silent but fast, before you know it – it's blown a huge hole in your backyard.'

'Or house.' Cherry added.

'Let's hope we boot the Germans out of France soon.'

'Yes,' he agreed. 'But I don't think it'll be yet.'

Cherry gave more water to those who could drink and tried to clear up the sick bags now they were flying level. To those who were on drips she checked on them and to those who were conscious went round and gave reassurance. She went to the young man who'd grabbed her hand as she went past. She consoled him and calmed him, fixing his oxygen and saying to them all loudly, 'Nearly home lads! Then you'll be taken to a hospital and you'll be fine then.'

Ted looked round and smiled, and she gave a thumbs up to him. She never would get used to dodging flak, but at least she could make it easier on the confused and scared patients who were in the aeroplane. She carried on chatting to the men who spoke to her. They were astonished to see a WAAF up in the air.

'Well done nurse for looking after us,' said a young soldier.

'I'm surprised to see a young lassie in the thick of it up 'ere,' said another soldier. 'Not many men let alone women would want to risk their lives getting us injured back home.'

Others around him agreed. Men who couldn't speak and were aware of what was going on stared at her. She felt they were looking at her for the first time. Some of them were in a lot of pain, some had their eyes covered or part of their head was covered. They were quiet but were they aware what was happening? She probably would never know.

'Just doing a job...' she said trying to sound confident. Goodness, if her mother and father could hear her now...She felt proud of all the air ambulance crews. She felt more confident than she'd ever felt, especially after what she'd been through. She would never forget the soldiers marching to the front near Caen. If they could be cheery then she would be too.

CHAPTER 23 - September 1944 - Belgium

The Mulberry Harbours were used to great effect the first few days of the landings and most of the infantry and tanks had landed. But bad weather on D-Day turned into a full-on storm battering the two Mulberry Harbours on 19 June. The American Mulberry harbour off Omaha Beach was bashed to bits and was unusable. The British Mulberry was saved where it was floating off Gold Beach near Arromanches, and engineers managed to secure it so that the continuation of ships and supplies could continue to unload and they could keep supplying the Allied armies right to the front.

With the French Resistance helping the Allies with their ongoing sabotage, the Allies slowly made their way south fighting, sometimes hand to hand with Germans who were dug in throughout the bocage in Normandy. Eventually, the German resistance was dwindling. On August 25th the Germans surrendered to the French Resistance and on 26th the American and French troops liberated Paris. Charles de Gaulle led the cavalcade of troops through the city as Parisians were wild with delight at seeing a Frenchman lead the troops through the centre of Paris.

On 11th September the British Second Army captured Antwerp. However, the Germans still occupied the Schedlt river with its canals and tributaries flowing into the southwest of the Netherlands, and controlling the port of Antwerp. To help the Allies gain access to the port, Canadians fought to clear the Germans from the Scheldt area. This wasn't easy, as the German army was well-trained, dug-in and well-resourced.

As the Allies advanced from France into Belgium, it was time for the field hospitals to move forward with the advancing Allied armies. The air ambulance units followed the front lines ferrying the wounded back and armaments and ammunition forwards.

Cherry and Ted flew into Belgium landing near Brussels in the first week of September. The area had just been liberated by the Allied troops. They heard reports of collaborators being shot, and women who had been friendly with the Germans had their heads shaved.

In October to help the Allies, who had re-taken the southern part of the Netherlands, the railway workers organised a strike to reduce the movement of supplies to the German army fighting on the frontline. However, with the Germans taking the local population's food supply to feed their army, and the Allied bombing campaign, the strike caused severe food shortages to all the inhabitants of Holland, causing an acute famine.

It was still a daunting time for the hospital units driving forward through the summer battlefields still reeking of death. Death lay in the fields; soldiers' faces with blue-black bodies were swollen and there was the constant sickly-sweet smell of decay. Cows lay on their backs in grotesque positions with four legs pointing to the sky. Flies fed on every hole of the head and body.

Cherry was surprised to see so many German horses had been relied upon to pull equipment and guns. Many had been killed and were still in harness, they lay on the ground their bodies swollen to a huge size.

The 151st Field Hospital was now established in Brussels. Cherry and Ted were ferrying the wounded from the field hospital to RAF Wroughton. The patients were mostly from the Grenadiers and Welsh Guards who had stormed down different routes in a neck-and-neck race into the city of Brussels.

'Hold tight. We're going to crash land!' shouted Ted from the cockpit.

Cherry hung on grimly and swayed violently as she clung on to the stanchions. The Dakota swung left and right and bumped and tossed her across the floor. In seconds they were landing on their second pick up near Brussels. The propellors of the Lady Susan were still spinning as they chewed up the turf and skidded to a stop. The Dakota swerved and spun ninety degrees, and the securing ropes of the cargo came adrift, the extra cargo slewed about from port to starboard just missing Cherry by inches as she flung herself away from it to avoid being hit. Her heart was thumping, they'd never had such a bumpy landing before.

The thuds of mortars were very close. Cherry wasn't particularly worried; she'd been closer than this to the front before. The crew climbed out of the Lady Susan and Ted and the co-pilot surveyed the damage.

As they walked unsteadily over the rough terrain a short distance across the field, Ted suddenly threw himself face down to the ground.

'Incoming!'

A whistling and whining sound so reminiscent of Normandy was the precursor to a huge explosion in a nearby field. Cherry joined Ted face down and the next second they were hit by a cascade of mud and dirt. It felt like someone throwing stones at their backs. They listened to the noises face down, then after a few seconds they stood up and brushed themselves down.

'Well, the V1's seem to be following us anyway,' she said. 'It's a good job that one fell in a field. I hope no one was hurt.'

They hurried to the nearby hedge where the bomb had landed and looked over the top. The field was full of dead, bloated cows. They looked across to the furthest field the other side. The huge tents of the British Field Hospital sprawled out in front of them filling up the field and going back as far as the eye could see.

'Jeesh!' Ted exclaimed. 'That just missed the hospital. It doesn't seem to matter where you are, the bastards'll try and get you!'

They saw a line of ambulances come careering down a lane at the side of the field towards them. Ted waved them down and pointed them toward the Lady Susan.

Two men jumped out of the first ambulance and opened the gate into the bumpy field they were in. The crew went to give them a hand unloading the vital supplies for the hospital and then they started bringing in the wounded from the ambulances.

As Cherry organised the patients into their rows in the Dakota, she checked on the drip lines for those who were seriously wounded. There were three patients on foot. One with crutches another one holding bandaged arms and one man had his whole head swathed in bandages with just eye holes to see out of. She helped him up the ramp and guided him onto a seat next to the door. As the Lady Susan started up another V1 came whistling overhead and the medical orderlies dived off the plane and ran towards their ambulances. It had been a mad rush to get the patients transferred to the aeroplane, but it was completed in minutes. Nobody wanted to hang around with the threat of a V1 bomb suddenly landing on you.

Cherry ducked even though the V1 whooshed overhead and exploded in a field beyond. A barrage of clogs of mud and bits of bomb pinged off the fuselage and the men in the Dakota went quiet. People held their breath. Cherry looked out of a window, her heart thumping.

'Ted that just missed us!'

'Let's get out of here! They seem to know we're in the area, it doesn't help the hospital.'

The Dakota swung northwards and Ted did a bumpy run up before the Lady Susan took a slow belaboured incline into the sky.

'Hold tight!' he shouted to everyone onboard.

Suddenly a burst of mortars fired on them. She heard the noise outside the aeroplane, the Lady Susan swayed about because of the weight, and she felt they weren't climbing quick enough to escape. Her heart was in her throat. The sounds of explosions sounded within metres of the aeroplane's undercarriage. The patients sitting on the end seats ducked automatically as they heard the rat-a-tat-tat of bullets and the sound of the cartridges pinging off the fuselage. Again, she held her breath, and comforted a young man who was lying on a stretcher.

'Won't be long,' she lied, and tried to swallow, her mouth was dry with fear. 'Nearly home now.'

Everyone seemed to be holding their breath listening to the violent sounds outside the Lady Susan.

'Bloody 'el darlin you do this every day?'

'Pretty much,' she answered, hanging onto the stanchions and squeezing her eyes shut at the chaos and fire erupting outside.

Cherry missed a step and banged her leg on the side of one of the stretchers losing her footing and landing on the floor between a row of stretchers.

'You all right luv?' he asked.

'Yes.' She got up stiffly, holding her shoulder.

'Then light us this fag will yer?'

As the Lady Susan climbed and then levelled off Cherry started to relax. She walked amongst the wounded and tended to them quietly. No one spoke. They weren't out of the woods yet.

She was too far away from the pilots to see how they were doing, Ted was concentrating on flying the aeroplane because he was silent too. She realised they had just had another near miss. How many more before they copped it? After a few moments, they flew over the white cliffs of Dover, she made her way to Ted at the front.

'I don't think we've ever come that close to being blown to bits,' she said.

'And I hope we don't ever again,' he said.

'We're home gentlemen,' she told everyone. 'We're just flying over the white cliffs of Dover.'

Some cheers went up at the back of the aircraft.

When they arrived back in the south of England, and the wounded were loaded onto the ambulances. One of the ground crew came up and spoke to Ted as they surveyed the damage.

The Dakota's fuselage was bullet-ridden.

'It's a miracle none of you inside were hit. They must know we're ferrying the wounded, why did they attack?'

'To the Germans, we're still the enemy,' replied Ted. 'Especially now we have their backs against the wall. We're pressing the Nazis back to Germany, they don't have anywhere else to go.'

The Lady Susan was out of action for the next few days, and Cherry and Ted had to use another Dakota. Ted was unhappy about using a different aeroplane, he was superstitious and didn't like the change. Cherry wasn't superstitious but she remembered the superstitions of the bomber crews at Finsham. Joe had been very particular about sticking his family photos inside his tunic, they had to go in exactly the same place every time. When she had laughed at him, he had told her he never went without them, it was his good luck charm. His friends, other pilots, and other crew were similarly superstitious. She remembered when M-Mother's crew had flown a substitute Wellington because theirs was damaged. That night, when M-Mother was in dock, and they were flying over Germany in another aircraft- the crew had been shot down. She brought herself back to the present and decided not to tell Ted about her past experiences, he would worry all the more.

A letter arrived from her mother which was surprisingly positive.

'Dear Cherry, You seem to be having a more exciting time than any of us dear daughter!'

(Dear daughter? Since when had she called her "dear" before?)

Sheila from next door and some of the other neighbours, Tilly and Esme, you know them, they brought today's newspaper to my front door and I opened it to find...you! A photo of you and your pilot working for the Air Ambulance standing next to the aeroplane. It talks about you dodging flak! And that you've been behind enemy lines. It's a good job you didn't tell me before you went, I wouldn't have let you go! But the neighbours are saying how proud I must be of you, and I suppose I am. I would never have dreamt you would have the wherewithal to have such a dangerous job when you joined the WAAF. I thought you would end up cleaning floors of spew like they get junior nurses to do in hospitals.'

We do that on a moving plane, mother, she thought to herself. And wasn't being Papa's assistant warden dangerous enough for you?

'Be careful. Tommy and I don't want to lose you as well. From your loving mother.'

She remembered the photo taken by the war correspondents near Caen after D-Day when Jim and Toby had taken them almost to the front line. That must've been the photo doing the rounds in the British newspapers. She would never forget the smell of death in the hedgerows that day. What she saw she would never be able to unsee.

The weather was damp, foggy and miserable when they flew to Antwerp. The Lady Susan's tyres bumped and skidded onto a landing strip in a frozen field on the outskirts of Antwerp. It was the end of September. Was this winter going to be as cold as the last? It seemed it was going that way. After the heat, smells and flies of Normandy, Cherry could hardly believe that it was getting this cold so soon.

This was the fifth landing the Lady Susan had completed on the man-made airstrip outside Antwerp. The field hospitals had slowed their advance now because the move to the Rhine had slowed, the Germans were making a stand against the Allies and digging in.

It was only twenty kilometres to Antwerp. Antwerp being the main port held by the Germans which the Allies needed to free so that they could bring more troops and resources to sustain the march across the Rhine into Germany. The Germans staged an effective delaying action - they flooded land areas in the Scheldt estuary slowing the Allied advance.

British armoured units had smashed across the Dutch frontier and reached the town of Breda twelve miles inside the border northeast of Antwerp. The German armies were dug in and defended at all costs. There were thousands of injured British troops to fly home to Britain that autumn, as the operation to thrust forward into Northern Germany capturing three bridges became a disaster. Thousands were killed or taken prisoner by the Germans. This came to be known as Operation Market Garden.

CHAPTER 24 - The Deserter

Cherry and Ted had orders to pick up wounded a few miles outside Brussels at the 51st British Field Hospital. They managed to land in a fairly flat field that had been prepared by the Engineers the day before, but the weather was closing in and they landed bumpily caught in crosswinds. What was predicted to be light winds, were now severe gusts. Ted swore loudly as they bumped and swerved to a halt on the field landing strip.

'Well done, Ted.' She said admiring his landing, noticing he'd broken out in a sweat on his forehead. 'If anyone can land on a thruppence, you can.'

While Ted and the co-pilot were checking the Lady Susan's undercarriage, Cherry walked in the direction of the field hospital which was two fields away. There were no trucks in sight and no sign of any loadings. It was deathly quiet. It was still very quiet when she looked over a hedge to see the top of the tents of the field hospital in the distance. A nurse came out as Cherry arrived at the entrance, she hadn't seen the nurse before.

'It's very quiet today. Where's Sister Fran?' Cherry asked her.

'Some people have had to go home for leave, they're exhausted. So, it's us new ones from now on. They've been going flat out. Sister Fran was the first one to leave, she didn't want to, but she went eventually. Now there are about twenty replacement nurses that have arrived.'

'Good for Sister Fran. The nurses showed me their living conditions after D-Day. They were terrible. Well, I hope your toilets are safer,' she quipped to the nurse.

A young medic hurried out of the tent over to Cherry. 'The patients aren't ready yet for a couple of hours and we've been radioed from your base the 'Meteorologicals' have seen a storm that's coming this way...and it's imminent. Best to be safe than sorry, you'd better stay until it's blown over.'

'Come inside,' said the nurse to Cherry.

'All right, but I'll go and tell my pilot first.'

She hurried back to the field strip and saw Ted and his crew checking different parts of the Dakota.

'Ted!' she called to him hurrying, closer. She could see the storm advancing towards them. Ted and the co-pilot crawled out from underneath.

'New staff have taken over. It'll be a couple of hours before they bring out the patients. And Ted, there's a storm on its way.' She pointed to ominous black clouds creeping towards them.

'Damn,' he said, observing the black clouds, 'I would have hoped to have left by then. It would've been good to be loaded and on our way.' He nodded to his co-pilot who went back into the belly of the Lady Susan.

'That's not going to happen, is it?' he sighed. 'Depending on how long the storm lasts. I can see we won't be up in two hours.' He wiped his hands on an oily rag.

Cherry was out of breath from running. 'Their regular nurses had gone on leave as they were exhausted. The newer lot seem to be slower and not as well organised.'

'Well, I'm not surprised,' he said. Then he pointed to an old barn in the next field. 'I'm going to smoke my pipe over there when it rains. I don't fancy waiting in the hospital today.'

'I think I'll follow you, I don't fancy going in today either.'

Ted walked over to a dilapidated-looking shed, leaving the rest of the crew to make their way to the field hospital. He stood underneath and looked up at the sky. A few plops of rain fell around him, he got out his pipe but a sudden gust of wind blew the match out. Meanwhile, Cherry made her way to a small farmhouse behind the shed. Raindrops fell heavily, it became very cold. She looked up, the rain was falling as sleet. She hurried towards the building. It was a ramshackle and empty-looking farmhouse, the curtains were hanging by threads in the kitchen window. No one had lived here for years. She tried the door, was it safe to go inside? The door creaked open it looked like it had been vacated long ago. The back garden had once been used to grow vegetables, now it was overgrown and desolate. Looking around it was a sad reminder of the occupation by the Nazis who had tried to starve people out of their homes.

With one foot in the kitchen and one on the veranda, Cherry knocked a few times on the back door. A tatty-looking curtain covered the dirty glass window in the back door. After a minute or two she pushed it open wide and walked in. It was then she smelled tobacco smoke. Someone had put out a cigarette recently. There was an ashtray on the table but no burning cigarette. But there were other things on the table – some crushed paper, some matches. It was as if someone had rushed away.

'Hello?' There was no reply, she walked up to the kitchen table in the middle of the small kitchen.

'Hello?' she said again. She started to feel uneasy. If there was someone here, why wouldn't they show themselves? As she continued to walk slowly towards the stairs. She had a feeling she was being watched. She was beginning to see evidence of life -there was dirty crockery on the kitchen sink and a full ashtray of dead cigarettes. Although the place had a broken window it felt warm in the room, as if someone was living there. Then she spied a packet of cigarettes next to the sink which was half opened, they had foreign writing on them which was probably in Dutch, looking again she realised it was actually German. Her heart sank. She realised there was someone there, watching her. Warning bells inside her head were telling her to get out of there quickly. She started to retrace her steps.

As she hurried towards the kitchen door, a man in a dirty German uniform, burst out from behind a door. She screamed as he launched himself at her. He was not tall but he was stout and his body was like a missile. He landed on top of her knocking the table on its side and Cherry hard onto her back on the floor. She lay confused, winded, trying to envisage what had just happened to her but before she could respond he hit her around her head with his hand as she tried to move. Stunned, she tried to push him off, but it was useless, he was as heavy as a ton of meat. A pain throbbed in her head. She twisted and turned her body to get out from under him but only managed to get her legs trapped. She screamed again. He tried to muffle her screams with a smelly hand. He started hissing at her in German. She didn't have a clue what he was saying. She shouted at the top of her voice.

'Ted! Help!'

The soldier grabbed her wrists and tried to twist her and push her face down on the floor.

'No! No!' she shouted and tried to push him off. She felt helpless, he was too strong. With one almighty effort, she twisted her right arm free swung it towards his head and punched him on the nose. He put his hand to his nose, and she was half up off the floor struggling to stand on both legs. With one foot she tried to kick him between the legs. He hit out at her hanging on to one arm and tried to grab and pull her down. She screamed again, as he tried to pull her hair and all she could smell was body odour and garlic.

'Ted! Ted! She yelled as she kept kicking and punching trying to escape from his grabbing hands and kicking out in all directions.

'Help! Help!' she yelled again, trying to wriggle and pull away. The soldier tried to smother her mouth, so she bit his hand. He swore and tried to grab her hair and pull her down again. She stumbled and landed back on the floor. She doubled over and his gasps and grunts showed he was flagging. Her heart pounding, it took all her might to fend him off by deflecting his blows as he tried bang her head on the ground.

Then there was a clang as the man slumped on top of her. Ted stood above them, he hauled the man back off her and threw the unconscious man on the floor. He had a long-handled shovel beside him. Some blood was on the spade end and on the man's head – the soldier was out cold.

'Cherry! Are you all right?' he said helping her up. She had blood running from her nose and cuts on her hands and neck.

'Thank God you came when you did!' she said, feeling sick. 'He was bashing my head on the ground I nearly passed out!'

'You were giving him as good as you got when I came in. This was behind the door outside.' He held the spade in his left hand. Her jacket and trousers were torn, and she was shaking uncontrollably.

'Ow!' she rubbed the side of her face which was red and sore. Her heart was pounding, she tried not to cry. A sob came out. Her ears and head hurt where he had hit her. 'Thank God you came in time, Ted!'

Ted grabbed the packet of cigarettes on the side, put his arm under hers and helped her towards the door and outside.

'Careful, take your time. Let's get you to the hospital.'

'Oh Ted, he was horrible. I think he was going to kill me!'

'He looks and smells like a deserter. Let's go and tell someone from the BFH to come and get him before he becomes conscious.'

Leaning against him Cherry and Ted made their way towards the field hospital. He picked his pipe up on the way back across the field. 'Dropped my pipe in all the excitement.'

She didn't feel the driving rain against her and by the time they got to the field hospital, they were both soaked through.

'We'll get you checked out with the nurses,' he said again. 'You gave me a fright! I wondered what on earth you were yelling about. Then, I heard terrifying screams – I thought I was back in Singapore. Then I realised it was you - I tell you, I've never run so fast!'

Cherry was gradually getting her breath back after her ordeal, she rubbed her head and neck. It looked like she was gradually getting the colour back in her face.

'Perhaps you'd better not go wandering off again,' he said, as they went inside the field hospital.

CHAPTER 25 - It'll be over by Christmas

Cherry occasionally met up with friends from the air ambulance team in her hut. But in the hut next door was an empty bed. The crew of another Dakota had gone missing over the English Channel. It had happened on their outward flight to Belgium, the whole crew and their Flying Nightingale had been lost at sea. There were no patients on board. It was hard to come to terms with the loss of one of their own. Cherry felt dreadful and had many sleepless nights. Dodging bullets and V1's, and now V2's were being sent over the North Sea to England. The V2's were even worse than the V1's.

Hitler launched his secret weapon V2 on Britain and Holland in October 1944. Unlike the V-1, the V-2's speed and trajectory made it practically invulnerable to anti-aircraft guns and fighters, as it dropped from an altitude of 62 miles at up to three times the speed of sound at sea level. It was the first jet rocket of its kind and no one could stop it on its death trips to Holland, Belgium and England. It was so fast people couldn't tell it was coming. No defences could stop it.

During the weeks before Christmas Cherry was flying almost daily. After a long weekend Cherry was ready to fly again. Ted suggested she have some time off, but she didn't want to. It meant she'd have time to think, about what had happened with the deserter. She wanted to keep busy.

In November 1944 Cherry and Ted landed easily on the more established runways of smaller airfields in Belgium and the Netherlands. While they waited for the wounded from the field hospital to be delivered to their plane they watched Allied troops playing football with Dutch boys in the middle of a large field. There was no warning and no pre-emptive sound. Suddenly there was a loud bang, and then there was nothing there. Just a big crater and bits of bodies, looking like bundles of old rags lying about. On the fringes of the field, men were lying bleeding. A V2 bomb had landed right in the middle of the pitch. The V2 came in faster than sound, so no one heard it coming, and there was no time to take cover. Everyone stood around in shock.

Hitler launched his V2's on Antwerp and tried to obliterate the whole port area and prevent its use. The rockets showered down, day after day. They fell within eight miles of the centre of Antwerp and thousands of civilians, servicemen and women were killed. As a result, casualties were increasing instead of decreasing by the planeload and a regular shuttle by the air ambulance teams was in process. Cherry and Ted tried to get in and out as fast as they could between raids. But there was no warning and it was a great strain on everyone.

On 4 December they landed on the outskirts of a small town not far from the mayhem of the River Schedlt, where the Germans had only just relinquished the estuary to the Allies.

The landing was slippery although the frost was melting gradually as the sun tried to force its way through the clouds.

Ted was not happy. 'This is lethal!' he exclaimed, as the Lady Susan ran on for longer on landing. 'The landing brakes aren't working. I wouldn't want to do that again,' he said to everyone.

'It's too dangerous to keep landing in this icy weather. We'll drop this off and pick up some casualties then go before it re-freezes.'

They waited for their injured patients. A little girl about eight years old was hanging around and was given some food by some of the injured. The patients seemed to enjoy having her around. Cherry kept an eye on her to see that she didn't get in the way as the orderlies put the injured aboard. She was stick thin and obviously hadn't had a good meal in a long time.

'What's your name?' Cherry asked her. The little girl shrank away as if she had done wrong. "I won't hurt you.'

'Emilie.'

'Thank you, Emilie, for talking with the patients,' said Cherry, she had noticed Emilie was offering sweets to thm, which someone had given her. It had cheered them up no end. Emilie looked guilty.

'Thank you for being nice to them. Would you like this sandwich?'

The little girl's eye looked longingly at the bread.

'Go on, take it. I don't need it. I've had enough,' Cherry lied. She had brought two sandwiches with her. But she and Ted had combined their lunch so Emilie could have something substantial to eat.

The Lady Susan's engines burst into life. It made Emilie jump.

'Where do you live?'

The little girl looked apprehensive but eventually pointed.

'Over there!' She pointed to a row of houses at the end of the field.

'Thank you. I hope we come here again and see you soon. You have a natural way with the patients.' Cherry said encouragingly, and the girl backed away as Cherry waved and closed the Dakota doors. As they took off the plane circled and passed over the airfield, the little girl was still there watching them as they climbed higher into the sky.

That week Cherry received a letter for the first time in months from her mother. It looked like a long one so she sat on her bed in the mess and read it while no one was around. She wondered what her mother was going to write about so lengthily. She'd never had a letter this long before. What she read from her mother was astounding.

Dear Cherry, I haven't been able to write for a while because I am still getting over your Papa's death. But I made a recent decision and it was to stop being lonely and go back to helping the WI. A friend came to me the other day and asked me to go back they need my help. So of course, I said yes. I received a letter from Sidney at last and he is doing all right. I wanted also to write and let you know that I don't blame you for Cecily's death. It was an accident. And I shouldn't have blamed you over the years, I am sorry, I just couldn't face up to my little girl not being here with us anymore. I still find it hard to talk about it. So no more to be said about that. Oh, and Mrs Newman had a baby girl yesterday they are doing very well. And the house was blown up opposite ours. No one was living in it thank goodness!

I am proud of you, I want you to know that. And I hope to see you soon. Be careful in France! Love from your Mother.

Cherry sat on the edge of the bed speechless and full of wonder. So her mother had kind of apologised for Cecily's accident. It made Cherry cheer up a bit as she'd been a bit down, with the winter months, the early darkness, and seeing Dutch children so emaciated. If her mother can start again, and let bygones be bygones, she was sure she could. She was glad her mother had written and was trying to get out of her depression. Well, wonders would never cease.

Cherry saw the little girl Emilie again when they landed back in her village on Christmas Eve. Cherry and Ted had been grounded on the Eastern side of Antwerp again due to bad weather. Although there had been flights during the cold sunny days, most of the time had been waiting for the Lady Susan's wings to defrost. The previous week icicles had formed after rain had re-frozen overnight on another landing ground in the south.

The winter of 1944 had shown itself to be a nasty one coming in. Weather reports weren't good but the air ambulance crews kept going as long as they could. Sadly, there had been another report of the loss of another Flying Nightingale.

No reason was given, no one had managed to bail out. It could have come down due to enemy fire or engine failure. Cherry didn't know the full story. She just knew that two of the girls had not returned. Their beds were as they left them, neat and tidy, ready for them to come home. Only they weren't coming home. The sadness hung over the huts. Everyone was quiet in the evenings. It was hard to talk when you knew two of your crew weren't returning.

Sometimes the flights were grounded, the next day if the snow had melted and it was sunny, they were allowed to fly. But on Christmas Eve Ted and Cherry had completed a late flight and it had snowed thickly after they'd landed. Although the snow had stopped, it had re-frozen, and it was now too frozen to take off again. They would have to wait until morning and hope it didn't snow again on top of the ice. Ted covered the windscreen of the Lady Susan with an old blanket, but the truth was it was so frozen to the windscreen it wasn't much protection at all.

As they couldn't get home that Christmas Eve, Cherry and Ted decided to join their old friends from the 51st British Field Hospital to give a party for the local Dutch children.

The Dutch had endured the occupation with great bravery. They welcomed their liberators and invited them to share in their homes during the Christmas period. They also laid on a

Christmas party for the town inviting their liberators and the staff at the field hospital. The ordinary townsfolk had very little themselves in the way of food.

Few people were on the snowy streets of Antwerp that night, not only because of the danger of V1's and V2's but because they were unfit to go out onto the streets. The Germans had taken most of their food during the occupation and thousands of Dutch people were starving to death.

They gathered in the local church. It was austere and cold and had hard wooden benches, but inside the church it was lit with candles and the warmth of the people. Groups of medical staff and members of the armed forces played games with the children. The children's faces were shining with happiness after all the hardship they had experienced and all the deaths they had seen. They called and shouted to each other, in a state of high excitement when the sweets and candy were handed out. For most of them, they had never eaten chocolate before.

Cherry thought of her little brother and her mother on their own this Christmas, and of their loved ones who had died. The people who were 'Missing in Action,' like Joe - would their bodies ever be found? She prayed that this would be the last Christmas under occupation and they all prayed in the church that it was soon coming to an end.

The village hall was dressed with simple garlands. Cherry watched the children playing games with her friends, and gasping with pleasure at the simple presents they had wrapped up of sweets and chocolate. The children were delighted because they hadn't seen such treats in a long time.

As they walked to the church from the hall, Ted put a hand on her shoulder and pointed up into the sky – it was full of snow. The darkness had descended early as it does in the northern hemisphere even though it was late afternoon.

They went into the church and there was a simple service, and although very cold outside, they were all crammed in and Cherry found herself warming up. Her throat felt constricted as the congregation sang 'Silent Night, Holy Night.' And because she was feeling lonely without her family, she joined in with the singing of the carol. It was beginning to feel like a real Christmas.

Cherry and Ted were spending Christmas Eve with Margarite and her daughter Emilie, the thin little girl that Cherry had met on the previous trip. Their breaths made clouds in the frosty air as they left the church after the service. The atmosphere was one of immense relief and happiness now that the country was no longer occupied.

Cherry realised how lucky she had been. Going without some food, but working in the WAAF she had been provided with rations even if there had been a shortage. She and her friends had complained about a lack of make-up, nylons, or new dresses. But here walking the streets of Antwerp she felt ashamed, because she saw how the Dutch people had hardly any food or basic necessities themselves. Food the locals had grown in the garden in the summer had been confiscated by the now retreating German army. The Nazis had taken it all.

'We're so glad you're here to liberate us,' Margarite told them. Ted offered her his arm and they crunched through the snow to the house. Emilie took Cherry's hand in hers, they were all smiling and in good spirits as they made their way back to Margarite's house. They skirted the big craters and rubble in the streets made by the falling bombs sent by Hitler.

Margarite led them into her house around the back gate and they kicked the snow from their boots as she led them into the house. It was a small house and very sparse. Ted built up the fire that had reduced to embers and they sat around it watching the warm glow and waiting for it to catch on the new wood as they warmed themselves. Margarite lit candles around the room, it seemed really Christmassy now, after all the gloom and doom.

Cherry had brought food with her on the Dakota; a fruit cake her mother had sent her for Christmas and some sweets. Ted brought some vegetables from his garden, and they gave these to Margarite and Emilie. Margarite made a thick warming soup with some homemade bread, and they had the fruit cake afterwards. Emilie was overjoyed to see such treats after such a long time, and marvelled at some sweets she had not seen before.

'They're called Bon-Bons,' explained Cherry. Ted added; 'I ate them too, when I was little. Emilie screwed up her nose as she ate one because of the initial fizziness and then jumped up and down with delight.

'They're lovely!

'Well, you can have them all, if there's any left, after Ted's eaten them,' said Cherry looking at him sideways. Ted and Margarite popped one into their mouths as well. They laughed and the warmth of the fire glow and the good humour made Cherry feel she was happy for the first time in a long time.

'What happened to your husband?' Ted asked Margarite.

'I do not know. He was taken away to work at a forced labour camp. Many of the men were taken, leaving the women and children on our own about a year ago. The SS came and took most of the men away from the village and put them on a train bound for Germany and Austria. There has been no word since.'

They sat quietly, thinking, looking into the embers.

'I wonder if there's any way to find out now, where your husbands have been taken now the Allies are advancing,' said Cherry.

'The men will be liberated soon. It's only a matter of weeks now before they are found and they can return home,' said Ted smiling at Margarite. Margarite smiled back.

He's giving her false hope, thought Cherry. *What happens if her husband doesn't come back? She'll be devastated.* She looked down at Emilie playing happily with a doll and sweets in front of the fire.

'Let's hope they find their husbands and fathers soon,' said Cherry thoughtfully. It's going to be a harsh winter.' Then wished she hadn't said it. It was all what they had been thinking. The snow was falling thick and silently outside, while the adults sat around the fire deep in thought.

When Ted checked his Dakota the next day, he had trouble clearing the snow covering the aeroplane. Volunteers came out to help him. Eventually, it stopped snowing but it wasn't until two days later that the airstrip was cleared of snow when the sun had melted it. Two days later they were able to say 'adieu' and 'au revoir' and the Lady Susan was able to take off, with the wounded on board. The next time they passed over it would be when the front had moved to Arnhem.

CHAPTER 26 - Holland and the Roads to Germany

In January and February Cherry and Ted hardly flew because of the freezing weather. The dreadful news of the Battle of the Ardennes was divulged in the newspapers. It was a depressing time when so many Allied soldiers had been defeated by the German army or had frozen to death by the exceptionally cold winter. The newspapers had made it known that the American 101st had no special winter uniforms, they were still wearing their battle fatigues from the D-Day offensive in June. The Battle of the Bulge, also known as the Ardennes Offensive, was a major German surprise attack on the Allies. It took place from 16 December 1944 to 25 January 1945. It was launched through the densely forested Ardennes region between Belgium and Luxembourg. Soldiers fought in brutal winter conditions with very little in the way of food, protection from the elements and armaments. Eventually, the Allies made a counter-offensive which caused the Germans to withdraw. By the time the Germans had retreated towards Germany, the Allies had lost 77,000 men.

After Christmas Cherry and Ted found themselves taking off at RAF Brize Norton landing in Holland at the 51st British Field Hospital.

The snow had melted but the ground was frozen and slushy mud was all that was left after it had defrosted in the sunshine. Ted heard his first familiar voice. The patient's voice was booming across the tent; 'Nurse!'

'Well, as I live and breathe if it's not Monty Brathurst!' Ted exclaimed as he went up to a patient on a trolley.

'How are you? Oh, an Air Commodore now, are we?' And shook the Air Commodore's good hand as the other arm was strapped to his chest.

'Shrapnel, old son,' said Monty as he nodded towards his incapacitated arm. 'What are you doing here Teddy old fellow?'

Cherry watched this exchange with interest. Monty didn't look like an Air Commodore. Monty had a huge bushy moustache almost completely grey and a lot of grey hair sticking out at right angles from his cap. His twinkling blue eyes spied Cherry standing behind Ted. He winked at her as she stood awkwardly behind him.

'And who's this fair maiden with you now, Teddy boy?'

It was a merry exchange, and Ted was certainly pleased to see his old friend. He introduced Cherry. Monty's hand was warm and gripped her hand tight and used it to pull himself upright.

'Well, hello,' his eyes fixed on her. 'I wouldn't mind flying with you.' Ted ignored the remark and said to Cherry. 'I haven't seen Monty, since Singapore.' He turned back to Monty. 'We're Air Ambulance crews now,' Ted told him. 'We pick up the wounded and take 'em home to Blighty.'

Ted read the tag attached to Monty.

'Nope, you're not coming with us, old son...you've not been wounded bad enough!'

'Well shoot me in the foot then, and I'll come with you!' And Monty roared with laughter. The whole of the marquee shook with the reverberations. The nurses looked and smiled at him. It was difficult not to. Everyone who could was looking his way. He seemed like a 'larger than life' character, jolly, and loud. Cherry liked him.

'How did that happen? Aren't you supposed to be holed up with the other brass in a bunker somewhere out of harm's way?' Ted joked.

'Normally old boy. But had to go out to view operations at Eindhoven, and this is what happened.' He nodded to his arm again. 'A V2 landed nearby and it blew us all to bits! You oughta see the others nearer the centre of the bomb, not much left of them!'

'I do believe it. You were lucky to escape. We saw the very same thing happen not so long ago. So where are you off to now Monty?'

'Hush, hush old dear, walls have ears.' He beckoned to Ted to come closer. Cherry felt herself automatically step forward with Ted to listen. Monty's whispering was as loud as Ted talking so everyone in the tent heard.

'Just come back from the border, nearly there, we were. The war will be over in a few weeks. We just need to take the Fuhrer in his bunker and we have the bastards!' He shouted triumphantly.

The Sister frowned at him from the doorway and put a finger to her lips. Monty ignored her.

'Then we'll move in through the country and get some of our people back if they're still alive!'

'What do you mean?' asked Ted.

'That's my job. To find out where the prisoners are.' Monty tapped the side of his nose with his finger. 'There are hundreds of prisoner-of-war camps. If they haven't already died of malnutrition, disease and cold, we'll find the poor old buggers and get them out! Jerry used all sorts of nationalities to do his dirty work for him!' And he leaned back on his bed suddenly exhausted. Cherry stepped back and let Ted talk to him on his own for a few moments. Then they were called away as the wounded were being loaded onto the Lady Susan.

Once they were in flight, Ted called Cherry to the cockpit.

'I knew Monty from the Far East when he was just a Group Captain. Capital fellow. Salt of the earth. I knew he'd go higher up, people like him always do.'

'He has lots of energy,' said Cherry.

'Yes, he can be exhausting. He's moving towards the front towards Germany and Austria. There are lots of POW camps that need liberating. I asked him if he could find out where the Antwerp villagers were sent to.'

'Do you think he could do that?'

'If we could find out where Margarite's husband and the others were sent we could help liberate them.'

A fleeting image of Joe passed in front of her mind's eye. And a plan started to form in her mind. She was so convinced and so positive about her plan, that when Ted said he was going to ask Monty to look for the lost people of the Antwerp village, she asked if she could go with him.

'Really? You didn't seem that keen on him before.'

'That's because he took some getting used to. And he's obviously a terrible flirt. But now I've got the measure of him I'm going to ask for his help.'

'How so?'

'If someone is captured and is a POW Monty may be able to find out where he is. I mean if Monty can't find out, then no one can.'

Monty was still wearing his sling when they turned up to see him, but was ready to be discharged and he would be sent back to Eindhoven.

Ted told him about the Antwerp villagers and then Cherry wrote down a name on a piece of paper for Monty with Joe's rank and last unit. Monty couldn't promise anything, he said, it would depend on which camps he came across.

'The Germans are renowned for keeping good records when they have to, however, they have also been reported as destroying them as we believe some POW's have been forced to leave their camps and march away from the Allies. If your fiancé is in one of the Stalag of which there are several spread all over Germany and Poland, I may be able to find something. If he's alive. And that's a big if. It's how long you say since Dieppe? Two and a half years? Anything could have happened to him in that time. And that's if he survived Dieppe. Don't pin your hopes up my girl,' he said and patted her arm.

'I know. It's just that I feel if he's still alive. I'll maybe not find out until it's too late...like when I'm fifty or something. If he's dead then I'll know if you can't find any record of him.

'If there's a record of Joe where he's going, Monty will find it,' Ted assured her.

'I hope it's not too late for some of them,' she crossed her fingers.

'It will be for some,' he said.

Two weeks after Christmas, Ted and Cherry loaded the Lady Susan up with food, and landed at the Antwerp airfield close to the village where Margarite and Emilie lived. But below them, as they were landing the scene was one of utter devastation. Cherry's heart sank. The V2 rockets had plummeted into this area and there was very little standing in the area of Margarite's house. All that was left was rubble and rubbish in what used to be her street. The two of them walked around in utter disbelief at the devastation around them. Only two houses at the end of the street remained. The walls of the church nearby where they had celebrated Christmas Mass were still standing, but there was no roof, it was like a shell. It was difficult to find anyone around. When they did find someone, a man nearby did not know if Margarite and Emilie were still alive. The dead bodies in the street when they had been bombed the week before had been taken away for burial where the ground wasn't frozen. But he felt that there were still dead bodies amongst the buildings. The smell of death pervaded the air and Ted and Cherry went back to the Dakota in a sombre mood. It seemed likely that they had either been killed or gone to another area for refuge. They didn't have time to find out. They had to pick up the wounded nearby at the field hospital and then fly back before bad weather set in, as had been forecast for later that day. They left the area with heavy hearts.

Cherry had a lump in her throat as they took off and looked down at the decimated village. She hadn't expected her new friends to be killed, or for any of the village to be bombed. Even though the Allies were advancing and everyone believed it was nearing the end of the war, Hitler still managed to inflict misery, death, and destruction from his bunker in the middle of Germany.

The Nazis, avenging the Dutch rail strike after the failed liberation attempt on the Allied airborne assault at Arnhem, imposed a reign of terror. The ports of Amsterdam and Rotterdam had been wrecked by demolitions. More than 120,000 locals were rounded up and sent to German labour camps. The Germans had systematically been commandeering food from the Dutch ever since the start of the occupation. Coal supplies, gas and electricity had been cut off. The Nazis tried to starve and freeze the Dutch into submission.

Food supplies were exhausted; many people were reduced to eating tulip bulbs just to try to survive. Fuel had run out and transportation was non-existent. Thousands of Dutch men, women, and children perished from starvation and cold.

In early 1945 thousands of families had died by late April. Buildings were torn down for firewood, and demolished by bombs, their timber was removed for fuel for the inhabitants of the towns. The Allies feared that an attack in Holland's north country would provoke the Germans into opening the dykes and flooding the lowlands. As people continued to starve, Britain looked on helplessly.

Bodies were piling up in the morgues and churches for the lack of coffins. But on April 29th RAF bombers dropped precious packages of food at sites near The Hague and Rotterdam. For those still strong enough it meant the long 'Hunger Winter' was over.

CHAPTER 27 – The Return of the POW's

Cherry and Ted continued to ferry the wounded from mainland Europe, although the trips were not as numerous during the Spring of 1945. The front lines and field hospitals were moving forward but not as fast as the Allied troop, and the Dakotas weren't expected to fly as far as Germany. However, the tide of the war had changed and instead of wounded flying back, the Air Ambulances were bringing home aircraft loads of displaced and emaciated soldiers and prisoners of war.

Ted met up with Monty before he went back into Germany. He told Ted of some of the terrible things he had seen in the camps. He had no news of the people that Ted and Cherry had asked him about. Those that were starving had been given food by the first Allied soldiers in the camp and without proper monitoring they would die a painful death, because the emaciated body would not be able to handle all types of foods.

Some of the people from concentration camps were put on drips and fed intravenously. As this was increased gradually, the men could get accustomed to the nutrients at a slow pace and the stomach would not go into cramps. This type of wounded was very different to those whom Cherry was used to.

The first starving prisoners of war on drips were loaded onto the Lady Susan from a British Field Hospital in Belgium. These prisoners had barely been able to last the journey from inside Germany. They were loaded onto trucks wrapped in blankets and unloaded in a fragile state, hardly able to walk. They were put on drips as soon as they got to the casualty clearing stations in Holland and Brussels. Some of them had been travelling on the trucks for hours.

The Air Ambulance crews ferried the patients from Holland and Belgium taking them to military hospitals across England. Cherry and Ted took their patients to RAF Wroughton, where the prisoners of war were cared for at the RAF hospital until they were well enough to take sustenance and had built up some strength. They were fed stews and broths after the intravenous nutrients, and when the body was able to take something more than liquids, they were then passed to other hospitals nearby to allow for other emaciated people to come into the hospital. Many of the POWs couldn't speak until they had built up enough strength to eat properly and then tried to remember who they were. Many misplaced people came from all nationalities through the Air Ambulance Service this way.

On April 30th Hitler and Eva Braun committed suicide as Soviet troops advanced towards the city of Berlin. Soviet troops captured the city two days later and the remaining German troops in Italy surrendered.

The sun was warming the land and Belgium and Holland were becoming green again. The spring flowers burst through after the coldest winter Cherry could remember. She was nearly twenty-two years old, she had gone through such a lot in the four years she had been a WAAF.

On their seventh trip that week they had a moment to sit and wait for the rest of the crew to arrive.

'It won't be long before we'll be asked to stand down,' said Ted. 'Have you decided what to do?' He leaned over the back of the pilot's chair and she came up and sat behind him.

'The trips are slowing down, we'll both need to make a decision about what we're going to do when the war ends. It won't be long now.'

'What will you do, Ted? Stay on in the RAF?'

'Not sure. What about you? Will you stay on or become a nurse, now you're over twenty-one?

'I'm not sure Ted. My friend Sally is staying on, for now. She wants to stay as long as she can to keep her busy. I feel the same. And I've looked into the Princess Mary's Royal Air Force Nursing Service - I may apply to them.

'With your experience, you shouldn't have any trouble,' he said.

'The irony is, Joe gave me the idea to be a nurse in the RAF,' she said sadly. 'And my mother wants me to return home.'

'You're not gonna do that are you?'

I can't do that after what I've experienced over the past four years.'

'Women are expected to go back into the kitchen and leave their jobs for the returning men,' he said. 'That's not going to go down well for some.'

'And what if there aren't enough men to fill the jobs?'

'Then I expect they'll ask the women to come back.'

Cherry shook her head. 'I couldn't go back to looking after my brother,' she said. 'There's so much out there now for women. We've shown what we can do. Look at the ATA, will they be expected to go back home and stop flying now the war is endin?'

'Same with the women in munitions, or on buses. And the Land Girls.'

'And wardens,' she added. 'We were good enough to fill the gaps during wartime. Now they want us to go back home without a fuss.'

'The war has changed women. My wife was a 'Gunner Girl' in the ATS, and still is, as far as I know. She met someone else and didn't come back.' He stared out of the cockpit windscreen.

'I didn't know Ted,' Cherry stared at him in a shocked silence.

'Something I keep quiet about.'

'I'm sorry.'

'Don't be. She's happy. They're mixed teams, men and women, the men are from the Royal Artillery, and that's who she met. I s'pose if you're thrown together all day, you get close."

'Goodness. What job does she do?'

'She's an Ack Ack girl. They're not allowed to fire the guns. The men do that. She'd find the height and range of the enemy planes. The men would do the rest.'

'So, they worked together? You'd have to be courageous to do it.'

'Aye, there's no flies on her. They get shot at and bombed. I suppose she found solace in the arms of a young RA. Even some friends of hers have been killed while doing the job.' Ted looked away into the distance. She waited for him to speak first.

After a period of silence, he said. 'She'd changed the first time, she was so chuffed to be helping to defend London during the Blitz. A week later she didn't come home.'

'What happened?

'War changes you. It changed me. Look at all the people we've looked after and all the places we've flown to. The incidents that have happened...'

Cherry rubbed her jaw where her bruises from the incident with the deserter had been. 'If you hadn't saved me in the nick of time from that German soldier. I could be dead and buried!' She often had nightmares wondering what could have happened if Ted hadn't been there to save her.

Ted was looking into the distance thinking of memories long gone.

'I've seen things that people my age don't normally see. I could never go back to the way things were. Especially after Singapore. I got out in time. Others didn't.'

They saw the rest of the crew walk towards the Lady Susan waiting on the tarmac.

'You'd make a good nurse,' he acknowledged. 'Especially with all the patients you've dealt with.' She agreed, she was used to being independent now, she knew there was no way she would return to her old life at home.

'What are you going to do, Ted?'

'Carry on until I'm demobbed. I have a plan to try and find Margarite and Emilie. I don't know what happened to them.'

'They may have been killed,' Cherry said tentatively.

'And they may not. I need to find out before I settle down, I just need to know what happened to them. Monty's doing his best to find out for me.'

'You should find out. You liked them a lot.' Cherry had seen Ted looking at Margarite last Christmas. 'I wonder what's the chance of the husband returning?'

'Not much, according to Monty. Thousands of prisoners have died since the beginning of the war. Of course, if he turns up, I'll be glad for her. But we don't think there's much chance of it happening.'

On May 7th the rest of Europe rejoiced with the end of the war in Europe. This became known as Victory in Europe Day. Everyone celebrated in the streets of Britain, and the celebrations went on all day and all night. But Ted and Cherry were in the air for most of it.

They landed outside Brussels on the outskirts of a town close to the German border. They were expected to pick up some POWs. There was no one about except some burned-out houses.

'Looks like the Germans burned everything before retreating,' said Ted.

They listened for signs of life amongst the ruins. But there was nothing. Not even birds. It had been a long hard winter and there was no food. The hedgerows and many buildings around had been flattened by bombs it was like a living hell. It had become a barren wasteland with burnt and ravaged trees sticking up on the horizon like black stumps.

Then out of nowhere, they heard the sound of trucks coming towards them in the distance. The growling of engines got louder. From around a corner, six trucks skirted around burnt-out vehicles and the shelled remains of buildings in front of them.

'Ho! Ho!' shouted Ted. He waved as the first of the convoy approached within shouting distance. It sounded its horn and pulled to a halt in the middle of the road.

'We thought everyone had gone!' he shouted to the driver in the first truck. His partner got out. 'You Air Ambulance?'

'We certainly are. We've been waiting for you.'

'Sorry about that. We have twenty survivors from a mix of concentration camps from Germany. They've had a five-hour trek from Germany and they're exhausted. Just tell us where to put them.'

Ted pointed to the Lady Susan.

'But we only have room for eighteen. We'll have to squash them in, can you do that Cherry?'

'Okey dokey,' she said hurrying towards the Dakota.

'The driver stuck his arm out the window and pointed forward, instructing the trucks behind.

The trucks unloaded their precious cargo, some patients were on stretchers and very emaciated, they were all too tired or ill to make a noise.

'They need their drips changing for the trip back.' The driver said to Cherry.

'I recognise you,' she said. 'Aren't you from the 151st?'

'Yes, it's hellish back there. I drop these men off then go back. Not only are we back and forth with the repatriation of our lot. But there are a lot of German civilians and children who are sick or injured. It's murder where I've come from in Germany!'

Cherry started replenishing the saline bags for the sick on the stretchers once they were in place. There was just enough room for two people to sit at the back next to the door. The two men were thin, but not as emaciated as the men on the stretchers. One of them made a grunting sound in the middle of the plane. Cherry went to see to the man who had been placed in the middle section of the stretchers. He was about hip height. She held his hand.

'Won't be long now,' she told him.

'Hold on tight!' she shouted to them all as she braced herself against the stanchions. 'We'll be back to Blighty in a jiffy.'

The man grabbed her hand and tried to speak, but it was difficult to hear. He had a bandage around his head and part of his face. His mouth was twisted, she could see that the left side of his face had melted. He was probably one of those poor pilots who'd tried to get out of his cockpit on fire.

Ted shouted a warning, and the aeroplane rumbled down the runway, lifting off slowly into the skies with her loaded cargo. There were a few twists and turns, as the wind was picking up. Everyone seemed to hold their breath, but Cherry was used to the different lift-offs now, she'd done it countless times.

The patient in the middle was struggling to sit up and ended up leaning on his right shoulder, he sounded like he was in pain but couldn't speak.

'No need to get up. You should lay down and rest. I'll get you a drink.'

The patient was weak and thin, he tried to reach out to her. The plane jostled about and there were groans coming from some of the other patients.

'Bit of unsettled weather we're going through at the moment,' Ted called to them.

'Would you like some water?' she asked politely. The patient nodded. He had no drip but a bandaged left arm in a sling. his mouth was intact and she helped him to sit up a little and tip water into his mouth. He tried to move but couldn't. The man seemed frustrated, grunted something and then lay back exhausted. He grabbed her hand and made a move for her notepad which she always carried these days in her top pocket. She gasped and pulled back wondering why he was reaching for her. She hadn't been expecting him to grab at her.

'Would you like some tea? I can get you some tea.' She said trying to wriggle her hand away. He shook his head and tried to lean on his right side, pointing with his left hand. He only had the index finger on that hand and he pointed at her notebook.

'Oh, do you need to borrow my notebook? Just a minute then.' And she passed him her notebook with her pen.

Someone vomited all over the floor at the rear of the plane. She had to pull herself away and go and clean it up.

'Here we go,' she said as she went back to the man who was trying to write with one hand. She gave him a cup of water.

'There's no tea at the moment. It's too rough.'

Cherry sensed he was desperate to make contact with someone. Someone else called 'Nurse!' and then was sick.

'I'll be back in a jiffy.' She dashed off to clear it up. After that, she went back to the man writing.

'Do you need help?' she asked him. Then others called her. The man didn't speak, so she went around with water and left the man to it.

It wasn't until later on that she realised the patient with the scarred face still had her notebook. He was struggling to lean on his right arm. He seemed like an old man but he must have been younger than that to be returning from a POW camp. She looked closer, he was a young man with skin that had darkened like he had been outside in the sun. He looked like he'd been through hell and back. He could barely sit up or keep his eyes open. But an extraordinary effort on his part made him reach for her and then lie back exhausted.

'There, there,' she said, thinking he was delirious and in pain. 'Do you need help drinking the water? I'll get you a straw. Just take it easy.' The man tried to sit up but didn't have the strength. She turned to assist someone behind her. Her back was to the patient, he reached up with a huge effort and tried to grab her jacket, he collapsed exhausted onto the stretcher again as she turned to help him, and then he stuck a piece of paper in her hand. She looked down in astonishment and tried to read what it said.

'Hold on, just coming into land,' Ted shouted to Cherry.

'What does it say?' she asked the man. He made a gruffled noise as he tried to talk. She couldn't make out the wriggly writing then realised it was her name.

C H E R R Y

'Yes, that's my name,' she gasped, 'how did you know that?' She stared at him again. She opened the note and read it again. He tried to grab it back - still with her pen he started writing something else. Her brow furrowed. This time he offered her the note. When she read it she felt dizzy and couldn't speak her heart felt like it was thumping out of her chest. He had written

J O E

She held her breath for five seconds. And released it all in one go. She held onto a stanchion gazing at the note as the Lady Susan's wheels bounced on the landing strip.

One minute she had no clue, then the next minute she was thinking...he's about the same height, age, and there's something about him that's familiar. But apart from that he looks nothing like Joe. He's emaciated. One side of his face looks like it's melted.

Was it really him? When she looked closer lifting the bandage gently above his left eye, she saw a dreadful scar down the left side of his face, interfering with his eye, cheek and left side of his mouth. His stubble made him look like a hobo and he was in civilian clothes. No, he didn't look anything like her Joe. His eyes looked startled, perhaps this man was still in shock. Although the injuries looked old. He was looking at her intently but he couldn't speak to her. She tried to calm her breathing and went about seeing to the rest of the men as the Dakota taxied to its drop-off point. She came back to the man, she looked down at him as he lay exhausted on the stretcher. His eyes were closed but she could see his face a little better. She stared at his face, still she couldn't say anything. A million things were going through her brain.

Cherry wasn't sure how long she'd been standing there with her mouth open looking down at him. He opened his eyes and stared at her. His eyes were a cloudless blue. She'd seen these eyes before.

'Joe?'

She didn't know what to say or do, her mind was in turmoil. Was it Joe? The man grabbed her hand and this time she held onto it.

The Dakota rear doors opened and the medical orderlies came to take the stretchers out of the Lady Susan. Two orderlies took the stretcher with Joe on it and her hand was pulled away and dropped down at her side. She swallowed and tried to breathe normally, her heart was pounding in her ears. It took a while to register what was happening. She tried to shout to the orderlies but no sound came out.

'What's up?' called Ted from behind her. 'You look like you've seen a ghost!'

'I have.'

'Who is it?'

'I think it's Joe,' she answered calmly. And pointed to the man being taken on the stretcher.

'Are you sure?'

'I think so. It feels like him. Although it doesn't look like him. This man is so thin and has had his face badly burned.'

'Did he speak?'

'No, he just gave me a photo.'

'Of whom?'

'Me.' She still held it in her hand and showed him. 'This is the photo I gave Joe just before he flew to Dieppe.'

By this time the orderlies were piling the stretchers onto the waiting ambulances.

'Wait!' she called to them.

The man wrapped in bandages was lying on his stretcher and was about to be loaded. He tried to turn his head in her direction. Cherry's heart was thumping. Her thoughts were all over the place.

'We need to get him off to hospital,' called the orderly impatiently.

'Go to the infirmary,' said Ted to her. Cherry looked around helplessly.

'Go!' he shouted.

It stimulated her into action. She jumped down from the ramp of the aircraft and ran as fast as she could. They were just loading Joe, if it was Joe, she still couldn't be sure. His hand was wizened the one that she had held, and the other hand in the sling was deformed with only a finger and a thumb. She had stared down at his hands about to say something. His hands would have been damaged like this if he had tried to get out of his cockpit with flames all around him.

Then he was suddenly pushed into the back of the ambulance. He was being taken away from her.

'Wait!' she called to the WAAF driver.

'What's the matter?' asked the WAAF.

'That's my fiancé!'

CHAPTER 28 - August 1945

Queen Victoria Hospital - East Grinstead Burns unit, West Sussex, England.

Joe got out of bed and Cherry helped him to put on his dressing gown. He moved slowly like an old man. She took his arm and led him through the ward out through the French doors into the late summer sunshine. It was the first time she'd managed to get him outside. He'd been reluctant before now, the pain of the last few months taking a long time to leave him.

They sat on a bench in the hospital gardens. Looking around, she noticed many of the patients had someone with them, a relative or a nurse. They were recovering burns patients to whom the now famous Dr Archie McIndoe and his colleagues had operated on. Dr McIndoe was doing pioneering work to help burn survivors mend quickly, physically and mentally.

Joe's face was unbandaged, he had had another operation the previous week to graft healthy skin onto his face. Recuperation was slow, and Cherry did her best to try and visit whenever she could. She was still serving in the WAAF, although her flights were getting less and less.

His black hair, now interlaced with grey, was free of bandages. His face was still scarred but his eyes didn't look scared. At this moment they were fixed on Cherry. It had been a quicker recovery than most because he'd been rescued by his girl whom he thought he would never see again.

Joe had more colour in his face than he had had for a long time and he was starting to put on weight. Months of near-starvation had made him stick thin. She suddenly felt an immense surge of relief that Joe had survived, so she put her hand either side of his cheeks and kissed him.

'I don't know how you can kiss me, or touch my face, its grotesque,' he said with a gravelly-sounding voice.

'It's not, don't be silly. Anyway, I still love you whatever's happened to your face. The doctor says it will get better, and I'm glad you're able to talk now. They've said I can come twice to see you this week.'

'It was more psychological, in that awful Nazi camp. I still have nightmares about it,' he said. He turned his face up to the sun and breathed in the air deeply.

She sighed. 'I understand. It's hard to unsee the pictures in your mind.' She looked into the distance thinking about the deaths she had witnessed. She squeezed his hand gently.

'I'm glad you didn't go with the others when they left the camp.'

'Some of us were too sick to go.' He looked above her head into the distance, thinking of his own distant hell he'd been through.

'I tried to find out what happened to them. There's no record. Perhaps we'll find out more once my friend Monty comes back from his trip.'

But she could tell he didn't want to talk about it. Not many knew the truth, as yet, about the thousands of POW's that had been forced to march by the Germans away from the advancing Allies and liberating forces. The Germans were using the prisoners of war as hostages. Hundreds were found dying of disease, starvation and exhaustion on the forced marches, already emaciated through hunger and sickness. Many still hadn't been found. She looked at his pale face, he was thinking about his comrades.

Joe shuddered. 'Thank God I was too sick to go. Otherwise, I'd have disappeared too. I hope your friend finds them.'

The sun was getting lower in the sky it was September tomorrow, but it was still warm. The tree above them was losing more leaves every time the wind blew. In a few weeks it would be Christmas. She thought of the awful past two Christmases, she didn't want those back again. She thought that this Christmas would be so much better.

'It's surprising how quickly the past three months have gone. I feel so much better since the doctor operated on me,' he said, a bit cheerier. 'It's nice that the other fellas here are in the same boat. I mean, I'm thankful I have friends here who understand. I've joined their club – it's called *The Guinea Pig Club.* There's a few of us - pilots with burns. Going through treatment.'

'Yes, I've heard about it.'

'The doctors talk to you about how you're feeling and try and get us to socialise more. The other pilots are allowed to wear their RAF uniforms, it makes them feel better. They've been through what I have. It's easier to talk to them. Talking is good for morale and healing,' he said. 'I'm only just learning to talk again after all this time.'

'I couldn't believe it when you stuck that note in my hand!' she said. 'It's a good job you did, because I didn't recognise you. I might have missed you!' she shuddered. It didn't bear thinking about.

'They starved us in the camp. I was dehydrated and my throat was dry. I'd had no water until I was on your plane. Now I'm drinking and eating I feel much better.'

'It's a slow process getting to eat better foods. You've lived on hardly anything for the past two years. She looked intently at the scarred side of his face.

'I don't know how you can bear to look at me,' he said turning away. One of the guards in the camp would call me names.'

'You're just as handsome to me now as you were then. You're still the same Joe inside.'

'Am I? I feel about a hundred years old after what I've been through.'

She looked at him fondly, he had become self-conscious, and he wasn't like the confident Joe she used to know. But that would come again in time. She smiled at him squeezing his hand. He looked away. 'I don't know how you can bear to look at me,' he said again. 'I can't bear to look at me in a mirror. I'm so scarred. You're so beautiful. Even more than when I last saw you.'

'That's what they all say,' she joked. He turned to look at her with a frown.

'I'm only joking. Don't be so serious,' she laughed at him.

'You seem different,' he said gently. 'Confident, much more self-assured, you even crack jokes. When I first met you, you were like a frightened rabbit.'

'I've been through a lot too. I've had to grow up quickly, a lot of us have had to. I've seen things young women don't normally see. I've changed too, for the better, I hope.' She squeezed his hand trying to encourage him to smile. He still sounded worried and had been getting depressed these past few weeks while he'd been having treatment.

'You're very different to the eighteen-year-old I met four years ago,' he said.

'Thank goodness for that!' she said jovially. 'Nursing has helped me. Now I'm joining Princess Mary's Royal Air Force Nursing Service. Do you remember ages ago suggesting it?'

'No. Never heard of them.'

'You said they had the Flying Angels in the US. Well, I inquired and it turns out they want nurses in the RAF. And I can do what I've always wanted to do.' She smiled. 'So, I'll be able to look after you.'

'Will you look after me? I honestly don't know how I survived in the camp.' He tried to screw up his nose in distaste but his skin graft was sore and he couldn't do it. He clenched his fist and closed his eyes, he sounded helpless even to himself.

'We'll be all right,' she said trying to sound positive. 'I'm here, and you'll be okay. You'll recuperate bit by bit, and put weight on as you get better. Forget about being sad, you're not in the camp anymore.'

'I wake up in the night thinking I'm still there sometimes. It's scary.'

'I'm so happy to get you back alive I don't care. They're sorting you out and at least it's keeping you in Britain. You're in the best place for burns.'

'It's a slow process taking skin from one part of your body and putting it on your face,' he said.

'Don't get despondent,' she said. 'Is it still sore?'

'A bit,' he said. 'The bit they took from my backside is sorer than my face. The saline baths help.'

She took his other hand and held them both in hers, even though his fingers weren't all there. He was the same old Joe. Still handsome on one side of his face while the other side looked like it had been pulled downwards, but the operation had given him a proper mouth so that he could eat better, and although the left side of his face was still disfigured it looked a bit more like his old face. She suddenly felt glad about his situation. It made him seem more real, more alive, to be in some pain meant the treatment was working, wasn't it? She felt a little guilty. Some small part of her felt glad he would be dependent on her, instead of the other way around. She had found her independence and was developing more nursing skills. One day he would become more independent and not rely on her so much, but that was further down the line when they knew each other much better.

'I can't tell you how glad I am not to be supping liquids now. I can eat without pain.'

He wasn't out of the woods yet, but it wouldn't be long before he was. A couple of birds above her in the tree canopy, whistled as if to confirm her feelings. She was so thankful she had found him. They were one of the lucky ones.

'I thought you would've given up on me and married someone else,' he said.

'Oh, Joe. Of course not. I thought you'd been killed in Dieppe! I didn't know what to do. I was distraught. The thought of you not coming back...'

'I spent some weeks recovering. It wasn't the best place to recover in a POW camp. But I survived.'

'After all this time I have thought about you,' she said. 'Even when you were missing presumed dead.'

'I woke up in a hospital after getting shot down, but everyone around me was speaking French and German. My hands were killing me; they were in so much pain. They had to give me saline baths because the burns went all the way down to my chest. But once they shipped me off to that prison camp down in southern Poland, they stopped with the baths. We had a British doc taking care of us there, but there weren't enough supplies to help heal our wounds or even feed us properly. We toughed it out in that camp for two long years, and there wasn't a whole lot we could do about it.

She could see he was tired, so she fussed over him a bit trying to make him more comfortable. This was the most he had talked to her since she found him.

‘Don’t talk if it hurts you,’ she said. He shook his head, he wanted to tell her what had happened to him, now he could talk.

‘There was this Brit medic over at the camp who slathered some Vaseline on my burns to keep 'em from drying out, and I gotta say, that stuff worked wonders. There was a point where I couldn't even see outta my left eye for a while,’ he said. ‘I couldn’t believe the number of us who had suffered burns in the camp.’

‘Oh Joe, I wish I could hug you.’ She reached out to him and took his hands. This time he didn’t shrink. ‘I don’t want to hurt you,’ she said. He took her hand and held it. A couple went by, talking earnestly. She waited until they had passed out of earshot. There was so much she wanted to tell him.

‘I couldn’t believe you were on my plane… I couldn’t get to you quick enough once I realised who you were. I couldn’t believe you’d come back to me!’

‘If I promise to behave and not act up, will you stick around? I might be able to get some more movement in my left hand, and if they keep taking skin grafts from my backside, I might eventually have a halfway decent face.’ He tried to smile but just looked intently worried. She could tell he was unsure of himself. His injuries had affected him.

‘I don’t care how you look’ she exclaimed. ‘I’m so glad to see you alive.’

'Are you happy I've returned then? I believe you are. Are you still my girl? Do you still want to marry me?' His voice was strained, a worried frown across his brow, and the scar on the side of his face was taut. She could tell the war had changed him. But then, she wondered, did any of us come out of this war unchanged?

'We should have gotten married regardless of how busy we were in the past,' he said sadly, looking at the ring on her finger. 'You wouldn't have hesitated then.'

She thought for a while longer, twisting the engagement ring on her finger. She had never taken it off. She observed his crestfallen face. But she didn't have to think long. She'd always been in love with him.

'There's never been anyone else,' she said. 'I never took your ring off. His eyes lit up.

'I need to finish my nurses training first, here in England,' she said suddenly serious. Whether we go to America together or we stay here - those things can be hashed out later.'

'I love that you've become such a confident young woman.' He took her hand and squeezed it with his strong hand. He took a deep breath. 'You've changed so much since we first met. You were so dang young...'

'Naïve...'

'Beautiful. Absolutely lovely. I swear, I love you even more if that's possible.' He flashed a warm smile and gave her hand a gentle squeeze.

She swallowed, a lump in her throat.

'And you'll need to finish your treatment, so you can go back to living a normal life,' she said pragmatically. She observed his face, his eyes were unsure.

'There's no rush,' she smiled at him. 'There's plenty of time.'

He nodded. Then he smiled, a quirky crooked kind of smile, it was the first smile she'd seen from him since she found him. Then she knew they'd be all right.

ALSO BY JANINA CLARKE:

SHE IS BEHIND ENEMY LINES
VICTORY IN NORMANDY

Janinaclarke.com

ABOUT THIS BOOK....by Janina Clarke

Thank you for reading my book about 'The Flying Nightingales.' It has been a project of mine for more than thirty years when I first read about them. I couldn't understand why there was very little information on these heroines. I researched their memoirs and decided to relay some of their adventures through my character Cherry Caldwell to make their adventures come alive again. It inspired me to write more about women in war. Women were told to forget what they had seen and dealt with and many of them suffered from Post-traumatic stress disorder. But nothing was done, they just got on with the rest of their lives.
In 2008, the Duchess of Cornwall gave lifetime achievement awards to the seven Flying Nightingales who still survived.

Thank you for purchasing this book **Cherry's War and The Flying Nightingales**. *I am extremely grateful. I hope you enjoyed it and learned more about some of our heroines in wartime. I would love to hear from you and hope that you could take some time to post a* **review**. *Either from where you bought the book or Amazon or goodreads.com. just type in my name and my books will come up. Your feedback and support will help this author greatly improve her writing craft and future projects.*

My author website has my blog about these women, please feel free to look me up at ***janinaclarke.com*** *and if you add your name to my mailing list I'll let you know when the fourth book is coming out.*

Thank you and happy reading!

Printed in Great Britain
by Amazon